WORKS OF MERCY

a novel

Sally Thomas

Wiseblood Books

Printed in the United States of America

Set in Baskerville Typesetting

Cover Design: Silk Sheep Studio

Paperback ISBN-13: 978-1-951319-73-1

1

On Mondays I cleaned the rectory for the good of my soul. I did it, too, in those days, for the good of Father Schuyler, who was young and untried.

"Were you a war bride?" he asked me, his first Monday in residence. He kept his head shaved, smooth as an egg, but his anxious face was a boy's still, flushed with the exertion of speaking.

I had come in with my handbag and was shaking out my old coverall apron. Even as we embarked on the customary conversational exchanges, I'd been thinking guiltily about some recalcitrant mildew stains in the bathtub grouting. All my bleaching had so far failed to obliterate them, and I wondered whether he would notice. Father Trotter had not noticed, but you never knew, did you?

Politely we had established that he came from Indiana and, while not unacquainted with farmland, still found this rural corner of the North Carolina Piedmont perplexing. How on earth had he got here? I wondered but did not ask. We had established, also politely, that I had been born in the Shetland Islands, which explained my accent, bent out of shape after forty years in Annesdale. How had I got here? To his credit, Father had asked.

Were you a war bride? The like of that, my Granny would have said. To this young man I must have looked as though I'd shaken hands with Moses.

"Heavens, it was nineteen-seventy-one, Father, not so long ago." I realized as I said it that to him, it was so long ago. His mother would have been still a child. Had he rubbed his cassock with sandpaper, to achieve that antique look about the elbows?

"We met on the train from London," I added. I was not given to chatter ordinarily, but the anxious silence tightening its screws between us made me plunge on. "Ranse—my husband, you know—was going to do some chemical research in a laboratory, on an overseas grant. And there was I in an empty train compartment, reading Robert Southwell—"

I broke off. Father's fresh face was all wide-eyed incomprehension.

"*Saint* Robert Southwell," I said. *What did they teach you in that seminary?* I nearly asked. Of course that was just the sort of thing an old person would say. "One of the Jesuit martyrs in Elizabethan England, a priest and a poet."

"Oh." Father raised his eyebrows. "A *Jesuit.*"

"Yes indeed." I felt sorry for him then, a little. Whatever the Jesuits might or might not be in these days—not knowing any personally, I couldn't have said—they had once upon a time made a deliberate point of being hanged and gutted for high treason and the old faith. At his trial, Robert Southwell is said to have declared that having been tortured ten times, he would far rather have endured ten executions. Not to know these things seemed to me a poverty. I turned my attention then to the bathtub grouting and other jobs of cleaning. Father followed me about the house, observing what I did. I tried to clean as if I knew my business.

We moved from room to room, not speaking. I was perfectly happy not to speak. At last, however, bending over the kitchen sink, I considered that I ought to try again. "And have you met many parishioners yet?"

Father picked up the lambswool duster I had left on the kitchen island and dusted a spray bottle of glass cleaner. "This isn't a big parish, but gosh, it seems like a lot of people. There were a number of children at Mass yesterday, a very large number of children, right at the back. I couldn't tell whether it was one family or several. They didn't exactly make noise, but there was movement." He shuffled his feet again. "I'm afraid I found it distracting."

I knew what children he meant. Even I, who kept to myself—even I knew the Malkins. In a parish like ours, they were difficult not to know.

"A little boy was waving his arms in the air, like he was *swimming.* And his mother just sat there. Maybe I should speak to them." He picked up a spray bottle I'd set on the kitchen island, swished it about for a moment, then set it down again. "I hate to put anybody on the spot. I noticed that the man didn't come up for Communion. The father, I guess." Again he paused, seeming to consider whether this, too, were a problem he should nerve himself to address. "Of course, people have their reasons."

I watched the bleach powder swirl down the drain. It was a lovely blue.

At last he wandered into the living room and began taking books from a box. Each book made a comfortable, papery *chunk* as he set it on a shelf. I went on with my work. After a time, perhaps intuiting that it was his turn to be worried by what we both considered to be a perfectly natural silence, he began to talk again.

"I was told—I had assumed—that this area was very—that there weren't many Catholics around here."

"No, Father. Relatively speaking, there aren't." My own husband, for example, had been a Baptist.

"But there are all these houses with Latin signs in the front yard."

"Latin signs, Father?"

"Yes, Latin signs. Out in the country. I keep passing them when I'm out driving around. I guess they're all parishioners. Some special devotion, maybe?"

I knew of no such devotion and continued wiping the kitchen counter.

"I can make out the first word. *Mater.* That's *mother*, of course. It's obviously something Marian. *Mother of Something.* Isn't that right?"

Wringing out my sponge, I agreed that it was.

"But the second word is giving me fits. I've been all through the Latin dictionary, but I can't find it. I don't recognize it at all." He pronounced it for me. "*Stah-kess.* S-T-A-K-E-S. Do you happen to know what that means?"

"I'm afraid not, Father."

I moved into the dining room to dust the sideboard. As I shifted a candlestick, suddenly the sign—which of course I had seen myself, all about the countryside—flashed into my mind. It wasn't Latin at all. It was, one might say, the very plainest English. Every summer people round Annesdale cut and sold those wooden posts for tying up tomato vines in the garden. *Mater Stakes.*

Should I tell him? Glancing through the doorway into the living room, I saw him absorbed again in shelving his books. Eventually the penny would drop, as my husband would have said, but did it have to drop today? I decided to let him accept those signs as a gift, an omen of good things to come. Or perhaps I merely chose the path of least resistance. In hindsight it is easy to laugh at him. I hope that time has brought him to a place where he can laugh at himself. But I rather think, glancing back on that day, that I too, scrubbing away at things, dodging conversation, watching the bleach cleaner circle round the plughole as if it mattered in the least —I too am ridiculous.

Finished with my cleaning, I tidied away my supplies. "I'm away home now, Father."

"Oh." Startled, he dropped the book he had just taken

from the box. "Oh, yes. Good. I mean, thanks." He wiped his hands on his trousers. "I'm sorry. I've already forgotten your name."

"Kirsty Sain, Father." With relief, as if I'd been sprung early from school, I took my leave.

* * *

The parish rectory was spare and plain. Red brick, shutterless, with a flat green-shingled roof, it was one of several hundred post-war two-bedroom brick boxes in a close-set neighborhood that had risen like an afterthought on the western edge of Annesdale. *Those new houses,* my mother-in-law had called them in the nineteen-seventies. Where the neighborhood ended, the town gave way to countryside. The church itself, octagonal, slit-windowed, with a low-slung roof of white corrugated metal, stood on a parcel of grassy meadow several miles out. It was an unprepossessing structure; Ranse always said that it looked like a farmers' credit union about to go under. The rectory had been purchased to silence the complaints of a previous pastor—two before Father Schuyler, if memory serves me—who had objected to living in a single room behind the tiny church office. He had pointed out that the parish council and the RCIA had to meet in that room, because there was nowhere else, except the church itself. He sat on his bed to preside at these meetings, and it was awkward. Priests are human like the rest of us, of course, but I have never met a stupid one. If he had merely griped about the smallness of the room, his successor would still be living there. He had played his hand shrewdly, however, with the consequence that money was found, or raised, or something, for the purchase of this modest house. The church gained a multipurpose room, and the pastor reveled in the expanse and privacy of eleven hundred square feet, with a short walk to the Korner Mart should he run out of milk or live bait.

Of the church I will say more later. Naturally it ought to occupy a higher place in my thoughts, but it was the rectory I had come to know with the curious intimacy of the cleaning lady. Absent a lover, what person penetrates the heart of a house's privacy more closely than the one who comes to clean? Often, after all, it is the outsider who sees things. Certainly I knew every inch of that house. I had touched all its surfaces with my rubber-gloved hands. With no effort at all, I can see the living room, a narrow rectangle containing a donated brown-corduroy sofa and matching twin armchairs in reasonable pre-owned condition. The room was dominated not by these, however, but by a massive, severe, walnut-veneer desk, rescued from some long-ago office, which stood beneath the picture window. Father Trotter, Father Schuyler's predecessor, had demonstrated for me how, when you opened a certain door beneath the desktop, a hidden platform sprang into view. If you were a lady secretary of the nineteen-fifties, this platform would hold your typewriter. Not being a lady secretary of the nineteen-fifties, Father Trotter had utilized this mechanism instead as a hidden wet bar, with a collection of bottles where the typewriter was meant to go. They clinked perilously as they leapt from their place of concealment. Father Schuyler had arranged the same desk as a sort of altar, with crucifix and candles, though it also habitually bore his breviary set, a tidy stack of books from which, I presumed, he extracted his Sunday homilies, and his slim aluminum laptop.

In Father Trotter's day, each of the rectory's two tiny, monastic bedrooms had contained a twin bed and bureau, with a crucifix over the door. Father Trotter had occupied one; the other, he said, he kept for the Pope. Immediately upon his arrival, Father Schuyler had converted that second bedroom into a chapel, draping the bureau with a green brocade cloth for Ordinary Time, introducing a tabernacle and monstrance, and importing a prie-dieu. Of course the twin bed remained; there was nowhere else to put it. It too, however, had been draped in what appeared to be a tablecloth, also green, so that if it did not exactly suggest an ecclesiastical furnishing, it no longer announced itself as a bed. I wondered what the Pope would do, should he find himself benighted in Annesdale. In the little dining nook off the kitchen, the plain fruitwood dinette table also wore a pristine cloth in the appropriate liturgical color. One would not profane this table, I felt, by setting a coffee cup on it, any more than one would commit the sacrilege of sleeping in the spare bed.

The rectory presented me with a morning's work, an extremely minor sacrifice with which to begin my week. Ranse had left me comfortably enough off that I didn't need to clean houses. He would never have rested easily, thinking that I'd been left unprovided. In death, as in life, he had been generous. As I saw it, cleaning the rectory was something to do by way of an apostolate. I didn't sing. I had never been fond of children. After so many years in Annesdale, I hardly even thought the word *bairns* anymore. Whatever you happened to call small people, in whatever language or dialect, I preferred to avoid them. I also didn't like ironing or, as a general rule, the company of women. That ruled out the altar guild. When Mrs. Kacszmarek, whoever she was, grew too old to clean for the priest anymore, the president of the parish council had somehow thought of me. "You'd be perfect for this little job," he had told me over the telephone. Well, yes. I did make the ideal candidate, for the obvious reason that I wasn't doing anything else. I was surprised that anyone had noticed what I did or did not do. I was surprised that the man knew my name. We were both surprised, I think, when I said yes.

But the work suited me. I did feel I should serve in some way. Although I attended Mass with assiduity, for too many years I hadn't *held up my end*, as Ranse would say. I hadn't been *taking one for the team*. The difficulty was that I preferred solitude to just about anything else. In fact, I had once said to Ranse that I craved loneliness. He had argued that this was impossible. "You can't want what nobody can give you," he had said. He had meant that I couldn't crave a negative. What I'd meant, meanwhile, was that I'd rather long for human companionship than have it. Had I been born in the right century, I might have made an adequate anchoress. I was in many ways a more contented widow than I had been a wife.

And truly, aside from churchgoing, I liked keeping house. Ordering, arranging, tidying: all of those endeavors satisfied me. I liked being at home and could occupy myself there endlessly. My house, though solidly built, wanted constant tending. Aging as I was, it consumed me with its little cares. Though I had long since reorganized the linen cupboard, still the sheets needed taking out and airing periodically. Though I had a place for everything, and everything stayed in its place—who was there to move it?—still everything wanted dusting. I could expend whole days, pleasurably, in taking out, looking over, polishing, flicking dust away, then putting back.

I had begun to understand my late mother-in-law, who had inhaled sharply whenever I opened the refrigerator door. She feared that I would open it too wide, or too frequently, inviting the germs in. Ranse had been trained to leave it alone. He would not so much as pour a glass of milk for himself. As a new bride, I had persisted in wanting to put things in, to take things out, to cook the dinner. "Let me do that," Mother Sain kept saying, until at last I realized that she mistrusted me. She took out the things I had meant to cook for dinner, then she cooked the dinner. At first I had been insulted. Finally I was amused. Now, had anyone else dared broach my refrigerator, I would have inhaled audibly and counted to ten.

Living alone, I cooked full meals for myself, planning them out carefully, meat and veg. I shopped meticulously and sometimes spent whole afternoons in the kitchen. Aside from the pleasure I took in cooking, I felt that it was important to make the effort. Food preparation, like cleaning, signaled my own existence. If I let that go—what then? But by the time I'd finished cooking, I couldn't bear the smell of what I had cooked. Though I had all my mother-in-law's dishware at my disposal, the thought of setting one place at table oppressed me. Surrendering, I would pack the meal away in the deep freezer, labeling it carefully with the date so that I should know when to take it out and transfer it to the dustbin. Making a sandwich instead, I ate standing up at the kitchen window, a book open on the counter beside me.

Great things had been expected of me in my youth. In my leisurely old age, the improvement of my mind seemed another suitable occupation. It made a change from the cleaning and the cooking, at any rate. I'd found, in the long, solitary evenings after Ranse died, that the books I had loved in young womanhood still spoke to me. Lines of poems, scraps of prose, rose to the surface, and I would say them over to myself, wondering why it was that I remembered them. Because I could never remember anything in its entirety, I went to the shelves to look out the appropriate text, last encountered when I was nineteen. After a spot of reading and meditation, though, I would improve my eyes by gazing through the window at the rigid line of Leyland cypress that marked the edge of our property. That too brought satisfaction. I was happy, or something like it. All my life I had lived among people. Now, although perhaps my days sound dull, I was well enough satisfied with my own company.

* * *

We were Father's first parish. In the halcyon summer following his installation, he had worked hard at being pastoral. He'd stood at the door shaking hands, trying in constricted earnestness to learn people's names. In his announcements at the end of his first Sunday Mass, he had informed the congregation, apologetically, that he was forced to adhere to a gluten-free diet. That was his word: *forced.* Nobody knew what was forcing him. He had declined to elaborate. He seemed to feel that the bare facts were imposition enough, and that he should not overburden us with more. He would accept dinner invitations with pleasure; he was sorry to be a nuisance. In the wake of this announcement, unsurprisingly, much conversation had ensued among the ladies of the parish. What would you feed the priest, hypothetically, should you invite him to supper? I overheard the murmured conferences in the narthex as I passed the little huddled groups. Did rice contain gluten? What about pot roast? In those brief early weeks, people did ask Father to dinner. When asked, he went, presumably with pleasure. He had not yet begun fleeing to the locked sacristy at the end of every Mass. In the summer, we had all—Father Schuyler, too, no doubt—entertained high hopes.

But the summer was over. Though weather was still

heavily warm at midday, in the mornings I wanted a cardigan. On this particular Monday in late September, Michaelmas nearly upon us, the empty rectory felt chilly. I'd let myself in and for a moment stood in the entryway, savoring the austere silence that greeted me, the stripes of light and shadow the blinds cast on the bare floor. The house smelt faintly of pipe tobacco, a welcome change from Father Trotter's cigarettes. I had seen Father Schuyler pulling on this pipe with a gravitas that I found both comical and endearing in one so young. Surely, given time, he would grow into both the gravitas and the pipe.

Setting down my handbag on the dining-room table, tying on my coverall, I went to work. Not that there was much to do. Father Schuyler lived lightly in that house. He seemed never to eat there. Week after week, the dishes in the cupboard looked not only clean but untouched. No crumbs littered the kitchen. Father Trotter had fancied himself a gourmet cook. Smears of tomato sauce on the cooktop, speckles of the same on the ceiling. For four years I'd scrubbed and scoured, scraping off the worst with the putty knife Mrs. Kacszmarek had bequeathed me. Oh, those crumbs: crumbs everywhere. Crumbs in the bed sheets. Round the toilet. Good gracious, that man. He weighed, easily, a good eighteen stone, waddling here, waddling there. I could imagine him eating with one hand, dropping ash in his food with the other.

Father Schuyler, *sed contra*—a Latin phrase I did know—belonged to the school of Leave No Trace. I had begun to wonder whether he ever performed the normal bodily functions that make cleaning necessary. It was Antony à Wood, wasn't it, who effected the total suppression of urine, for reasons I can only wonder at, not having read him myself. But perhaps Father Schuyler did the same. Or that, not eating, he didn't perform the other thing. Every fixture in that bathroom gleamed like wedding china. Still, I cleaned it again, leaving a chlorinated smell which, for better or worse, overlaid the lingering, fruity fragrance of pipe tobacco.

With a lambswool duster I flicked non-existent particles from the relics that stood on the mantelpiece in their little brass reliquaries: minuscule chips of Saints Francis, Thérèse, Padre Pio, and someone else whose name I always forgot. Stiffly, feeling my age in my knees, I genuflected at the open door of the bedroom Father had converted to a chapel. The room was made shady by an overgrown pyracantha outside; even in daylight, the sanctuary lamp shone brilliantly red. Though I dusted the prie-dieu, I didn't have it in me to dust the draped bureau-altar, or the tabernacle. The nuns at school had intimated dire consequences for any girl who dared approach the Blessed Sacrament in its holy housing. Father Schuyler's tabernacle would hardly be dusty, anyway.

Genuflecting again on my way out, I took the hoover from the hall cupboard and skated it over the hardwood floors, still slick as an icy pond from their refinishing after Father Trotter's departure. I was making a show of replacing the bag, though I knew there was nothing in it, when the kitchen door banged, and Father Schuyler walked in.

"Sorry, Father," I said. "I'm just finishing."

"That's all right, Kirsty. Don't hurry on my account." He stood at the kitchen island riffling through the post. Riffle, riffle, went his fingers through the letters, over and over. He must have read each envelope three or four times. On his account I did hurry. I bundled the hoover away in its cupboard.

It always surprised me to be called *Kirsty*. Even now, it catches me off-balance. Of course, *Kirsty* is my name, or at any rate my name's diminutive. It's a good job, too, that I'm called by it. Here in Annesdale, I would have been forced daily to spell out my full Christian name, *Kirstaine*, popular in Shetland in the seventeenth century, but not here, ever, to put it mildly. It hadn't been popular there, either, in the postwar years. Inexplicably my parents had settled *Kirstaine* on me at a time when all other girl infants in the islands were being given pin-up names, *Betty* and *Peggy* and *Norma,* which everybody had seen painted on the fuselages of American bombers. At any rate, my own name feels incongruous to me now, too girlish, as if I'd tried to wear my favorite dress from the year I turned eighteen. Quite correctly, Father Trotter had called me *Mrs. Sain.* As my mother-in-law used to say, "To anybody under the age of sixty-five, my name is *Mrs. Ransome Sain, Senior.*" Granted, there were certain younger people, Ranse's childhood friends, who made bold to call her *Miss Annaluree.* I thought her Christian name exotic and beautiful; nevertheless, I had called her, dutifully, *Mother Sain.*

As I shut the cupboard door on the hoover, I glanced at Father Schuyler. He was wearing, as always, his carefully-aged cassock. He had told me that strangers in the supermarket liked to say, *Nice dress, dude*, and then laugh as if the joke were original or witty.

"You've had a quick day out, Father," I ventured to say.

"Yes." He went on leafing through the post, over and over, as if he were treading water.

"I hope everything's all right?"

He looked up at me, startled and anxious. "Is there some reason why it wouldn't be?"

"No, Father," I said. "Of course not. It's just that I don't often see you on a Monday."

"Yes, well." An envelope quivered in his hand. "I went to the church to pray for a while, since nobody's there. And then I felt that I wanted to be at home. Alone," he added falteringly. "That is, I'm sorry, but really. I don't feel like talking."

"Yes, Father. Of course, Father. I was just going." Obscurely chastened, I took up my handbag.

I drove away into the brilliant morning. The rectory neighborhood lay on the town's fringes; one highway bend, and I was back in the country. I passed the church, low and brown, set far back from the road. The incongruous white cross on its metal roof ventured up like a periscope from behind a screen of unmown meadow grass, and made a silhouette in negative on the dark trees beyond. Only the big concrete crucifix at the foot of the drive, clustered with hot-pink knock-out roses, announced itself without embarrassment.

Farther along, the trees, still green except for the wild dogwoods purpling in the ragged stands of timber, crowded close and reached across the road. I drove over their shifting shadows. All the woods looked dustier, washed out, in the concentrated light of early autumn. When the view opened again, the land for many miles rose and fell in great, gentle, undulant waves, an ocean whose fawns and golds and faded dry greens were its own and did not reflect the sky. At the edge of this ocean, to the west, the mountains hung like low blue clouds. Above them, real clouds, cumulus thunderheads, were piling like darker, more substantial mountains. Somewhere to the east, the radio said, a hurricane was churning ashore. This sunshine would be brief. Over the new subdivisions along my road—whole neighborhoods risen from cotton and tobacco fields once owned and farmed by Sains—the light was stark. The sharp-gabled pink-brick houses stood out from the landscape in startling relief.

I let myself into my own house, a box of a similar vintage to the rectory, though larger, with a second story. After the Second World War, Ranse's father had gone straightway to university on the GI Bill and come out with an engineer's exacting mind. On marrying Ranse's mother, he had erected this house where I now lived. It was a pretty enough house, with its white clapboard, its black shutters, its twin dormer windows protruding from the roof like a frog's eyes, its screened front porch where in the summer so often Ranse and I had sat longing for a breeze. Mr. Ransome, Senior, had spent his career designing highway overpasses; the house was well built to the point of inevitability.

I had spent all my married life in that house, first with Ranse and his widowed mother, then with Ranse alone. Now that Ranse was gone, I might have sold the house. I might have moved into town, been less isolated. I might have gone back to gold-lit Shetland, so vivid at the back of my memory. I might have returned to the English university town of my brief youth. I might have begun some entirely new life in a place of my own choosing. With no ties and nobody to stop me, I might have taken down the world atlas from the shelf, opened it at random, shut my eyes, and asked the Holy Spirit to point my finger.

Instead, I had stayed where I was. After Ranse died, I had had the thick old wall-to-wall carpeting stripped, the dark paneled walls repainted a fresh cream. Ranse would have asked why; by *why* he would have meant *don't*. In his mild-mannered way, he had been sometimes autocratic, as I understand that children can be. I had lost many arguments over the years to Ranse's Intractable Law of The Way Things Are. Mind you, in life, he never raised his voice to me. In death, too, he never seemed to accuse me. But at times, as I pottered about the house, I fancied I felt him grieving. As soon as his back was turned, I'd got rid of the carpet, painted the walls, and made myself at home.

* * *

Ghosts like the waning of the year, and it is then more than ever that they creep out of their corners. I was haunted by my own share of ghosts: Ranse, of course, but others as well. Even the ghost of myself returned to me, that silly girl so fleetingly, foolishly happy. In the university Michaelmas Term, through the brief afternoons, the cold early nightfalls, the dry smell of electric fires, the smutty scent of coal, the rains that shone on the cobbled courts, that provincial girl with her silly little ambitions had fallen in love with her tutor. Oh, Dermott, she had sighed, day and night. Between tutorials, she had wheeled her bicycle over the wet cobbles in Saint Hilda's lane, beneath the walls of his college, hoping for a glimpse. Though she was supposed to be clever, she had dressed herself in the same stupid things all girls wore in those days: mini dresses, white vinyl boots with chunky heels. In the mornings she tried to iron her hair straight. The moment she stepped outside it sprang up again, a fat red cloud expanding round her freckled face as she pedaled across town against the wind. Her nose was always raw. You'd think that she might have been used to weather. She'd grown up, after all, with rain and gales and the incessant lashings of the winter sea. As a child, she had not been oppressed by any particular desire to be pretty. Now, poor ghost, she was.

"Hallo, lovely," Dermott had said, meeting me at the door of his rooms. "How's my scholar today? Not still homesick?"

I stepped out of the dark stairway into the lamplit room. "No, not at all, thank you. I'm quite adjusted."

Of course I was adjusted. Hadn't I always been adjusting to something?

Still, he seemed pleased with me. "That's the ticket. Let's see what you've got for me today." He studied me briefly, and his cheek twitched. He had a trick of smiling without smiling, as if he shared a secret with you. "I do like that dress," he went on after a moment. "Of course as a general rule I don't notice what girls wear, but blue suits you."

He directed me as usual to sit in the moss-green-patterned Morris chair with its low, deep seat. You couldn't sit straight in that chair. Its angle canted the body back, cocked up the knees. As Dermott read my essay, I studied those knees of mine, too shiny in nylons. My new blue dress, which had looked all right when I'd put it on that morning, now felt jarringly bright. It didn't go with the room's fusty colors, all the greens and browns. Even the golds were dull with learnedness, modest in their intimations of achievement. My dress was too short as well as too bright. I had *tried*; that was my mistake. Oh well, I told myself hopelessly, I could hardly go home and change it now. When I thought Dermott wouldn't notice, I tugged at the hem. Still my shiny knees exposed themselves.

Now and again, reading, Dermott smiled to himself and underlined something with a pencil. People laughed at Dermott and his pencils. In lectures, he took out whole bundles of pencils and sat sharpening them with a little knife, dropping the shavings all round his chair. Too anxious to laugh, I watched him turn over another page. I could see, as I hadn't seen when I was writing it, that anything I wrote was bound to be stamped with the pathos of youth, and also with the enduring mark of Sister Bede, the sixth-form English mistress. I wanted terribly to be clever. Though Dermott behaved as though I were clever, already the traces left by the nuns had amused him more than once.

He had laughed when I'd proposed Robert Southwell as

the subject for my essay. His area of inquiry was the sixteenth century, but a different sixteenth century from the one I thought I knew. His Tudor era was full of girls named Stella and Corinna, of Maying and lutes and lost maidenheads. C.S. Lewis, he told me, had categorized poets of this era into two sorts: "golden" and "drab." He had his own set of goldens and drabs, not necessarily Lewis's. In Dermott's reckoning, Milton was a drab. Dermott's favorite, Thomas Campion, writer of lute songs and masques, was golden. "Though he was a bit of a moralizer," Dermott said. Southwell, naturally, was a drab. Dermott thought: All that time and talent wasted, skulking about in those ridiculous disguises, saying those secret Masses. Why? Think—Dermott thought—how great he might have been, if only he'd let the bloody Baby burn. Now where'd Corinna got to, with her jolly old lute? I could hear him say it, as clearly as if he had said it.

At last he glanced up at me. "I must say, this is good. Of course it's good. You've got the makings of a real mind there. But it's a bit *credulous* in places, don't you think? You don't believe all that silly nonsense, surely?"

Dermott's eyes, set high in his pale oval face, were long and narrow and gray. He'd a habit of crinkling them when he was amused. In the early twilight—*the mirknen*—I could see one strand of silver shining in the straight fall of dark hair on his brow. Everything about him was long and straight: his white fingers with their gleaming nails, his legs crossed carelessly, his narrow feet in their antiquated wingtips. He must have been thirty-five, then, or forty. Possibly he was older. I never knew. I didn't care.

In addition to more edifying things, I had read my share of paperback novels beneath the bedclothes after lights out. In those novels I had made the acquaintance of the older man—a nobleman, generally, though why shouldn't he be a don?—who nurtured the foundling until she came of age, whereupon a wedding occurred. Generally the wedding was preceded by some crisis, some saving act on the part of the nobleman—but why not a don?—which culminated in a declaration of love that was not after all completely paternal. Then the wedding came to pass, tied off like the denouement it was. Of course, I told myself, what I daydreamed about Dermott was about *minds.* I'd the makings of a real mind: hadn't Dermott just said so? And minds might marry. *Let not to the marriage of true minds admit impediments.* There was Jane Eyre, too, wasn't there, and Mr. Rochester in his blindness. My thoughts grasped in confusion at these more literary examples.

How did Sister Bede's Jesuit fit into the vision I was trying to form? Well, a girl in my college, a postgraduate in theology, was engaged to her thesis supervisor. These things did happen. People talked, but she went about with her ring and her small secret smile. I should smile my own smile, of course, but I should also find a Jesuit to perform the Nuptial Mass. We might have lute music after. I should wear, not this stupid dress I had chosen for my tutorial, but a heavy Elizabethan gown, crusty with pearls. I should have my red hair spun out down my back. I should, in fact, look entirely too like the young Elizabeth I for the comfort of any Jesuit, but I meant my marriage to be a peaceable kingdom. That I had never known any marriage to be remotely a peaceable kingdom did not matter a jot to me. I should do things differently, that was all.

I tugged again at the hem of my dress. Even through the nylons, my knees tipped up before me were red with cycling in the cold. I saw now that I'd laddered the nylons, just above the top of my left boot. A great ragged rent in the sheeny suntan-colored fabric; through that rent, my white gooseflesh.

With a gesture of sudden renunciation, Dermott cast down my essay and looked at me. "I don't believe any of it. I think we die. That's it. No resurrection. No heaven. Nothing." His gray eyes crinkled. "You're a clever girl. You'll soon put things right. Is it time for a drink?"

I supposed that it was. The cut crystal sparkled in the lamplight. It was all so beautiful, all so very much what I wanted. And what of my Jesuit, about whom I had written so credulously? One way or another, I'd soon put that right. I had the makings of a real mind. Dermott would help me make it. Full of visions, I brought the glass to my nose and smelt the brown peaty scent of what was in it.

"To poor old Southwell." Dermott tipped the lip of his glass to mine. "And to clever old you."

We drank and drank again. There was more talk. I remember none of it now. At some point Dermott rose from his chair, and I thought he meant for me to go. I struggled to my feet, tugging openly now at the hem of my dress. Instead of showing me the door, Dermott took my hand. This was the true door opening, I thought, the door to my new, true life. Rain struck the window. Everything was beginning.

* * *

Sometimes it seems to me that all my memories begin there, in those rooms. It seems to me that I must have sprung into the world as a young woman, fully formed, and leapt straightway into disaster. But of course that isn't so. I'd had a childhood, ordinary enough, though I suppose that to anyone in Annesdale, it might have appeared hopelessly exotic: a wind-scrubbed island of crags and quiet bays—*heogs* and *houbs,* the Shetlanders say—a little village clinging to its rocks, winter darkness lit by the great green and amber striations of the Northern Lights, golden sunshine breaking through the *haar,* the thick sea-fog, on Midsummer Night, to shine on the skin of the sea. Our village was so small that we hadn't our own Up Helly Aa to mark the end of the long Yuletide season, but some years my father went over in his boat to Lerwick, where the Catholic church also was, to march in the torch procession.

The Shetland Islands are as Norse as they are Celtic, perhaps even more so. My father's name was Ivar, and in the rare photographs of his youth he looks the part, a giant with sleeked-back pale hair, glittering light eyes. There was a bit of the berserker in him, something that made him, every now and again, set down a teacup so hard that he broke both cup and saucer. My mother came from Aberdeen, was round and red-haired, and as a girl had had the fleeting superficial beauty I hadn't recognized in myself until it was too late. I remember her face and hands as always chapped. The salt winds rubbed her raw, summer and winter. In my memory, naturally, she is never young.

Even now in the island's life turns on fishing, though oil and petrol have made their inroads. The croft people still graze their sheep on the brilliant grass, startlingly green in the hazy northern sunlight. The greatest herring shoals, the shoals of legend, had faded away thirty years before I was born, but in the village of my childhood there was nothing but boats and fish. My father, in the war, had been damaged in some invisible way, so that although he was a fisherman he did not go out regularly with the rest of the men, bobbing away in their boats across the clear swells in the early morning. When he was at home—as far as I could tell nobody was keeping him there—he brooded as if he disliked being inside, away from the mackerel and herring, from wind and waves and danger, which signified life for every man we knew.

My mother, meanwhile, was village postmistress. She learnt, imperfectly, to understand what the Shetlanders said to her in their dialect with its echoes of Norn, the old Scandinavian-influenced tongue. At home she spoke Scots English to me, and I to her. We lived round the bend from the little red post office, in the gray stone house of my father's birth, where my father's mother lived with us, or we with her. Granny Astrid and my father belonged to a local biblical sect, exponentially nonconformist, that met of a Sunday not in the plain white chapel up the hill, but in the house of Magnus Wilson the boatwright, down by the harbor. I never knew what went on there. I imagine that of popery and its outrages something was said, within the righteous walls of Magnus Wilson's front room. At home there were Shetlandic mutterings, for my mother was a Catholic. So, by what seemed to me some wholly mysterious tacit agreement, was I. On Saturdays when the gales didn't blow to keep us home, my father put my mother and me in his boat and puttered us across the sound to Lerwick. With a great show of concession, he handed us in and out of the boat. Leaving him, my mother and I walked from the harbor into the streets of the town, where we would stop the night with my aunt and go together to Mass in the morning.

This aunt was my mother's spinster sister, also round and russet but with a softer, less wind-scrubbed face. As a young woman, Auntie had come from Aberdeen to Lerwick to teach in the infants' school; there she had remained, geographically and otherwise my mother's nearest relation. There were a host of aunts and uncles and cousins in Aberdeen, I was given to understand, and even grandparents, but somehow we never saw them. Some rift had occurred, before my time, and now only my Lerwick aunt spoke to my mother, or my mother to her. Auntie's given name was Catriona, but from infancy she had been called Lass, and that was the name I knew her by.

Saturday nights we passed with Auntie Lass in her bedsit, in a gray street where the winds could cut the Sunday roast, as my mother said. My mother slept with Auntie on the divan beneath the window. It was narrow, they were not, and occasionally whoever was on the outside fell onto the floor in the night with a thump and a cry. I slept on two chairs pushed together. When I grew too long for the chairs, I had a pallet of blankets on the floor.

In the morning we walked to the church for confession and Mass. Until I was old enough to make my own confession, I would sit with Auntie Lass in a pew while my mother vanished into the mysterious cupboard. I kicked my legs and studied the carved wooden reredos above the altar, set at back of the sanctuary alcove with its Gothic arch. Ancient, it looked, though the church had only been built in 1911. When my mother reappeared and knelt beside me, I studied her as well. She prayed her penance with ardor, her eyes squeezed shut, her entire body palpably tensed. While my mother prayed, Auntie Lass took her turn in the queue for the cupboard. When she came out again and sat on my other side, I noted with interest how she drooped romantically at prayer, like the Lady of Shalott in the print that hung in the wallpapered entryway of the house where she lived.

Afterwards, through the Mass, I gazed at the clear mullioned windows, holding the early light in summertime. Their crosshatched shadows fell over people's sun-bright faces; their glow turned the plain-washed walls to gold as the priest's Latin whispers fell on the air. When the Mass was ended, we walked Auntie Lass back home and stayed to break our long fast with her. Even then, my aunt's room was like an old lady's, with net curtains, white lace on the little table. Before her simpering painting of the Immaculate Heart, done by herself as a girl at convent school, we prayed a rosary together. After that, and a spell of tepid gossip, we would have a sort of early tea with cakes and sausage roll. Then my mother and I had to hurry away to the harborside to meet my father.

He was always impatient, even when we were there ahead of him. I remember standing with my hand in my mother's, the wind tearing our hair back as we watched the little blue boat dip and crest across the silvery swells. As he approached, and we could see his face, it was possible to read his lips before we could hear him. Though the wind scoured his words away and whirled them inaudibly past us, he would be shouting, "Let's get slick home, then." Though it was in silence, generally, that we let him hand us down into the boat, he was always exhorting us not to fuss and take on. "Dinna make a wark about it. Now, sit." Sometimes he would add, smiling bitterly at my mother, "My jewel at du is," which meant, *my dear.* Bitterly she would smile back at him, the wind cracking the sore skin of her lips.

At eleven I went to Aberdeen, to board and go to school to the nuns as my mother and my aunt had done before me. Presumably I had other aunts who had been at this school; presumably I had cousins my age who might have been there. Though I had intuited, from whisperings between my mother and Auntie Lass, that I had an entire Aberdeen family who might have spoken to me if they'd chosen to, in all the years I went to school I never saw them. Once there, I never gave them a thought. My mind was too full of other things. Unlike my aunt, I never painted any pious pictures, though certainly the life was like that: up in the dark and into

Mass with unbrushed teeth, so perfectly did the nuns keep the Communion fast. Though it stood against the remains of a medieval priory, the convent as I knew it was of Victorian origin, all heavy red brick and ponderous Gothic-style arches which seemed not to soar but to lour at us schoolgirls as we knelt in the waft of incense.

Our chaplain in those days was Father Burke, who was tall and gaunt and rather Spanish-looking, in the way of the Black Irish, with soft dark curls that fell across his forehead. He looked as if he'd fallen out of bed to say the Mass, and we were all in love with him. In the candlelight we studied the glint of gold thread decorating his fiddleback chasuble. We admired the elegant fingers, like ribs in a vaulted ceiling, lifting the white host as the altar boy, some negligible figure dragged in from our brother school across the way, shook the silver notes from the sanctus bells. We knelt and received the Body of Christ, light and dry and vaguely salty, on our outstretched tongues. After that we went to our breakfast of tea and bread and margarine, and when we had done with that, our lessons.

Later, when Father Burke's reign had given way to that of Father Bogart, who was short and acne-riddled and had orange hair that stood up from his head like a Pentecost flame, I fastened my love onto Sister Bede, the sixth-form English mistress. Perhaps I loved her only because she had, inexplicably, taken a liking to me. I'd always been the sort of lumpish, tongue-tied child with whom teachers grew impatient. Even nuns, I think, prefer beauty and cleverness. Until I reached the sixth form, I had never been popular: not with my classmates, who thought me a bumpkin, and not with the sisters. To be fair, Sister Bede, too, could and did speak sharply to girls who exhibited dullness. But, for some reason beyond my understanding, she smiled on me. Naturally I bloomed a little in the light of Sister's approval, though I also admired her, disinterestedly I hope, for herself. That self was defined by two things: love of God and love of poetry in the English language. Another girl might have been inspired by her to seek the religious life. But it was the other thing in her that spoke to me.

Growing up, I had absorbed, like nutrients, all the poems and songs and stories in the Shetland dialect. Nobody in my family was educated, unless you counted Auntie Lass, but these were things you didn't go to school to know. They just came into you, like the wind or the summer light, out of the local air. Everyone breathed; everyone knew the fiddle tunes, the stories about witches and fairies, which we called *trows*. Though I was a Catholic and a Shetlander, not brought up to sympathize with the English, still I cheered for the Papa Stour Witch, whose wind-summoning had driven away the ships of the Spanish Armada, to save us all from King Philip and his Jesuits. So Granny Astrid told the story, shooting my mother looks the while from beneath her white brows. My mother, to her credit, at these times kept her eyes on the stocking she was darning—Granny's stocking, often enough. Our house did not have books, but we did have the Bible, which Granny Astrid read aloud in the evenings, after she had done with the other stories, flavoring even the gorgeous English words of the Stuart era with Norn. All that, I suppose, had given me the taste, or the ear.

Sister Bede was English, from Shropshire, she said. She had been at Oxford. Her postgraduate studies had been interrupted, so she told me, first by the war, then by her call to religious life. She had been writing on Robert Southwell, S.J., whose name she had later wanted to take in religion. Southwell being as yet uncanonized, she had had to settle—though it was hardly settling, she said with a laugh—for the

Venerable author of the first English history. Bede, after all, had told the story of Cædmon, the first English poet known to us by name, and of the inspired singing of his Hymn. Still and all, it was Southwell, the Elizabethan Jesuit, who had been Sister's first and most abiding human love.

Even now, without trying, I can transport myself to that school room, with its weak yellowish lights, its wintry smells of wet coats and galoshes and coal smoke, at the end of the autumn term. I can hear her voice, beautiful as her face was not, speak lines I would struggle to get by heart. They say that smell triggers memory, but it is those words that bring with them the smells of the particular lost day when I first heard them.

* * *

At Kings Cross Station, the air smelt of cold and diesel exhaust. So too did the air of the train compartment: someone had left the window open. I got up, shut it with a decisive bang, and sat down again with my book. I was trying, without much success, to read as I waited for the train to start. All the Christmas holidays—interminable, spent at home with my mother—I'd meant to be writing an essay on Southwell's "Mary Magdalen's Funeral Tears." Perhaps I might say, having finally read this remarkable prose piece, though I did not read it that day or for many years after, that what its author strove to do was to answer the Lord's own question: *Woman, why do you weep?* He joins the Magdalene at the empty tomb, where she grieves to find the stone rolled away, the body gone. In his sympathy he affirms to her, over the course of some pages, that while she weeps with the fervor of love, hers is a short-sighted love, looking for death, not life. It has gone to the cross, then the tomb; there it has stopped in its imaginings. In the morning light she has come to love a corpse, but now even that is taken from her. Her tears will turn to joy, but only after my Jesuit has explained to her—exhaustively, patiently, penetratingly, leaving no stone, as it were, unturned—why it is she stands weeping. In his pastoral effort to console her, to explain her to herself, he extends priestly absolution for her sorrow. All of this means something to me now.

But as I sat in the train, waiting for it to start, I had not read all that. If I had, what would it have said to me? I kept trying to read and think, but other things pushed in somehow. Some of them were things that I felt, on the whole, I should not let myself think about, and the effort of not thinking about them kept me from thinking at all. The holiday was over, the book hardly broached, the essay unbegun. In the dark of the previous morning, I had taken leave of my mother. All one long steely day I'd come across on the ferry from Lerwick to Aberdeen. From there, overnight, I had taken the train, the old Aberdonian, down to London. Now, in the morning, in a bleak, sleety weather, I sat alone in a second-class compartment, waiting for the train I was on to start east into the fenlands. My book lay open on my lap. As the train idled, almost empty at this hour, I shivered in my corner seat and watched the frozen rain fall on the lines outside.

The compartment door banged open, and with a rush of cold air a young man put his head in. I glowered at my book. People in trains were always banging in and out. You didn't notice them until they spoke to you. Then you were polite; still you didn't exactly notice them.

"Where is this train headed?" the door-banger said.

I looked up then. The voice was American, but not at all

like the American voices in the films I had seen. It emerged slowly into the air between us, sounding almost furred in its diction. I might have found it beguiling; firmly I took hold of myself. Nothing would beguile me, ever again.

I told him where the train terminated, a nondescript town at the end of the line, where East Anglia petered out into the North Sea.

"I don't want to go there," he said forlornly. "I don't even know what that is."

I took pity on him then. "Where is it exactly that you do want to go?"

He named my own destination.

"Yes, then," I said. "You've got the right train."

"Do you mind if I sit here?"

"I didn't pay for the whole compartment."

He looked puzzled. Perhaps my accent gave him difficulties.

"Sit where you like," I said, a shade more kindly.

He came in then, swinging an enormous suitcase, which he heaved into the rack above my head. With a thud he sat down across from me, rubbing his hands. "Sure is cold."

Suddenly my book was interesting. *Sorrow is the sister of Mercy*, I read.

With a jerk and a bang the train started. Outside, the tracks slid away, the trains waiting at other platforms. There were gray walls, then a tunnel, which made the lights in the carriage suddenly urinously bright. Then we were out again in daylight, brown houses and draggled gardens flashing past us, faster and faster, in the rain.

My companion leaned his head back and closed his eyes. With luck, I thought, he'd sleep for an hour. But even as the thought flickered through my mind, he opened them again and said, "Are you a student?"

"Yes." I was beginning to wish that this American had found another compartment to go banging into, another girl to interrogate. Of course a girl on public transport expects to be chatted up, especially if she is wearing the tiny black skirt she has bought herself for a belated Christmas gift during a lull before the train at Aberdeen, and wriggled into in the lav on the train. Today, though, I was in no mood for chatting.

"I'm Ransome Sain," my companion said next. "In high school they called me Handsome Ransome." When I didn't laugh, he looked anxious. "It's just a joke. I know I'm not handsome."

I granted him one fleeting, disinterested, unencouraging glance. Flick, and away. "You're not so bad."

It was true, he wasn't. Brown hair, a little bushy, with sideburns, which everyone wore in those unfortunate days. An overnight growth of beard. Hazel eyes, not green, not brown, but a bit of both. A round chin like a little boy's, a mouth that curved up with it. A face made for smiling, I thought. Real smiles, that meant something. Not the almond-eyed twitch that told me Dermott was laughing: Dermott, whom I loved, though he laughed at me. Laughed at me or, worse, didn't think me important enough to laugh at. I didn't want to think about this boy on the train. I wanted to think about Dermott. Again I applied myself to my book, the essay I meant to write for Dermott, whose pencil corrections were indecipherable and who did not care what I did.

We left London behind, with its clusters of terraced houses. The train stopped at Stevenage. My companion noted that this was where Vincent motorcycles were manufactured; perfunctorily I agreed that it was. Industry interested him. It did not interest me.

He remarked that he ought to have been in Vietnam, not England. "Got turned down. Diabetes."

I pretended to read my book. *Sorrow is the sister of Mercy.*

Gradually, even in the cold, the world along the railway lines began to be green, not gray. The houses gave way to woods, fields, cricket pitches, greener and greener, though the trees stood bare. In the little stations the train idled, again and again. In our carriage, nobody got on or off. Nobody looked into our compartment.

"That looks like an interesting book you're reading."

"Quite." I glared at the page till the words ran together.

Opposite me, my companion had shut his eyes again. He must be just off the plane, I thought. I had heard of jet lag, but I had never traveled by airplane, never gone far in any direction, never crossed any time zone. Though France lay across the English Channel, close enough to touch, I had never been there. Though Germany, Holland, and Denmark lurked just over the North Sea, though Shetland was closer to Norway and Iceland than anything else, I had never seen any of those places, either. On that particular day, I had traveled only the vertical length of Britain, yet I felt as steeped in exhaustion as if I had been to China. I would have shut my eyes, too, if I hadn't been afraid of sleeping through my station. Once asleep, I feared I might never wake up. I sat upright, steeled myself against the train's drowsy rocking, and trained my eyes again on the page. *Sorrow is the sister of Mercy, and a maker of compassion,* I read. I was sorrowful; might I then also become merciful? On balance I thought not. I felt too numb for mercy. Mentally I went through the contents of my handbag. I'd spent my last silver between trains at Kings Cross, on a skimpy cheese sandwich and a cup of tea. No taxi for me when I got off the train. No bus, either. I should have to walk the two miles back to my college.

With a sigh I returned to my reading. *Sorrow is the sister of Mercy, and a maker of compassion; weeping with others' tears and grieved with their harms. It is the salve and smart of sin.* Yes, well. I could have done with a bit more salve, a bit less of the smart I'd felt of late.

Now we had reached the edge of the fenland. We were coming through black winter fields, flat and flatter, threaded with ditches, water mirroring the sky. At last we were approaching our station. As the train slowed, my companion awoke.

"Where are you going, once you get off this train?"

Coolly I named my college.

In return he told me his lodgings, in a street I didn't know. "Is that anywhere near where you are?"

"No idea," I said.

"How do you get where you're going? Do you take a bus, or what do you do?"

"There's a taxi rank outside the station. That's the safest way if you don't know the town, and easiest if you've got luggage."

"Are you taking a taxi?"

I smiled an unfriendly smile. "I'll walk. I know my way, you see."

Once off the train, he extended his hand. "It sure was nice to meet you. I'll be here all spring. Maybe we'll run into each other sometime."

"That would be lovely." Of course I didn't mean it; it was something to say, that was all. Turning, I shouldered my rucksack and stalked off down the platform, leaving him to find his way. At that hour the station crowd was sparse, but I attached myself as best I could to little clumps of people headed out, so that he wouldn't see me strike off up the Station Road towards the town. I'd a sense, I suppose, that if I didn't put distance between us, he would want to attach himself to me. Perhaps he would want to help me. I was in no mood just then to give or accept any kindness.

The rain had slackened to a fine frozen mist that clung to my hair. Turning up my coat collar, wishing I'd something thicker on my legs than nylons, I trudged out to the Mill Road and began my long walk in earnest. In the bag on my shoulder, my book lay like a stony heart. I was colder than cold, and so tired. At the end of my walk, no one would receive me with any particular warmth.

I plodded up the road past the little shops—electronics, books, buckets of cellophane-wrapped flowers and knobbled stalks of Brussels sprouts, set outside shop doors to be rained on. I passed the grimy red-brick Anglican church of Saint Bartholomew, then the Salvation Army. Cars and buses, meanwhile, were passing me, spraying up cold water in great gray fans. I paid them no mind. I paid no mind, either, to the rattle of a taxi, until it had drawn up beside me and someone was leaning out of its door.

"For goodness sake, get in." It was my companion of the train.

"I'm all right," I said.

"You're going to freeze to death."

"No, I'm not. And —" I was too tired and cold for pride. "I've got no money with me. I can't pay."

"Do you think I'd let you pay? Get in."

The taxi man screwed down his window. "Get in or don't, love. Meter's running, and I'm stopping the traffic."

"I don't want —" I began.

But my companion had got out in the rain and was relieving me of my rucksack. "Get in the taxi, ma'am. You won't owe me a thing. I'm not about to let a lady get wet."

Mind you, when he said I wouldn't owe him anything, I chose to believe him. But when the taxi let me out, he noted my college. Though I managed to be out when he called round and asked for me—I was in hospital, in fact, for a stretch of that time—and I failed to return his telephone calls, still he knew how to find me.

In the spring of that year, as the days stretched out, golden at either end but still frigid, I began to talk long walks round the town, following the loop of the river. It was what I did instead of research, instead of writing, instead of tutorials. It was what I did by way of convalescence from an illness, but really, there was more to it than that. Though I hadn't yet gone down from the university, I had abandoned all hope of staying. I'd set Southwell aside—that drab, my old love. I considered that we'd parted ways forever. Alone, in the cold, I walked along the Backs, past the college gates, beneath the trees, then up a lane and over the quayside and down along an open common where cattle grazed, rained on and buffeted by the bitter March winds. On the far side of the river, daffodils grew from a college garden down the bank, to the very hem of the rain-roughened water. I pulled my hood up till my face was lost in its shadow, and I walked and walked.

Frequently, walking the towpath, I passed a particular pub, the Fort Saint George, which had a terrace giving onto the river. In the bright days of early autumn I had sat outside there, with friends, watching the boats, in a former life I hardly recognized as having been lived by me. When had I last seen the friends? Before Dermott. I'd cared for them only until he began to care for me. By the time he stopped caring for me, so had they. Presumably, just then, they were all going on with tutorials, reading, writing. They were waiting for the golden Trinity Term to roll round with its rowing, its garden parties and croquet, its Sunday afternoons on pub terraces in the sun. I had stopped the tutorials, the reading, and the writing. I had ceased to think about the summer. As far as I was concerned, the wind would always blow cold.

If I'd been capable of any emotion at all, I might have been surprised to encounter Ranse outside the Fort Saint George. Somehow he was always just going there, for a quick pub lunch or a drink. Being a Baptist, he drank nothing stronger than tea, preferably with ice, but he had developed a fondness for the Fort Saint George, he said. Always it seemed an accident, his catching me up on the towpath by the pub door.

"Oh, hey there," he would say.

I would answer with a monosyllable.

"I was fixing to go have me one of those ploughman's lunches. Have you eaten?"

Another monosyllable. I had not eaten. I didn't want to eat with Ranse. Really I didn't want to eat at all.

"Sure is cold, isn't it?"

I would agree tersely that it was. Perhaps he would intuit that I didn't want to talk to him. I hadn't the energy to say it.

"That coat's a pretty color. Makes your eyes real blue."

Grudgingly I thanked him. It was the sort of thing I would have given my life to hear Dermott say. Even then, when I knew there was no hope, I would have given my life to hear Dermott say anything. I would have offered my firstborn child, if such a thing had been possible, to have Dermott wait in ambush on the towpath.

"How's that book you're reading?" Ranse might ask as we walked. I didn't look at him, but I could feel him beside me. I could smell the wet down of his jacket.

"Which book?" I would say. "There are lots of books."

"You were writing a paper or something, weren't you?"

"Oh that." I would laugh harshly. "That's ancient history."

Another time, Ranse might command me to say something.

"Say something? Say what?"

"I don't know. Say *whistle.*"

"Why should I do that?"

If I said it, he would laugh. I could read the train timetables, all those place names, he told me, and he would listen to me all day long.

If I refused to say the word he wanted, he would still laugh. "I like your spirit."

"How I talk isn't a quirk of my personality," I told him. "There's an entire nation of people who talk like me."

"But they're not all you," he would say.

"Lucky them."

"What makes you say things like that?" He would stop, take my arm, and turn me so that I had to look at him. "See this pub? Come on in with me out of the cold. You think they'd make me a glass of iced tea?"

"I think they'd think you'd come from Pluto," I heard myself answer. I'd resolved not to speak to Ranse any more than was absolutely necessary to get rid of him. I was done with men, that was my line. Now he'd made me laugh.

"Why don't we go in and find out?"

I had to admit that it was interesting to watch him make this request. Several times already I had witnessed the round-eyed incredulity of a barmaid with her hand on the tap. Ice? In *tea?*

Tucked up round a corner table while the wind blew outside, he told me things about himself. I was reminded why he'd come to England, when he might have been tramping through the jungles of Vietnam.

"Isn't sugar poison for diabetes?" I asked, watching him pour a steady stream of it into his glass. White sediment filtered through the layered ice cubes, to lie an inch thick at the bottom.

For answer, he drew a little vial of insulin from his pocket.

"Sometimes you have to get the blood sugar *up*. But I also have my magic potion, just in case. Want to watch me take it?"

"God, no. Stop. I can't look."

I did not drink tea, iced or otherwise. Because he was paying, I ordered not a ladylike half, but a full pint, crowned with foam. When that was done, I asked for another. He would never drink with me, but cheerfully he paid for whatever I wanted and sat with me while I drank it. When would he tire of buying beer for me? Never, it seemed.

For some reason, I couldn't find it in me to refuse Ranse outright. I wanted him to go away, I told myself. When opportunities arose, however, I could never say it, not to his face. I went into the pub with him one day, then another and another. He sat over his iced tea; I sat over my Old Speckled Hen. *Now,* I kept telling myself as I had a second, then a third. *Say it now.*

But he was too busy talking about where he came from to have heard me. It was a small place, he told me. "Everybody knows everybody, pretty much. If you moved in any time after 1635, you're a newcomer. People look at you funny. Or else they think you're the new Methodist minister. They change out every four years."

"I know places like that," I said.

Eventually I found I'd accepted an invitation to dinner. I drank wine; he pressed the long-suffering waiter for sweet tea with ice. No sweet tea? Well, tea. Yes, cold, with ice. And lots of sugar on the side. I laughed at him. He laughed as if my derision, of all things, charmed him most. By that time the days had lengthened out into endless chilly sun-washed twilights: April, then May. I was still walking the loop of the river every day, but I no longer walked it alone.

On one of these walks, almost by accident, Ranse let spill

the information that he would be returning to the States at Midsummer. Perhaps I would go with him?

"What do you mean, *go with you*? You know I've got no money to travel like that."

With elaborate patience, he said, "I *mean,* I wonder if you'd marry me."

I looked away at the river. The spring had been wetter than usual. The moored narrowboats rode high and bumped the grassy bank. Above the weir, a swan and two gray cygnets paddled implacably against the surging current.

"Why not?" I said at last.

I felt, rather than saw, his eyes on my face. "Now, look. Don't just say what I want to hear."

"I'm not saying what you want to hear." It was true. What he wanted to hear was that his proposal had caught me up into the third heaven. I would not say that.

He jostled me with his elbow. "You know what I like about you? You don't flicker your eyes around and act all, I don't know."

"Act all how, exactly?"

"You know. However it is girls act. Like you're supposed to read their minds. You just say things straight out. No buttercream frosting on the cake."

No, no buttercream frosting on the cake. At the time, I'd never heard of buttercream frosting. And of course there was much I didn't say. But I had told the truth, as far as it went. I didn't mind the idea of marrying him. I thought him kind and honorable. If I could manage some semblance of kindness and honor in return, then we might both do worse. Having read the paperback novels, I had taken it as a matter of course that I would find what people called *The One*. If finding *The One* had not been precisely what I had gone up to university to do, still I had entertained the possibility. Now

I did not. If I had not exactly come to disbelieve in the existence of *The One*, I no longer believed that I would meet him.

Or more precisely, I had met him, but I had turned out to be one of those unlucky people who are doomed never to be loved in return. To want someone was to be, myself, unwanted by the very person I would have died to have. When I roused myself to think of the future at all, I saw before me a long twilight, full of shadows, unwinding endlessly from the time when I'd been alive, reaching toward the moment when I could finally declare myself dead. Meanwhile, in the heedless world of the living, spring was lengthening into summer. The river filled with punts and laughter. People went to May Balls and lay about on the grass in stages of undress. Transistor radios set up their tinny wailings. *Love the one you're with,* went one new song, over and over, everywhere I turned in that weather. *Love the one you're with!*

I might as well, I said to myself at last. I might at least try.

When we landed in Charlotte, after a hasty registry-office wedding, a dash for the airport bus, and a largely silent transatlantic flight, we were greeted at the gate by Ranse's mother and a girl who looked at me once, then looked away. I later learned he'd gone to the senior prom with her. Behind the rail they stood waving frantically as we staggered from the plane. Big square Mrs. Sain had worn a green belted pantsuit, daring for her. In all the time I knew her, I hardly ever saw her in trousers, but for Ranse's homecoming she had acquired this almost fashionable outfit. The afternoon light through the concourse windows lay on her powdered cheeks as it might lie on an undusted sideboard.

Not that any sideboard in her house would ever accrue the slightest grain of dust. I would come to find that out. In hindsight, I am surprised all over again to find her wearing neither hat nor gloves. Perhaps the girl had talked her out of them, that girl in her yellow baby-doll dress, pale hair teased high and sprayed. When we emerged from the jetway, Ranse gripping my hand in a spasm of pride and possessiveness, both their jubilant faces froze into identical expressions of horror. Ranse, always frugal, had not rung his mother between the registry office and the airport. In fact, he appeared not to have rung his mother at all that spring. Or written to her. If he had written, he had written selectively.

I climbed into in the back seat of the blue Buick, all gleaming white interior. I sat beside that girl with her bubble of blonde hair, her smile hardened into place, her gaze fixed on the scenery sliding past. I looked at the scenery, too, though I saw none of it. Up front, Ranse drove while his mother told him all the Annesdale news. We let the other girl out at the foot of her driveway. Though Annesdale is a small place, by the grace of God I have managed never to see her again.

A subtler man might have realized that this was no way to begin a marriage. Ranse wasn't subtle, and he noticed nothing wrong. He called goodbye to that girl as cheerfully as if we'd all just been on a picnic together, and I said to myself, I have ruined my life. Mind you, I'd nothing to go back to. I'd gone down from the university. My mother was dead. I had only my aunt, to whom my mother had left her house. I didn't want to go back there. Auntie Lass had spent her life sending children from the safe haven of nursery out into the terrible world. It was for my own good, I told myself, that I went forward, not back.

But I was stranded on the wrong side of the world. I'd only the clothes in my rucksack, the same rucksack Ranse had taken from my shoulders, that frozen day. Clothes, a necklace, one earring—I'd lost the other clip-on in the plane. On the third finger of my left hand, a simple gold ring bought in a charity shop. Did I mention that Ranse was frugal? I had those things to my name, plus a box of books and oddments I'd had sent by slow boat. And the man for whom I had done all this was too simple to see that the girl striding to her front door in high heels had expected to marry him herself.

Women often say that men are like children. Over and over I made the mistake of thinking Ranse simple, but he wasn't. Once, I came upon him teaching himself Russian for his own amusement. He liked crossword puzzles, number puzzles, birdwatching, biographies of American Civil War generals. In his working life, he developed new sorts of synthetic textiles, better and more wearable polyesters. His Charlotte firm, to which he commuted daily from our house in the country, had an office in Düsseldorf. He traveled often. He was not a stupid or unsophisticated or uninteresting man. But he had a child's openness, an instinctive trust that you would deal as honestly with him as he dealt with you. This meant that he could be hurt. Knowing that he could be hurt, I kept myself under careful check, so as not to wound him. When I might have spoken, I was silent. When there were things I might have told him, I kept them to myself. If I held myself at a distance, I reasoned, it was because I loved him, not because I didn't. Did I tell myself the truth? That I wish I knew.

* * *

Though Ranse was dead, death hadn't rendered him absent, not exactly. I could find his pocketknife in a drawer by now and not want to weep. Still I often felt him about me, a mild presence, sometimes reproachful. After he died, as I've said, I'd had the carpeting taken out, the wall-to-wall his mother had regarded as a luxury. To me the carpeted house had felt suffocating, a woolly cocoon. Despite my mother-in-law's constant hoovering, and mine, it never felt clean. I missed the uncompromising stone floors of our house in Shetland, lashed to a shine by Granny Astrid's broom. Also, I'd been shown early snapshots of this house. I knew that there were good wood floors underneath that smothering of carpet. Mr. Ransome, Senior, had demanded the best of everything, including the narrow red-oak planks whose waxy sheen was evident in the multicolored light of various photographed nineteen-fifties Christmas trees. Ranse had not cared about the oak floors, which he knew were there. In timber country like this, all those years ago, oak had not been a luxury. Carpeting was. Mama had bought herself that wall-to-wall after Daddy died. It was still perfectly good. Ranse liked the way it felt underfoot. If I experienced a niggling guilt as it was cut apart, ripped up, and carried outside in rolls and shreds, I also felt intensely satisfied to see the true floor beneath. I thought Mr. Ransome, Senior, might share my feeling. But at my shoulder, I could feel Ranse chiding me. *Why?*

One damp late-September evening, as the rainy twilight shone on my beautiful floors, I discovered that in other, less pleasantly mournful ways, I was not alone. As I idled at my kitchen window, eating bread and butter for my supper, trying after all these years to recite "The Burning Babe" from memory, my eye caught a streak of movement across the floor.

"*A pretty Babe all burning bright*," I said, and stopped.

Something about that movement did not suggest a palmetto bug, one of those big hard-shelled cockroaches which regularly invaded the house in wet weather. Though Ranse had repeatedly assured me that they were harmless and no reflection on my housekeeping, I hated them. I took grim delight in sucking them up with the hoover, hearing them scratch and rattle as they went up the tube. This, however, seemed bigger than that, darker and more solid. I thought I might have imagined it. But later, after I'd set my book aside, snapped off the light, and lain back in bed to wait for sleep to find me, I heard a whisper of movement in my closet, an infinitesimal scrabble of claws.

"Damn," I said out loud.

2

Annesdale was, and is, a small town. When I first took up with it, it was the sort of town that seems smaller than it is. At that time it was larger than Lerwick by several thousand souls, yet it looked shrunken, fallen in on itself, all empty storefronts and redundant textile mills. To me as a *peerie lass*, Lerwick had seemed a vast city. Buildings on buildings, it ascended the gentle rise that sloped back from the harbor. Most of the houses, the churches, and the public buildings were built of stolid Scots granite, but some had the look of Norse longhouses, painted in brilliant red or blue. I don't remember a time when my world lacked a view of Lerwick rocking toward us over the clear, creaming water as we sat waiting for it in my father's boat.

At some point, of course, I began to know that it was we who moved, Lerwick which stood and waited for my father to hand me up to it from the boat. My mother would reach down her hands to me. I would reach up to her. The town went on rising before us, rumpling and gray against the dim cold land: houses, houses, houses, crowded together beneath the marbled sky.

I can still hear myself marveling at it. "Are there so many people in the world, then?" I can still hear that rare sound, my mother laughing aloud.

No one would ever marvel this way over Annesdale. Even now it's no better than a bedroom community, an oversprawl of nearby Charlotte. *Near the City, Near Perfect,* the town's motto goes. *Near* is one way to put it. People move into new houses built on old farmland. They come and go from those houses, transient. They sleep in Annesdale, but their lives occur elsewhere. The empty storefronts have filled up with antique malls and florists, the sorts of businesses that cater to day trips rather than daily life. The largest of the old textile mills has had its decaying brick painted over and become something called a *brew pub.* As clearly as if he were here, I can hear Ranse pronounce those words. *Brew? Pub?* He would mean *a place where you can't get sweet tea.* I merely wonder what other sort of pub there could possibly be.

When I first came to Annesdale, it felt less like Lerwick than like my own straggled village, which in my childhood had already begun hemorrhaging its young. Mostly people went to Lerwick, of course: not far, but the village felt their escape. Sometimes they went to Aberdeen, or even Glasgow. Sometimes they went so far away that nobody knew where they'd gone, or spoke of them again.

Along the one-lane island road, the central houses, including our own, stood solidly inhabited. Farther out from the village, many of the old stone croft buildings had emptied and begun their slow collapse. When I was born, the island population had numbered perhaps thirty. By the time I left, it had dwindled by half. Even the relatively prosperous stone cottages clustered round the post office, the pub, the chapel, and the empty-shelved general store, stood out defiantly in a general atmosphere of absence that had settled on them like bad weather.

I might, then, have felt almost at home in Annesdale. The down at heels Main Street with its vacant-windowed storefronts could have been my own road, translated to an oceanless landscape that shimmered with alien summer heat.

The white ashlar-stone courthouse, all Greek pediments and columns and weather-stained grandiosity, was only a more self-conscious suggestion of our island's low, white-framed community center, which held dances and wedding dinners and had at various times served the village as both hospital and jail.

As a child, Ranse had known the shops that had occupied the Annesdale storefronts. He had wandered in and out of them with friends, and into the cinema on Saturdays. To me none of it had a history. Those blank windows held Ranse's memories, not mine. Having come upon the town in its decline, I saw it as having been always in decline. Nothing was, anymore, what it had started out to be. A church, for example, occupied the old Main Street cinema. The Exodus Church, it called itself.

"What's up with this Exodus Church, anyway?" I can still hear a woman's ringing voice inquiring of the narthex at large, one weekday noon after Mass. I can still feel her hand on my arm, her fingers communicating urgency, though she didn't seem to be speaking of anything in particular, to anyone in particular. Her hand had reached out; it had landed, by chance, on me.

"I keep passing that church on my way here, and then I can't stop thinking about it. *Exodus Church.* All through Mass, I'm thinking about the Exodus Church. What the hell do people do there? Get up and leave?"

It was by chance that Janet Malkin had seized on me. Holy chance, someone more pious than I might call it. Not that I felt that anything holy had occurred. A trap had been set for me, and I had been caught in it. Ranse was newly dead. I had begun to turn up for Mass every day at noon. The worship of God had seemed preferable, just, to stewing away the day alone in bed. I merited no reward for my efforts, but now God had seen fit to grant me a dubious one. He had sprung Janet on me: Janet, new to the parish, joggling a serious-eyed baby against her breast, waiting at the door to pin down someone with her conversation. I was not entirely gratified to be that someone. I wanted to go home. With some envy I watched other women walk out in twos and threes, talking impregnably among themselves. There I was, meanwhile, alone and vulnerable, pinned down.

Joggle joggle went Janet's arms, holding the baby. Blink blink went the baby's solemn eyes. Talk talk went Janet, for a long time, while I was conscious of having forgotten to eat any breakfast. What was up with the Exodus Church? Why was the Bi-Lo supermarket called *Bi-Lo,* when Food Lion was cheaper? Why did people in Annesdale call pine-needle mulch *pine straw?* It wasn't straw; it was pine needles. What was up with that? And if anybody knew how to lose forty pounds without going on a twelve-hundred-calorie diet, she was all ears.

As I soon learned, Janet was a repository of questions and commentary, a conversation in search of something to be about. She was a compulsive talker, I a compulsive—I was going to say *listener*, but that's going too far. I was a compulsive non-talker, which was good enough for Janet. As we stepped out of the church, day after day, week after week, year after year, she would turn to me and begin to talk. There would go the next hour. By the time I got home, I would be starved for my lunch, but strangely over-sated with something else.

Janet and her husband Howard were the parents of a large family, a whole human gamut ranging from a twenty-year-old in a mantilla to that blinking baby in arms. At Mass they were difficult to miss, as I might have mentioned. Even for Catholics, the number of children they had was unusual in this age. I never was certain how many children there were. In the back pew their number seemed continuously to expand and contract and scintillate. I could never get them in focus. Out of church, they separated and ran wild with other children, dissolving into the general atmosphere. It was impossible to count them.

Howard, a large, gentle-eyed man, habitually wore a yarmulke, which everyone must have noticed but nobody wanted to ask about. As Father said, people did have their reasons. As I myself had reason to know, many people—perhaps more people than not—made incomprehensible marriages and spent their lives, in one way or other, unequally yoked. If Howard's actual convictions remained a mystery, still he came compliantly enough with his wife and children to Mass. In this he was one better than my father, even than Ranse. If Father Schuyler noticed that Howard didn't present himself for communion, the rest of us politely averted our eyes. Any of us might have had our reasons. I went forward with my gaze fastened on my clasped hands, resolving to notice nothing but the state of my own soul, which was mostly boring in the extreme.

Janet and Howard came from a leafy, affluent New Jersey township whose name meant something to people from New Jersey. They had gone through years of school together, Moriarty behind Malkin in the alphabetical seating chart.

"The year Monica Meraglia was in our class, that was a bad year," Janet said. "I spent the whole freaking year trying to burn a hole through her head with my eyes. I thought if she even *spoke* to Howie, I was gonna deck her. Seventh grade. What a time."

"Even then she loved me." Howard's heavy-lidded brown eyes made him look always half-asleep. His chins had begun to melt into his neck. Looking at him, a grown man in a too-big flannel shirt whose tails hung nearly to his knees, I was hard-pressed to imagine the boy for whom Janet would have decked poor Monica Meraglia. Howard liked to lay his large, warm hand on your arm when he spoke to you. He made prolonged, significant eye contact, behind which you sensed a certain amount of effort. Janet, her curly hair standing out wildly round her head, dealt with their many children in a casual way that almost shocked me. If a child fell over in her presence and scraped its knee, she said, "You're okay. Up you get. Run along." If Howard saw a child fall over, he would kneel, put his arms round it, agree solemnly that the scrape had hurt, and propose to buy ice cream for everybody. Janet said that this was why their children were always falling over and getting scrapes. "Every kid in my house knows: if you want something, wait for Dad to come home. Then start bleeding and cry."

"Yeah, yeah," Howard would say. Always he stood to one side, round-shouldered, anxious, a little disconsolate, clustered with children. Invariably he added, for emphasis, "I don't *like* for people to be sad."

"We were a match made in heaven," Janet would tell me. "Nice Jewish boy: socially bar mitzvahed. Nice Irish girl: socially baptized."

I could think of worse matches, myself.

"You can imagine how much our parents loved us. As *us,* I mean, as individuals we were fine. As people who got pregnant with each other on grad night, not so much."

If you wanted to know what Janet was like, I would tell you: *He got me pregnant in the bushes by Kimberly Cohen's pool house.* It was a story all her children knew by heart.

"Howie's mother came to see me," Janet said. "She's some kind of doctor. Like his brother's an eye doctor. That's the kind of people they are. All doctors and lawyers. His mother told me, *Babies are nice—when you've made partner.* That was the plan. Howie was in at Yale, perfect test scores. I mean, look at him, *obviously* he's brilliant. I was very much not part of the plan."

That I could imagine. Still my mind said: Stop! Already I had learnt far more than I ever wanted to learn about Janet and Howard. Don't tell me, I often longed to cry. Relentlessly, in the church narthex or the car park or the rosary garden, nursing her baby, then watching him toddle about, Janet unwound her life story for me. Don't, I kept wanting to implore her. It's too much. I wanted to say the things you say when people offer over-generous gifts: when you've sent a Christmas card, and they respond by buying you a refrigerator. I can't possibly accept such a thing. Or when they urge food on you, and you choke at the thought of one more bite. But always I found myself too mesmerized, or paralyzed, to say anything at all.

Janet, naturally, interpreted my silence as a signal to keep going. "Howard's parents grounded him. They took away his driver's license. All my dad said was, *It's your rope, go hang yourself.* And then he got remarried to some woman he met at a gas station. Couldn't pump her own gas. He had her five kids and a bunch of her grandkids, and now he's gone, and I don't know a soul of them."

Janet spread her hands to show me how empty they were. What are you gonna do, she meant. Indeed, what were you gonna do? I had no good answer.

Janet and Howard's answer, at the age of eighteen, each of them armed with a high-school diploma, had been to run away and get married. "I drove," Janet said. "I had this old banged-up silver Toyota my dad had handed down to me so he wouldn't have to take me everywhere. Howie was still grounded. He climbed out of his bedroom window, and off we went."

All this was another story their children knew by heart. The county office building's janitor had stood witness for them. Married, armed with their combined graduation cash, they had embarked on a life together, roving about, following whatever jobs a young man who might have gone to Yale could secure. Currently Howard worked as some sort of manager in a factory that made dishwasher components, a position that at least came with health insurance, Janet said. As a sideline to his factory work, he refurbished and resold old cars. Janet had told me that in their driveway, at any given time, there were six or seven cars in various stages of dismantlement, out of which Howard perpetually hoped to construct one car that ran. This too I felt I could imagine.

"We never really went to church," Janet told me. "My family, I mean. Like, I made my First Communion, because they have to have the picture of you in the white dress and the veil and gloves, holding your rosary and looking all prayerful, to hang in the stairwell with all the pictures of your sisters in the same dress and veil and rosary. Except I didn't have any sisters. It was just me. One gigantic picture of me. And then it was like okay, punch the card, clock out, goodbye. I went to Catholic school until halfway through third grade, but then my mom died. After that, my dad believed in the public schools. I gotta hand him that. If he hadn't, I would never have met Howie."

"Our whole family got *married* in church, though," her daughter Lucy might put in, if she was within earshot. "The ones that were born, anyway. I was flower girl. Mom let me wear this pink tutu we'd found in a thrift store, and fairy wings. Moshe was ring bearer, only he lost the ring, and Dad had to use the ring off the car keys until the real one turned up. Moshe had put it on his toe, inside his shoe, for safekeeping, but then he forgot it was there. Mom pushed Dominic down the aisle in a stroller."

"*And* I was pregnant with Hannah. That was some wedding. I'll have to show you the pictures sometime. Howie was a good sport." Janet laughed. "I mean, *legally*, we were married already. But I had had this conversion experience, or whatever, and I put it to him that it was get married in church, or he was my brother. We both like sex a little too much for that."

Stop, I wanted to say. At the same time, for once I could nod with actual understanding. When Ranse had met me, I had been, in practice, a non-churchgoer, if not actually an unbeliever. Though he kept many Baptist opinions to himself, he had assumed without asking that, as his wife, I would accompany him and his mother to church. It was in the natural order of things; that was his view. In the short time I had known him, I had not thought to speak of being a Catholic, for the simple reason that I had ceased to think of myself in those terms. Having no church of my own, then, he reasoned, I could only benefit by going with him to his. As my husband, it was his job to do things for my good. As his wife, it was my job to say, *yes, dear*. Though I might have chafed at this state of affairs, I could see no good reason to argue with him about church. I had gone with him, dutifully enough, Sunday after Sunday, year after year, until one Sunday I jarred him with the news that all on my own I had gone to the Catholic Church, to Mass. I had made my confession. I had received the Eucharist. I wished to continue to receive the Eucharist, as I had slipped out to do first thing that morning, while he was still smiling over the funny papers.

"Well, that's fine, I guess, if it's what you really want to do." He had looked honestly perplexed, and a little hurt. "I still think a wife ought to go to church with her husband."

"Of course I'll go with you," I said. "Mass is at nine. I can be in and out and back home by a quarter past ten. You'll be drinking your coffee. You won't even notice I've gone. But there is one thing."

I had expected him to balk at the notion of a marriage convalidation. I could have predicted what he said. "I meant it the first time. I don't see any point in saying it all again." In the end, however, I talked him round. That I had gone uncomplainingly to church with him all those years struck home.

"All right," he said at last. "If it means that much to you, we can do that marriage thing. But you never said a word about it before."

"I'm saying it now," I told him.

How and why do we come to these moments? Again: someone more pious might call it holy chance. That, and the mark of your baptism. It can fade like a childhood scar, so that you forget it's there. But then, without warning, something happens to it. You knock it against something and feel the twinge. Ah, yes. There it is.

I did not raise the possibility of a Josephite marriage with Ranse. Did we like sex too much for that? We didn't dislike it. If it hadn't seemed exactly an adventure—if its outcome was always certain—if there had been children, if things had been different—well. It was nice enough. Let's leave it at that. Like going together to the Baptist church at eleven o'clock of a Sunday, it was one more thing that married people did. Ranse, I feel sure, would have insisted that this was so. To my own credit, I did not make him say it.

Janet said, "Every time I had a baby, the doctor would ask me if I wanted my tubes tied, or if my husband was getting a vasectomy this time, or if, you know, something, because obviously we didn't know where all these babies were coming from. And I always said no, even though, I mean, I don't know why. Maybe it was because every doctor sounded like Howie's mother. And I guess we just thought, well, we like sex, and if we make these new cool people to hang out with, fine, no problem. It was fun, you know? It wasn't anything religious. It was just, I don't know. We like living dangerously. You know what I mean."

I did not, as it happened, know what she meant at all. I'd not the faintest idea what Janet's version of living dangerously felt like.

"But then. Then!" Her sea-glass eyes widened. "There was this one time. Things were, you know, not good. In the financial department. Like really not good. We went with all the kids to this shelter deal that served dinner, and it was in this inner-city Catholic church, like in a neighborhood where you'd get knifed if you had to stop and change a tire. There were a lot of places like that."

Living dangerously, I thought.

"So we ate the dinner in the parish hall, and we said thank you for the diapers and stuff they gave us, and we were leaving, but before we left, I just—I don't know. I went into the church by myself. I don't know why. I just did. It was like something had called me, and I had to go see what it was. Howie and the kids were outside, in the car, like come on, come on, we want to get out of here before we get knifed. I'd told them I had to go to the bathroom. Instead, I sat down in the church in the dark. I looked at the tabernacle up there behind the altar. I felt like what was in the tabernacle was sitting there looking at me. And I thought, all right. Screw this. You're real. You win."

Always I wanted to push her talk away from me. Thank you, but I've had enough. I couldn't eat another bite. But day to day, week to week, year to year, her conversation continued to wash over me, a surge tide that never turned.

The Malkins' life presented itself continually as a jumble of removals, rented houses, First Communions with one mislaid white shoe, scrambles to pay for Confirmation retreats. From all this, over time, I learnt a lot about Janet. Howard I knew only as the good sport. Dutifully he appeared at Sunday Mass with his brood of children, his ill-fitting clothes, his yarmulke on his head. What were his actual beliefs? I wondered, but I would never have asked.

As it was, I felt I'd already learnt far more than was strictly my business. I had made a point of not noticing whether Howard, or anyone else, went forward for Communion. Hadn't I, after all, sat through decades of Sunday services at Spake's Fork Baptist Church? Hadn't that been one of the inevitable compromises that make a marriage happy enough? Hadn't I received my own compromise in return? As Father Schuyler had rightly pointed out, people did have their reasons. They made their arrangements, and their peace. I thought of my father handing my mother and me onto the quayside at Lerwick, the blue boat turning to nose its way home across the clear rumpling water. It was better, most of the time, not to inquire too closely—better, or easier.

"How ya doing?" Howard would ask in passing. He always wanted to know how you were. He seemed to feel he *had* to know how you were. I would murmur some response, but somehow I never found out how *he* was. Howard was quiet, the audience for Janet's talk, the occasional word in edgewise. Only once in all the time I had been acquainted with the Malkins, had Howard and I ever managed more than the most cursory exchange.

It was before the Easter Vigil, the spring after Ranse had died, or possibly the spring after that. A late Easter: the dogwoods were blooming. The congregation, that remnant who liked long Masses on Saturday nights, had gathered outside the church. Father Trotter, who was to light the Easter fire in a little brazier, was nowhere to be seen.

We clustered round the church door with our unlit candles, remarking on the fineness of the weather exactly as if Jesus Christ of Nazareth were not about to rise from the dead. I didn't know I was standing next to Howard until he touched my shoulder.

"Do you ever miss where you come from?" he asked me.

What a question. Did I? Taken off-guard, I floundered for a response. "Of course, I've been a long time away," I said at last. "I wouldn't recognize it now. It wouldn't be the same place at all."

"Yes, but do you miss it?"

Where was Janet? Home with some unwell child? Had she been present, she would have rescued me. "Oh, Howie," she would have said. "Don't ask people such personal questions." Janet, who had no privacy to speak of, was fierce when it came to the privacy of others. *Tell,* was her policy. *Don't ask.*

I might have welcomed the interruption. As it was, I had to fend for myself. "Yes and no," I said. "There are always things you miss, aren't there? Smells, even. Things that surprise you—"

I forgot that I was talking to Howard. In that instant, I was lost in the toss of the boat, the silver sea, the gleam of the westering sun as we went over, my mother and I, my father at the tiller, to Lerwick on Holy Saturday in the afternoon, for the Easter Mass in the morning. After that Mass and a quick, hardly celebratory breakfast, we'd hurry down to the pier again, in time to meet my father as he came from his own early service. His sect didn't observe Easter, that foremost of the traditions of men. Still, Sunday was Sunday. But it was the Saturday I remembered, coming over the sound into the harbor, the town and its low blue headlands before us, the wake creaming behind us, the gulls and skuas skating across the air, a seal's bright glance from the mercurial water as we hurried along the harborside and into the streets, the long cold golden dusk of the northern springtime.

"Right now I miss Passover," said Howard.

Startled out of my thoughts, I turned to him. But at that moment Father Trotter emerged with the altar servers, the Paschal Candle, the lighter fluid and the box of matches. The fire blazed, and whatever Howard might have said next went up in its smoke.

* * *

On Saturday afternoons I went to confession. Like many older people, I imagine, I had long since run through my stock of active mortal sins. I had no more fornication to report, no killing of any kind, literal or metaphorical, no mother or father to dishonor, no child to provoke. I kept the Sabbath holy enough, I felt. There was nothing anyone else had that I particularly wanted: not goods, not donkeys, not husbands or wives. I was habitually truthful and did not gossip. What I had to confess was only what lies at the root of anything anyone has to confess, which was that I did not love God with all my heart, soul, mind, and strength, or my neighbor as myself. All I ever had to say in the confessional was some mundane variation on the theme of original sin.

By September, Father Schuyler had begun to alarm the parish. Already the new was burnishing off, and he was, to all appearances, wearing thin. It wasn't just that he looked thin, although he did. *Does that man not eat?* In Mass I heard the whispers, as Father advanced into the church like Christ at the gates of Jerusalem, heralded by a flock of nervous-looking small altar servers, all boys. Previously we had had girls on the altar. Several prominent families had made a great show of leaving the parish when Father dismissed their daughters from service.

At first there was whispering. Then there was muttering. Then there was alarm and bewilderment. Before Mass, Father displayed himself in church, praying in apparently unassailable silence. "You hate to bother him," people said. There was something holy and unexpected about the sight of the priest on his knees, alone before the altar. Father Trotter had certainly not behaved in this fashion. He had stood round the church door smoking and talking until it was time to vest.

When Father did finally arise from his prayers, people at the back of the church gathered themselves to spring at him, but he was too quick for them. Straightway he ducked into the sacristy and locked himself in. The choir director had to guess whether or not Father would anticipate an introit before the entrance hymn. The faith formation director was forced to consider when else to announce a mandatory parents' meeting, if not at the end of Mass. Altar boys had to hammer to be let in for their cassocks and cottas. After Mass, again Father rushed away into the sacristy, and again locked the door. This entire ritual was repeated later for the Spanish Mass. Avoidance, I thought in bemusement, was underappreciated as a universal language.

It was also rumored that Father no longer accepted invitations to dinner. *Well, he doesn't eat anyway,* people said. More and more Father's thinness had begun to look like gauntness, and even people who didn't like him, which by now was practically everybody, were worried. As I suppose is drearily and everlastingly the norm, it was the women who talked. "Is Father just going to waste away?" I had heard one lady ask another recently, as we all emerged from daily Mass. "Into thin air?"

"Not before he's got us all speaking Latin," her companion had responded darkly.

A third lady added, "It's the young people I feel bad for. They won't know what any of it means."

Had we, when we were young people, known what any of it meant? I had wanted to ask, but of course I hadn't. They were talking to each other, not to me. It might have been school all over again. But then the question of whether he was a drinker or a drugger raised itself. At that point, recalling my Monday occupation, groups of women I'd never exchanged five words with would turn to me in the narthex corner, to confirm or deny this whispered hypothesis. Though I too found Father mystifying, the eagerness in their eyes made me angry.

"I've seen no evidence of anything like that," I would say in my chilliest voice, then proceed to the car park while the women looked after me, shaking their heads and wondering aloud what bee I'd got in my bonnet now.

But for all his obvious discomfort with the human race, Father was good at confessions. His more severe homilies, in fact, emphasized our universal human need for forgiveness, and as a result, more of us had been rattled into discovering this unexpected talent of his. There were always queues for confession now. Behind the rattan folding screen, a piece of jumble-sale detritus that had migrated to the former janitorial cupboard grandly rechristened as the *Reconciliation Room,* Father heard our confessions with a great and surprising gentleness. He praised Jesus for the graces of a good confession, offered us kindly if rigorous counsel, and absolved us, giving the tenderest emphasis to the words, *Your sins are forgiven; go in peace.* Possibly it was there, at his most invisibly *in persona Christi,* that he felt safest and most himself.

On that September Saturday, Father heard me out, assured me of God's love and boundless mercy, and sent me on my way with the Joyful Mystery of the Visitation as my penance. Relieved, though I hadn't considered myself to be in serious danger, I came out clutching my rosary and knelt in a pew to pray. In other pews, a few other people also knelt. The votive candles shivered on their metal risers before the statue of Our Lady to the left of the sanctuary, and before Saint Joseph to the right. As I performed my penance, a woman came in with a little girl. She pressed the child's shoulder to remind her to genuflect before the tabernacle. There was a clank of coins, and they lit a candle together, the woman's hand guiding the girl's as it held the taper. The air smelt of candles and also, faintly, of last Sunday's incense. Despite the ostentatious congregational coughing that accompanied it, Father was obdurately generous in wafting our prayers about on thick resiny clouds whose aftermath lingered.

There, as always, stood the blond pine table that served as our altar. There, as always, was the matching wooden tabernacle, its door veiled with what looked like Auntie Lass's net curtain. On either side of the tabernacle hung stained-glass sanctuary light boxes, each representing one of the Four Evangelists, which waited to be switched on, blink blink blink blink, to signal the start of Mass.

In his early weeks, Father Schuyler had preached often on the need to offer God our best. Clearly he had meant to lay groundwork for a radical renovation, if not a whole new church. The parish could afford neither of those things. Anyone could have told him that. Anyone could have told him, further, that people had given money for those Evangelists and were attached to them. In the meantime, he had quietly instituted some smaller and more ephemeral changes, to which nobody could object. The Gregorian chant, for example, unspooling serenely in the quiet from a CD played over the sound system, changed the complexion of things remarkably. It seemed to me as much a building material as brick or corrugated metal. If people's complaints amounted to a set of home truths, nevertheless Father deserved some credit, I thought. The chant CD was a stroke of insight. As I bent my concentration on Mary and Elizabeth and the babes who greeted each other, womb to womb, from the back of the church came a wordless murmur of human voices like waves on a distant shore.

Coming out of the church I met Lucy Malkin holding her little brother's hand. Lucy was the eldest of Janet's many children. Though the children ran together in my mind, I did know Lucy at one end, Henry at the other. At twenty-three or four, Lucy was pretty in the natural way of young women who take their freshness for granted and never recognize it as beauty. Only in middle age, coming across old photographs of themselves, are they shocked, too late, by this realization. Seeing Lucy, I could easily imagine how Janet had looked at the same age, with black curls, a clear freckled skin, eyes like sea glass, not green, not blue.

Lucy was old enough to be out of the house and doing something. She should have gone to college, but there was no money for college. At the moment she worked as a cashier in the Bi-Lo supermarket. The rest of her time she spent, cheerfully enough it seemed, with her family at home. Henry, aged four, leaning now at her side, had the same enormous light eyes as his sister. While Lucy's eyes sparked—all of Lucy radiated energy—Henry's were quiet and full of thought. I remembered those eyes going blink blink, like the Evangelists, as Janet joggled him up and down against her breast. Henry had been a grave, courtly, elderly sort of infant. In the intervening years he had grown taller, but his demeanor was much the same.

"How's your mother?" I asked Lucy, for Janet was pregnant again. I asked as a matter of convention, expecting no particular answer, for Janet seemed always in excellent form.

In her carrying voice Lucy said, "Well, she's been having some vaginal bleeding."

If you wanted to know what Lucy was like, I would tell you: *vaginal bleeding.*

At once I was paying attention. "Is she all right?"

In my childhood I had known babies to be lost, women to die. Grownups never whispered such things in the presence of children, but said them right out, as cautionary tales.

"She is all right?" I repeated, as Lucy had stopped to dig a wadded mantilla out of the pocket of her jeans. She and her sisters always wore mantillas in church and, on Sundays, tiny dresses that showed their white thighs.

"Dad took her to the hospital last night and stayed with her. He called home just before I left to come here and, you know, so far so good. Lots of tests and ultrasounds, I guess, but he didn't sound too worried."

"Are *you* lot all right?" I heard myself asking next. And then, more daringly still: "Do you need anything? Food?"

Lucy laughed. "Mom had just done this monster shopping trip when the bleeding started. She got literally five cases of frozen pizza. And other stuff. Ice cream. Marshmallows. Hershey bars. We're going to have a bonfire tonight and make s'mores, if I can find the graham crackers. I legitimately think we'll be okay."

I remembered that she had seen many brothers and sisters born. Doubtless she knew when to worry, and when not. Sometimes chaos is its own form of competence;

presented with this evidence of self-sufficiency, I felt my shoulders relax. Again I fell into the polite conversational formula. "Tell her I asked after her, now."

"Will do, Miss Kirsty. Is there a big line for confession?"

All this time, Henry had been gazing up at me with his thoughtful eyes. "We have loud kids and we have quiet ones," Janet had told me. Henry was a quiet one. When he spoke, it was because he had something to say. Sometimes, kneeling during the Prayer of Consecration, I would glance over and see him standing on the kneeler, hanging onto the back of the pew, resting his chin on his white-knuckled hands, peering this way and that with bright eyes that catalogued all that he saw. Or I might see him on his stomach, on the floor, arms clenched to his side, writhing beneath the pews like a snake. "Henry gets a little caught up sometimes," Janet said. Even when Henry was *caught up,* as his mother put it, a peculiar sense of purpose seemed to emanate from him. Whatever he was doing, you hesitated to interrupt. It always looked important.

Henry's speech, likewise, tended to take the form of a pronouncement. "Did you know," he said now, in his little clear voice, "that there is a kind of tick that has a star on it, and if it bites you, you will never eat beef again?"

Lucy glanced down at him as if she had forgotten that he was there. "A *tick,* Henry? Are you sure?"

"Yes." Someone had just gone over his head with clippers, and his black hair prickled and bristled in the narthex's fluorescent light. "A tick."

"How can a tick do that, Henry?" said Lucy.

"I don't know. But this one does."

"How did you find that out?"

He shrugged. "I just did."

"I see," I said, a shade too brightly. "That's very interesting, Henry."

He held up a hand, a little don quieting his lecture hall. "Also. Also. I am taking swimming lessons now."

"Very good," I said. "Swimming is a life skill."

"At the big pool at the park," said Henry. "In the wintertime they cover it over and it has a heater, so even if it is snowing, you can swim. I would like to go swimming in the snow. Like this." He windmilled his arms.

"Yes." I nodded, hoping that I looked grave and sincere. Henry was a person to be taken seriously. "I see you've been practicing."

Lucy tugged at his hand. "We have to go in now. Henry, I want you to sit in the pew and *not move one muscle* until I come out. Do you understand?"

"Of course I understand." Henry sighed and shrugged his shoulders, an old man's gesture of resignation. "I will not move one muscle. Except to blink. I have to blink."

"All right, you can *blink,*" Lucy was telling him as I moved away.

* * *

That same evening, Wylie Springfield called on me. "Brought you some pears," he said, handing me a crumpled paper sack. "My neighbor give 'em to me, and I'm not gone eat 'em."

I had known Wylie for ten years, at least. I had, in fact, been present at his baptism one Easter Vigil, early in the Father Trotter epoch. Wylie was a convert from the Baptist Church who somehow had never got round, as he told me, to being born again in his youth. My presence at his baptism had, for reasons I am at a loss to explain, attached him to me. After Ranse died, it was Wylie who had torn out Mother Sain's carpet, painted over her paneled walls, and refused payment for his labor.

"You just give me money for the paint and shit. *Stuff*, I mean," he had said. I had laughed, as I seldom did, and given him the money. I did not like to be in anyone's debt, but Wylie made me feel as though I were the one doing him some good turn.

Fortyish and solitary, Wylie was by now a fixture in the parish. He was a handyman, a builder and repairer, a patcher-together of whatever came unglued. He was not, by any normal measure, a good Catholic. That is, he was an enthusiastic Catholic. He made Holy Hours and went on pilgrimages. A wreath of rosaries swung from his truck's rear-view mirror, to be handed out to anyone he might happen to meet. On more than one occasion, encountering Ranse in the town, Wylie had urged one of these rosaries on him. Ranse, invariably polite, had accepted the gift with grace, thanking Wylie kindly and asking Wylie to pray for him. Later he would hand the rosary off to me, saying, "Here's another one for your collection."

Periodically Wylie would ask after Ranse: "He using that rosary I given him?" And I would have to say that I hadn't seen him use it, but you never knew, did you?

Indisputably Wylie loved his neighbor, and he was fond of God. But he was not what I suppose you would call regular in his observance of religion. His Mass attendance was a matter less of obligation than of what he felt like doing. Also, he liked to smoke things that afforded him visions, which he described to me sometimes at great and frankly tiresome length, so I shan't repeat them here. In recent days, more than once, I had come upon Father Schuyler as he tried doggedly to induce Wylie to tell him how bad the plumbing situation was, how long the roof repairs could wait, or whether Wylie had time to build a new altar in a more traditional style. But what you wanted to talk to Wylie about was not always what you did talk to Wylie about. I might have told Father that. Wylie was a good man, though, always ready to mend what broke. He was mindful of the widow and the orphan. I liked him more than I liked many people.

"Look at them floors," he unfailingly commented, whenever he came round. "Damn if you can't see your face, ever time you look down. *Darn* if you can't."

Wylie lived in a trailer in a little ragtag enclave down by Houser's Creek. At home the word was *caravan,* but somehow, with its whiff of the Spice Road, *caravan* failed to apply in this context. I had seen those trailers, a clutch of washed-out blue, yellow, and apple-green corrugated shoeboxes, nested in kudzu at the foot of a gullied red-gravel drive that fell away downhill at a certain bend in the highway. I drove past that place regularly, but though Wylie lived there, in company with many Spanish-speaking members of our parish, I had never stopped to call on anyone there.

Wylie's neighbor in this sprung-up community had waded the Rio Grande in the bowels of the night, then had walked for days, carrying her newborn baby, until she got to anywhere that was anywhere in America. The baby, Wylie had told me, had been afflicted with what he called *the yellow jaundice,* but in the desert there had been no help for it, and now the boy lived in a wheelchair, his hands and feet folded back on themselves. He could not speak. I had not known that jaundice could do this to a person, but Wylie swore to me that it was so. It was what Maricruz had told him, at any rate. At Mass I had seen them, the tiny woman pitting her weight against the wheelchair where the boy, half-grown now, reclined, nodding and gesturing with his cramped hands. During Mass he offered responses according to his own liturgy, deep sighs and groans like those we are told that the Holy Spirit offers as intercession on our behalf. During the day the boy went to a special-education classroom at the middle school, and Maricruz worked at a produce stand. At the end of every work day she was allowed to bring home whatever would spoil before morning. She brought any extras to Wylie, who ate only what he could procure at the Taco Bell drive-through. So, with the regularity of ritual, he brought the fruit to me.

I took the sack. "I think I've got mice, Wylie. Come in and see what you think."

Wylie went all round the rooms with me, poking in corners, looking for spoor. In my closet, moving my shoes aside with his foot, he showed me the little black pellets like seeds. In the kitchen he moved the refrigerator, and we were appalled together at the quantity of matted hair and droppings beneath it, and at the hole in the wall. There were more hair and droppings, and another gnawed portal, behind the cooker.

"Good heavens," I said in despair. "I thought I kept a clean house."

"Don't matter none. When it's wet like it's been, or cold, mice'll just come on in." Wylie took down my broom and swept where the refrigerator had been. "Mice just do what they do. Ain't no reflection on Miss Kirsty and her pretty clean house."

But I felt it was a reflection on me. On me and all my house.

"Will you bring me some traps? I'll pay you for them, of course."

Wylie removed his tractor cap and smoothed down his slick blond hair. "I got some glue traps with me now. You don't have to pay me nothing. I get mice and shit too, sometimes. Stuff. But you know what you ought to get you? Is a cat."

"Where in the world would I get a cat?" I said. In my

childhood, though we'd always had cats, we had never acquired one voluntarily. They had simply materialized out of the air and gone back into it again. They took up with us for a time, then they wandered away again into the vastness of the universe.

Dermott told me once that the ghost of a sixteenth-century cat still haunted the passage that joined the building where he had his rooms to the parish church next door. In the early fourteenth century that church had served as the college's chapel, and even in my day, if you wanted, you could access it via this passage, which would set you down, Dermott said, in what was now the toilet beside the sacristy. He said that in the night sometimes you could hear this ghost cat yowling to be let in or out. Of course, I was never there at night and never heard it. In those days his college did not admit women, and if you were female, even if you weren't sleeping with your tutor, still you went in and out with your head ducked, the hood of your duffle coat drawn up to hide your face. The last thing you wanted was to hear mewing at the door.

Now Wylie said, "If you want you a cat, I can find you a cat."

"Why not?" I said. Why not indeed?

"I'll be back," said Wylie.

* * *

On Sunday after Mass, I approached Howard Malkin, as he stood clustered round with children in the narthex, and asked after his wife.

"Janet?" he said, as if he might have had multiple wives and wanted to be sure we were discussing the same one. "Oh, she's home. They let her out last night. They're worried about the placenta, though, how it's lying or something." He gestured with one hand to indicate some aspect of internal female anatomy. "So now she's on bed rest."

"Which is a drag," put in one of the girls, aged ten or eleven. "We have to keep yelling at her to lie down."

Howard smiled fondly. "She's going nuts. She says she wants to lie in bed and be waited on hand and foot, but really she wants to be up making Halloween costumes."

"Halloween costumes?" I said.

"She likes to get an early start." Howard smiled again. One massive hand rested on his son Henry's shorn and prickling head; he had been patting Henry absently as he spoke.

"Excuse me," Henry said now.

Howard looked startled to find a little boy beneath his patting hand. "What is it, Henry?"

"I wanted to tell Miss Kirsty something."

"Yes?" I said. *Miss Kirsty.* Wylie Springfield also called me that, and I rather liked it. It was a Southern American affect, I knew—Ranse had referred to all Annesdale women of his mother's generation as Miss Christian Name—but though it intimated a certain distance between ages or social strata, still it sounded friendlier than *Mrs. Sain.* It sounded, in fact, a good bit friendlier than I was. I wasn't sure how Janet and Howard's children, who came from everywhere and nowhere, had picked up this habit of speech, but they had.

"It's about that tick I was telling you about. The one that makes you so that you can't eat beef ever again."

"Yes?" I said.

"Well, the name of the tick is the *Lone Star Tick.*"

"Like Texas," said Howard.

Henry looked up at him with severity. "It is the *name* of this *tick.*"

Howard's hand resumed patting. Over Henry's head he said, "I don't know how he finds these things out."

I wanted to tell him not to apologize for Henry. I wasn't much drawn to children as a demographic, but it did seem to me that they were people, and that surely the things they had to say were no more irrelevant or inane than the things larger people said. Over my shoulder, at that very moment, I could hear one woman telling another in what shop she had bought the shoes she was wearing and what she had paid for them. By what social contract had shoes become an inscribed topic for polite after-church small talk, I wondered: shoes, but not ticks?

"Why don't you come see Janet?" Howard was saying, meanwhile. "She's bored at home with nobody to talk to."

I wanted to laugh at this, but beyond Howard I could see Wylie Springfield beckoning to me. Vaguely, noncommittally, I replied that I would come sometime. Not proposing a day, even to myself, I edged away through the narthex crowd.

On that brilliant autumn day, Wylie was wearing an even brighter shirt, short-sleeved, resplendent with red and gold tropical blooms, ironed crisp as a wafer. He had combed his flat fair hair with water; though it had dried, the combed ridges still showed. As I stood next to him I breathed the scent he exuded, at once leathery and woody, so potent it made me blink. With him he had Maricruz, his neighbor, and her son in his wheelchair.

"You've been a good boy today, Wylie." I felt I ought to praise him for observing his Sunday obligation. To admonish the sinner is one of the Spiritual Works of Mercy, but I had never had much taste for that. The best I could manage was to encourage the sinner when he did something right.

Wylie nodded at Maricruz, who stood apart, deep in conversation with another woman. Their Spanish syllables clicked softly together like beads in prayer: a language, but wordless to my limited ear.

"She wanted to come," he said. "And it's easier for her to get here if somebody helps with Miguelito."

"Well, you're a doubly good boy, then."

"You know, them teachers at that school, they say there ain't nothing wrong with his mind. He understands good as you or me. She says they tell her she's got to stimulate him more, you know, read to him and take him places and talk to him. I figure if he could understand that sermon we had, well, sir, that's some stimulation right there."

I agreed, a little dubiously. The homily, taking the teachings of the *Humanae Vitae* encyclical as its theme, had been extrapolated with some straining from the day's readings. The alert listener for whom artificial contraception posed no temptation might still have discerned a broader application to his or her own life, some sense in which he or she was endeavoring to interfere with the divine will. I had not listened alertly, however, and had done no such discerning. I had simply wondered how long Father could go on talking, talking, talking. Instead of worrying about my failure to cooperate with God's plan for my life, I had worried about the chicken I'd set out to defrost before Mass. The cookery books warn against such practices.

"How's them mice?" Wylie said.

I sighed. "One down."

He had given me a stack of glue traps, and before going to bed, instead of taking the chicken from the freezer to thaw properly in the refrigerator as I'd meant to do, I had set out these traps, per his directions. Several hours later, sure enough, a shriek had shaken me out of my deepest sleep. Slipping from beneath the refrigerator, the mouse had failed to look both ways and had blundered right into one of my trays of goo. Then, naturally, it had struggled. I had found it splayed on the gluey surface like a dissection specimen pinned down. Its sides heaved; its black seed-like eyes bulged hysterically. I could see where it had gnawed the edges of the tray.

Taking up a pair of kitchen tongs, I had advanced it. "I'm sorry," I told it. "You'll just have to weep and gnash your teeth in the outer darkness."

With the tongs I seized the trap by one corner and carried it outside. I dropped it twice on the back walk and had to pincer it up again in the dark. On the shining black glue surface, the mouse squealed and shivered. "God have mercy," I said, and dropped it into the dustbin beside the back gate. I dropped the tongs in after it, but I didn't care. Shuddering, I trotted back into the house, and for a long time afterwards I lay wide-eyed in my bed.

"You gone be home this afternoon?" said Wylie.

Again I was present, and grateful to be there, in the bright narthex and the bracing smell of aftershave. "Where else would I be?"

"Because I got something for you. Let me get Maricruz and Miguelito settled, and later on I'll bring it around to the house."

At home, I dropped my chicken into a stockpot, topped it off with water, and sliced a carrot, a stalk of celery, and an onion to add to it. The chicken reposed in the water like a fat little child at its bath. When it was cooked, I would have some of the meat on a sandwich for my supper. The carcass I would remove from the stock and cool, saving more meat for future sandwiches and adding the rest back into the pot. Perhaps by the time Wylie came round I'd have some soup to send home with him: recompense for the pears, the glue traps, whatever it was he was bringing me in the afternoon. Tomorrow, too, I could take soup to Father Schuyler. Perhaps he might be induced to eat some.

The house filled with the simmering chicken-soup smell.

For the moment I forgot all these cares. The sun leaned in at the front windows. Outside, the bristling dark centers of black-eyed Susans offered themselves to the goldfinches, which scissored the air in their bright, flashing flight. After I'd eaten an egg and toast, I took up my book and sat down in the living-room rocker. Lately, for reasons I couldn't articulate, I'd been trying to put myself through the reading of my university days, the work I had abandoned so long ago. It was hard going, I was discovering. Either my mind was not so agile as it had been in my youth, or I'd lost whatever knack I'd had for penetrating to the heart of things. Still, I'd got out Southwell's *Collected Works* and begun battering myself against it, as against a locked door.

Once more, on that golden afternoon, I endeavored to read his prose piece, "Mary Magdalen's Funeral Tears," which I'd never finished, never written on, in the days when I read and wrote to please Dermott. *Passions I allow, and loves I approve*, I read in the preface, which addresses the young woman, later a Benedictine nun, who was the essay's dedicatee. *Only I wish that men would alter their object and better their intent.*

Struck then by a longing, I turned from the prose to the poetry. My eye fell on the familiar lines of "The Burning Babe."

My faultless breast the furnace is, the fuel wounding thorns,
Love is the fire, and sighs the smoke, the ashes shame and scorns;
The fuel Justice layeth on, and Mercy blows the coals,
The metal in this furnace wrought are men's defiled souls–

At once I was back in the sixth-form English classroom in Aberdeen, on a dull day close to Christmas. I sat in the row next the window and could feel the chill seeping in through my uniform blazer. Though the seats by the window were cold, the fire in the grate made the air dry and peaty, laden with smells of wool and rubber galoshes and the yellowing pages of our books. At the front of the room, beneath the weak lights, framed against the blackboard in her white habit, stood Sister Bede, reciting. She was a plain, hard-faced woman, but when she opened her mouth to speak poetry, the words that issued were ardent, full of music, so wholly beautiful that she herself was transformed. When in the summer term she'd read bits of *Beowulf* aloud to us in Old English, she had made a point of saying, with a smile in my direction, that the story was more Norse than English, strictly speaking. She had read us, too, Chaucer's Prologue to the *Canterbury Tales* in Middle English, before assigning us the first eighteen lines to get by heart. Later we heard Wyatt's translations of Petrarch, then his own sonnets, and Surrey's, and Sidney's, and Shakespeare's.

But it was Southwell she loved. Of them all, he was her hero. She told us his adventures, how he went about England for six years in disguise, shadowed by the Queen's pursuivants. Sometimes he went disfigured as one Tom Cotton, a beggar. At other times he was a young lord with a falcon on his wrist, and falconer's terms he was always in danger of muffing. He feared that this latter disguise would betray him. In fact it was a woman, Sister said, her little lashless eyes narrowing at us in accusation. Anne Bellamy, a cousin of that Bellamy executed in connection with the Babington Plot, had fallen into the hands of the Queen's chief pursuivant, Richard Topcliffe. Fallen into the hands, was all Sister would say. Later I realized that this was a euphemism. Topcliffe had raped and impregnated Anne Bellamy, then used her shame —for naturally it was her shame, not his—as a lever. Who was the strange young gentleman about her father's house? A priest? Yes? Yes. She named Southwell, and Topcliffe stooped for the kill. It was, as I might have intimated, a slow slaughter, with rounds of torture in Topcliffe's own gatehouse, before Southwell's father intervened. His son was, after all, if a traitor, still a gentleman. Father Robert—his own prophetic childhood nickname—was removed to the Tower, and from there eventually taken to be drawn and quartered.

"Love is the fire," said Sister Bede. Her voice kindled on the stifling air.

3

Towards evening, the doorbell startled me from my rocking-chair sleep. Wylie stood on the screened front porch with a shoebox in his hands. "Told you I'd find you a cat."

"What? Now? In that box?" I blinked sleepily. Whatever was in the box, it made neither movement nor sound. "It's alive?"

"Sort of."

"What do you mean, *sort of*?"

"Let's go in the kitchen," said Wylie. "Light's better."

He set the box on the kitchen table and removed the lid. Inside lay something, a darkness on a bit of folded towel.

I peered at it. "What is that thing?"

"I been working for this man I know, wanted to clean up some rental property he's got. The people that lived there trashed it bad. You wouldn't believe. I'm not gone lie to you. I seen some gross in my time, but that was the grossest place I ever seen. Them people would have been lucky to have mice."

I peered again into the box. As I looked, the something resolved into a definite, if mystifying, form. What I saw might have been a very small gargoyle in some dusty blue stone—except that it was alive. Tiny breaths inflated and deflated the secret lungs, in the stark birdcage of its ribs. It was not stone, but something animate, a creature. The blue stuff was its skin.

"It was out in this back shed where they had a whole bunch of cats locked up. Some big mean feral ones was still alive. We called Animal Control on them. But a bunch of dead ones. I mean to tell you: smell? I hope to God I don't ever have to smell nothing like that again. This was the only little one alive, so I fetched it out."

"Dear God," I said. "That's a *cat*?"

"I took it to that vet that's in the church, you know who I mean, that Dr. Morrow?" My blank look prompted him to fill in this outline. "Little skinny man? Big eyes? Saturday night Mass? Aw, you know him—"

"Go on," I said, for I did not know him, and it seemed pointless for Wylie to describe a person I had never noticed in my life.

"Well, he does big animals, you know, horses and goats and cows, not cats, but he cleaned it up for me and give me some kitten milk. I thought you'd give it regular milk, but he said no, that'd make it sicker. I been nursing it a couple of days, and it ain't dead yet, so I brung it to you."

"Why hasn't it got hair?" I asked.

"Dr. Morrow just thinks because it was in all that dirt and wet and shit. Sorry. *Stuff*."

I waved away his niceties. "It could have any sort of disease, Wylie."

"He done a skin scraping, you know, to see if it had mites or fungus. It's all right that way. And he give it some medicine. He said for something that ought to be dead, it was doing pretty good. It's a few weeks old, so if it gets strong enough it can eat some solid food."

If. We both stood looking down at it. Puff puff went the tiny lungs.

"But there is one kind of bad thing." Slipping his hand into the box, Wylie scooped up the little creature. It lay limply on his palm. I could see the translucent unretracted claws, the furrowed forehead between wide winglike ears. Wylie tilted the triangular face towards the light.

"Oh God," I said.

It had no eyes. The pointed face bore two impressions like thumbprints in dough, nothing more. No blood, no gore, no blinding of Gloucester, only those shallow hollows, velveted like the rest of it in slaty blue. As Wylie's gentle hands maneuvered it, the mouth opened, startlingly pink, and a breath came out. No cry, only a breath. *Giving up the ghost*, I thought. Then it did it again.

"What's happened to it?" I said.

"Don't know. Bugs or something might have ate the eyes out. Or a infection. But Dr. Morrow thinks it was just born that way."

"And this cat is supposed to catch mice, Wylie? The mice will dance on its grave."

"Well, you know, cats is smart. They can smell real good. I reckon this one could figure out how to hunt."

"If it doesn't die in the next five minutes," I said. "Why didn't Dr. Morrow put it to sleep?"

"He asked me if I wanted to. And I did think about it. But I don't know. Seemed like kind of a shame. Poor little thing's lived this long. Maybe with some loving it'll live longer."

My shoulders tensed. For some reason, again, I saw myself backing away from Howard Malkin and his phalanx of children. "I am not going to love that thing, Wylie."

"But do you want him? Because if you don't, I'll take him home and feed him myself." He gazed at the little crumpled bat-looking thing in his hand. "He's so ugly, damn if I don't think he's right cute. *Darn* if I don't."

"Oh, stop it," I said. "You don't have to put on your drawing-room manners for me."

"Take this cat, and I won't put on no kind of manners."

He handed me the kitten. It was warm in my hand. As I

held it, the pink mouth yawned again. The little claws scraped weakly at my wrist.

In late-medieval altarpieces, triptychs and diptychs with folding wings and multiple painted panels, sometimes Saint Joseph is pictured separately from the rest of the Holy Family. In the central panel the Blessed Mother cradles the Christ Child, in the stable with shepherds and magi adoring, or in a domestic interior with ecclesial overtones, to suggest that the Church herself presents the Bread of Life on the altar of her blue-draped lap. Saint Joseph, meanwhile, occupies some side panel depicting his workshop. Here he has retreated, out of the glare of angels, and engages in some work with his hands. Often he is shown making mousetraps.

"Mice symbolized the devil, you know." Dermott pointed to the page in the glossy book we were looking at together. Indeed, in the image on the page, where the workshop wall met the floor, a little brown mouse nosed for a crumb. Dermott's eyes crinkled: oh, the credulity of it all. To him, the devil might just as easily have symbolized mice. All the same he said, "It's not something trivial he's doing there, out in the cold. He's keeping the house clean, you see: spiritually clean."

His eyes crinkled again. Then he turned the page, and we looked at something else. Dermott's interest in the Holy Family was academic and fleeting. It certainly wasn't spiritual. We were sitting, just then, propped on pillows beneath a mountain of blankets, with no clothes on. The gray early evening seeped in at the window. Soon Dermott would have to rise and dress to dine in hall. Now, as he turned another page, he was joking about sending me through the passage into the church next door, with the ghost cat to lead me on. Most likely, I thought, I'd run up against a locked door on the church side and be stuck there with the cat for my own pitch-black eternity. My cries would be the yowlings of another ghost. In a sudden panic I flung back the blankets and rummaged on the floor for my underwear.

I got up twice in the night to feed the little eyeless cat. In the morning it was still alive. I fed it again with the needleless syringe Wylie had given me and watched its soft bald stomach expand as the tinned kitten milk went down. It didn't drink, exactly. Wylie had warned me against letting it aspirate milk into its lungs. "Make sure it's swallowing," he had told me, "not inhaling." I didn't know how you'd tell the difference, but then again, I hadn't killed it yet. I emptied the last syringeful down what I hoped was its esophagus and laid it back in the shoebox. By the merest degree it shifted itself on the folded towel, as if it cared, just a sliver, in what position it lay. Its skin rumpled loosely over its bones. Still, it lived.

I set the shoebox on the floor beside the cooker and turned the oven on low. Wylie had said to keep it warm, and the poor thing had no hair to help it. Praying that it would live another hour or so, because I didn't fancy coming home to a corpse, I poured off some of my chicken soup into a Mason jar from the inexhaustible supply Mother Sain had bequeathed me. Then, taking the jar with me, I went off to clean the rectory.

In the rectory driveway I found Father Schuyler unlocking his car. He wore, as usual, his tatty day-off cassock and his harassed look.

"Oh, hello, Father," I said.

He started. "You're early."

"I was up. I've acquired a sad kitten, you see, and it wants constant feeding."

"Ah." He fumbled with his keys. "Well."

"Off for a nice day out, I hope," I said.

"Yes. I hope so." His voice trailed off a little sadly.

Desperate, I brandished my Mason jar. "I cooked a chicken yesterday, Father, and I took the liberty of bringing you some soup. With the autumn coming on, you know. Colds and flu."

"Colds and flu. Yes. I see what you mean." Perhaps both of us were wondering how any germ might manage to transmit itself to him. It certainly wouldn't get at him through personal contact. He opened his car door.

"Oh, Father," I said, feeling a great fool, but seized with a sudden conviction. "Janet Malkin is ill and on bed rest at home. A complicated pregnancy. Perhaps her husband has already spoken to you, but it might be nice if—"

From the driver's seat he gazed at me in bewilderment. "*Who* is this?" There was a note of panic in his voice.

Be patient, I rebuked myself. *He can't remember everything.* "That great family in the back, Father. The little boy who swims." I heard myself nattering on and on. "You know what people I mean."

"Oh, yes, of course," said Father uncertainly. "And this is the mother? Is it an emergency? Life or death?"

"No, Father, not an emergency, I don't think, as such." It occurred to me that even in the face of death, the Malkins would build a bonfire and roast marshmallows, rather than ring the priest.

"No immediate danger of death?"

"Not so far as I know, Father, but—"

"Well, I only answer actual emergencies on my day off." He delivered this prepared speech in some haste, like a schoolboy wanting to have his recitation over with. Then he slammed the car door, thrust his key into the ignition, and shifted into reverse. The car idled. As if entertaining second thoughts, he put the power window down again. "If there is no immediate need for the sacraments," he continued in his most precise manner, "the Anointing of the Sick and so forth, then it can wait until tomorrow."

Up slid the window. Away he went. There were round white decorative stones edging the driveway. I wanted, rather, just then, to pick one up and hurl it through the retreating rear windscreen.

In that moment I felt something like my mother's rage at old Father Goudie after my father died. Father Goudie had appeared on the scene belatedly, only when the emergency was over, my father already scattered ash. Of course, my father hadn't been a Catholic. Naturally he wouldn't have wanted my mother ringing for a priest. It was also entirely possible that Granny Astrid's berserker reputation preceded her as far as Lerwick. If I had been Father Goudie, I might not have come knocking, either, thinking myself unwanted. On the other hand, my mother had been going to Mass at Lerwick all her married life. She had given money for Masses for a brother who'd been lost in the war. She might reasonably, at the time of her own bereavement, have expected the priest to come and minister to her.

But then it had all happened so suddenly. My father had gone out fishing, as he sometimes still bestirred himself to do. Why he chose to go out that day we would never know. He'd come in late in the afternoon, beached his blue boat on the harbor stones, walked up the village street to our door, put his hand on the latch, and fallen dead on the threshold. That was that, which was more or less how the Mother Superior broke the news to me, when I was called away from calculating the area of a circle. Both my mother and Granny Astrid repeated this story, once the friend of my father's who had fetched me in his boat from Lerwick deposited me on that same threshold. Next day we'd had the service at the crem, and I'd been sick on lemon-curd tarts after.

"Shop tarts," Granny Astrid said in disgust.

All that was over by the time Father Goudie arrived. I had

known him at a distance all my life, and in the anonymous intimacy of the confessional, but this was the first time I had seen him up close: a bent, bleak little man with a face like a shriveled apple and a Jansenist outlook. I was introduced to him. We established that I was at school in Aberdeen, that I liked it there, and that I would shortly be returning to the nuns. He received this intelligence with a twitch of his lips, then I was sent to the kitchen with my book, to sit with Granny Astrid.

"As for that," she remarked, though I had said nothing. *What did you expect,* she meant.

She had taken up a broom and was lashing the floor with it, for the floor's own good. I sat down in the chair by the fire. In silence I watched her sweeping. I felt glad to be living in the twentieth century, when people didn't habitually go about cleaving each other in twain with battleaxes. In an earlier era, Granny Astrid would have been not merely intimidating, but dangerous.

I heard the front door slam. A moment later, my mother appeared in the kitchen, seething over something Father Goudie had said to her. I never found out what it was, though in hindsight I could guess. Father Goudie was fond of the gorier dreams of Saint John Bosco, in which schoolboys were pulled into hell by demons for having made bad confessions. He might well have intimated to my mother that even the doors of Purgatory were barred to my puritan father. Or he might have refused to say a requiem Mass for him. In any event, Father Goudie went back to Lerwick, ferried by that same friend of my father's, who had gone specially to fetch him. This was a good deed for a man who believed, as my father had done, that Catholic priests were part of a worldwide conspiracy to destroy the Christian religion. Meanwhile, my mother, whom I had never known to smoke, produced a packet of cigarettes from somewhere about her person, lit one from a jet on the gas range, and dragged on it as if it were her only source of life.

"Tell no me," said Granny Astrid. *Did not I prophesy?*

At school there had been snipping and sniping and scoffing at my Shetlandish idioms. While I didn't exactly talk like Granny Astrid—there was never any call for me to prophesy—still my diction bore the island mark, and the echoes of Norn, the old Norse-influenced Shetland tongue. I had stored up much knowledge through the endless winter nights, when Granny Astrid, or occasionally my father, would tell stories: the tales about trows, the famous Papa Stour Witch who summoned the wind. I knew the poems and songs that my village knew. I knew only what everyone knew in the whole world, or so I thought. At school, however, I had discovered that my knowledge was not knowledge at all, and that, an outsider among the Aberdeen girls, I was the butt of jokes.

All the same, while I was away home, all I wanted was to go back. If I had no talent for pious paintings, still I longed for the dull rounds of Mass and classroom, the comfort of calculating a circle's area. It was as if, after all, you could measure that eternity which was always opening out, enormous and windy, filled with magic and supernatural doings, in my Granny's imagination. It remained eternal, of course; still you had acquired some language for defining it.

Therefore I was alarmed, in the wake of Father Goudie's departure, to hear my educational future called into question. I sat in the corner, hiding behind my book, as my mother drew on her cigarette. Granny Astrid watched her gloweringly. At last the outburst came.

"What does she want anyway with those nuns?" My mother blew smoke, blue and bitter. "All she'll do in the end is come back here. She'll be postmistress after me. What else is there? What else am I to do with her? If I hadn't listened to those nuns, *and* those priests, all my life—"

I expected Granny Astrid to agree. At last, I presumed she must be thinking, my mother was coming to her senses: *if* she had any, which Granny Astrid manifestly doubted. At last I was to be freed, whether I wanted to be or not, from the yoke of popery and superstition. It was as if the Protestant wind, summoned by the Papa Stour Witch to blow away the Armada and the Jesuits, were rising even now about our house. In another moment Granny Astrid would fling the door wide, and that wind would come into the kitchen, catch me up, and whirl me away to the secondary modern school in Lerwick, then back to the village post office. I was to be postmistress after my mother. It was settled. All I had to do was wait for it to happen. Holding my book before me like a shield, I braced myself to receive that blast.

But Granny Astrid only said, as if nothing mattered, "Never bail out dirty water afore the clean comes in. Those nuns, they're no sae ill. She's right enough where she is." The next thing I remember, I was back at school, and it was as if I had never left.

I have reflected that, though my mother and I had been too preoccupied to see it and might not have believed it if we had seen it, that moment in the kitchen marked the first last gasp of Granny Astrid. I'd assumed she would go on forever, but hadn't I begun to learn that nothing did? I returned to school, and though six weeks later I was back on the island again to see Granny Astrid, in her turn, reduced to smoke—of course you never saw it happen, only the coffin sliding away through the doors, the faint flicker beyond—truly, I had got away.

Nothing went on forever. The island could not go on forever, not for me. Now I knew it. *Postmistress?* Not I. That was the first time I can remember thinking: I am not someone else's, to be done with. What I will do, *I* will do. Later, perhaps inevitably, I thought of God what I had first thought of my mother. I was not His, either, to be disposed of. I was my own, and what I would do, *I* would do. Though I'd long since come to see the lie in this, still—particularly in conversations with priests—sometimes the ghost of the berserker arose in me and looked about for an axe.

Well, Father Schuyler was hardly Father Goudie, not yet, at any rate. Young priests were like babies: all alike in the beginning. They came, they experimented on us for a season, and they went away again. What they would become we did not see. That was for the next parish, or the next one, or the next. Our parish, as I put it to myself, was a first-or-last parish. Our pastors were either old, like Father Trotter, checking in one last time on their way to retirement, or else, like Father Schuyler, just out of the egg.

These pastoral assignments recurred in a rhythm that had become familiar to me over time. A young priest would arrive and immediately insist on upending established parish habits. Before Father Trotter, we had had Father Poletti, who introduced Communion by intinction and sprinkled ashes into our hair on Ash Wednesday, instead of smearing the customary cross on our foreheads. Everybody groused, until eventually we all forgot that things had ever been otherwise. When Father Trotter appeared, having long since run through his own stock of innovations, he had endured a period of mourning for Father Poletti Who Was So Spiritual. Now that we had Father Schuyler, people's complaints about him tended to wax into eulogies for Father Trotter. You would have thought that Our Beloved Pastor had been assumed bodily into heaven, not removed to a comfortable patio home at the Ave Maria Manor in High Point, and that the Bishop had sent the Antichrist to take his place. But Father Trotter had been no better, not really. "Monday is my day off," I had heard him growl during the end-of-Mass announcements. "Unless you or someone you love is clinically dead, don't call me on Monday."

On balance, for all their painful seriousness of purpose, I preferred the younger priests, not yet hardened into their vocations. My dear Jesuit, in the youth of his short priesthood, had written an *Epistle of Comfort* to the Earl of Arundel, exhorting him and his fellow Catholics to prepare for the martyrdom which he himself expected, sought, and feared. Of course, even in our easy times, the priest's life was lonely, exacting its costs. These young ones in their first assignments, left to themselves in parishes they tried to transfigure overnight: they would find it out. Time and again we watched as a young one found it out. Then we let him go, to receive in turn the old priest who had found it out, put up his guard, and grown tired.

Meanwhile, as I washed and swished and swept the immaculate rectory, I seemed to step outside myself, to observe with bemused curiosity the stout frowsty-haired woman in sagging blue jeans and coverall who bent to these largely unnecessary tasks. *The house won't clean itself,* my mother used to say, but these days, the rectory did more or less just that. It shone with self-sufficiency. *I have no need of you,* it said to me. In Father Trotter's day, on being asked to take up the rectory cleaning, I'd shuddered at the recollection of that venerable tradition: priest's housekeeper as priest's *de facto* wife. To my relief, Father Trotter had called me *Mrs. Sain,* keeping me properly, with decades of practice, at arm's length. The trick with the desk and the bottles was his one intimate gesture; I had the feeling he performed it for everyone who entered the house. He would have sprung his bottles on the Pope. Beyond my predictable amusement at the secret of the desk, he seemed not to consider that I might have any thoughts at all. Why would I? I was the cleaning lady, nothing more. This was only meet and right.

I smiled to think of my younger self, who certainly never imagined for one instant that she would end as a cleaning lady. *Of all things*, she would have said. If *postmistress* was beneath her, *cleaning lady* hardly registered as a human category. Cleaning ladies existed only dimly in the peripheral vision of clever girls like me. Invisibly the college bedders moved from room to room at midday, while we were out. They shook the tumbled sheets, ran their carpet sweepers over the floors. At night we returned to find our disorder righted. Expected to find it so, through no effort of our own, as we expected to find oxygen in the atmosphere. This was the rule by which the universe operated. Some houses did clean themselves. Cleaning had nothing to do with me. This, at least, was what I thought. At least, it was what I thought I thought.

Ranse had to show me how to operate the hoover, how to change its expanding paper bladder when it got too full. We hadn't had one at home. Our household had approached electrical appliances with caution. When we got television, shortly before I went away to school, Granny Astrid insisted on unplugging it at bedtime. Mrs. Moodie across the way, seeing the blue glow through the curtains of an evening, had worried that we would leave it on all night and burn the house down. In one of their muttered conferences in the middle of our street, two old ladies clutching string bags full of shopping, she had voiced this worry to Granny Astrid. Granny Astrid had thought it entirely reasonable. Never mind that she went to bed at seven o'clock. As she told my father, there was nothing on the telly after seven o'clock that was worth burning down the house for. In truth, there was never much on at any time, that we could count on being able to see. I had to stand holding the antenna this way and that above the squat gray box so that my father could perceive a football match through blizzards of static. As for house-cleaning conveniences, hadn't a broom been good enough for our ancestors? Well, then.

I'd been hopeless with Mother Sain's hoover, and laughed at by Ranse.

"If you aren't the cutest thing," he said. "I never did meet a girl who couldn't run a vacuum cleaner."

I glared at him. "Tell your mother about this, and I'll be on the first bus out of this place."

On cue, Mother Sain appeared in the doorway. "Tell me what, now? Ransome, what did you all do to that thing? Your daddy bought the top of the line, and in twenty years I've never had a minute's trouble with it, until you came home and started messing with it."

"Just changing the bag, Mama. Kirsty doesn't know how these American ones do. Vacuum cleaners are different where she comes from. Now." He straightened and winked at me. "She ought to run just fine. You touch that switch there, and let's see how she does."

Of course I had my small triumph in the end. I mastered the hoover and no longer called upon him to help me. Over time I taught myself to out-clean his mother. What exactly I won in this prolonged skirmish I am still not sure—other than a sense of my own competence, which was not nothing. I could open the refrigerator all I wanted; no germs would dare rush in.

"Don't you want to make the bed?" I asked Dermott once. In spite of myself, I was shocked that he should rise from it in the afternoon and leave it crumpled and tossed beneath the window. To me, so new to everything, this neglect seemed as scandalous as what we had just been doing. There had been no hoovers in the convent, any more than there had been at home, but we'd all been drilled in bed-making. If to leave a bed unmade was not in itself a mortal sin, still it was an outward sign of something inwardly disordered. So I had been taught.

A crinkle of the eyes: amusement and pity. If Dermott had been given to words like *cute*, I might have been the cutest thing, just then.

"The woman will see to it," he said. "In the morning."

"But what will she think?"

"Think?" He stared at me.

* * *

As I unlocked the front door at home, a cry came from the kitchen. I broke into a stiff little old-lady trot. *What now*, I thought. *What now?* But even as I hastened, the cry came again, and I realized that it meant good news. It was one thing better than hunger. It was being able to say *hunger*, in whatever tongue. In its box by the cooker, the kitten no longer lay like roadkill, but crouched, actually on its feet. It had had a piss—I could smell the metallic tang of it—and left a small black curl of poo. I should have to procure a litter box for it, and some cat litter.

"Well, you. Looks as though you're still not dead." The head tilted towards me. The empty eye-hollows stared. Already I was finding those non-eyes less alarming; at least they were clean and dry. Scooping the kitten from the box I felt, through the soft wrinkling skin, the heart throbbing against my hand. The kitten mewed again in its rusty small voice. This time, when I put the syringe to its mouth, the pink tongue flickered and lapped.

Father Schuyler's reluctance to visit Janet Malkin made me feel, uncomfortably, that I should visit her myself. Mind you, I did not want to. Visiting people, entering their homes, seeing how they lived, in their very presence: this was a level of intimacy I could, and did, perfectly happily live without. I might come to clean a house. I did not want to know the people who'd made the mess. The thought made me squeamish. But Howard had asked me to come. *She's going nuts with nobody to talk to*, he'd said. Well, for half an hour, I supposed, I could enter the foreign country of Janet Malkin's house—not the church narthex or the car park, or the bench beneath the apple tree in the rosary garden, but Janet's own house—and be talked to by her there. I could do this for half an hour, or perhaps twenty minutes; it would not kill me.

I continued to mull over the prospect for a day or two. Surely *nobody to talk to* was an overstatement. There were too many people in that house already. I should only be in the way. I should not know what to say, what to do, where to look in all that sprawling humanity. *I shall pray for them,* I thought. Taking up my rosary, I piously did so. But the anxiety at the back of my mind did not ebb away.

One afternoon, then, because I still had more chicken soup left than I could possibly choke down myself, I poured off a gallon jar of it for the Malkins, screwed the lid on tight, and set it in a basket Mother Sain had used to hold her crocheting. I hoped that a gallon of soup would be enough. How much did children eat? I'd no idea. I leafed through the latest parish directory, for which we had all been photographed, by express command of Father Trotter, back in the spring. On my appointed day, I had shown up in a spirit of grudging resignation, to be jollied intolerably by the photographer and to enter my name and address on the appropriate paper form. In that issue of the directory you can find me still, looking every inch the retired lady berserker, my faded hair standing out in puffs either side of my face. My expression betrays the itchiness of my best moss-green wool dress and the lameness of the photographer's jokes. I am recorded in those pages as the worst species of witch, who eats children for breakfast and enjoys every mouthful.

The Malkins on the other hand were not the sort of people you expected to fill out forms or appear in coordinated outfits for photographic opportunities. As I had anticipated, the directory lacked a Malkin family photo. But to my surprise and ambivalent relief, their name did appear in the back pages—*Malkin, Janet, Howard, others*—under the *Not Pictured* heading. Beneath it, an address on the other side of town. It was a sign, I felt, my final excuse struck down. I set the kitten on the litter box I'd procured for him, then returned him to the plastic tub from which I had emptied Mother Sain's collection of newspaper clippings. Already he was showing signs of wanting to explore his surroundings; when I was absent, I thought it wise to keep him contained.

Above the fading trees, wheeling in and out of the sun, two hawks hunted or courted, I couldn't tell which. Their cries rose and died as they tilted on the brilliant sky. Climbing into my car, I thought again of my Jesuit poet and his hawking terms. He'd feared, quite naturally, what would happen if he forgot them. He never feared the people who opened their houses to him. Or else his love overshadowed any fear he might have felt. And here was I, all unhunted, trembling to take soup to the Malkins. I couldn't meet my own eyes in the rearview mirror.

They lived on the east side of town, where subdivisions built in the optimism of the late nineteen-fifties thinned and gave way to country again. Out that way, the houses sat their acre lots like trailers, as if they'd been not built but dropped and left where they landed. Every now and again a plain brick ranch-style house would be tricked out like an estate, with white rails or pickets, or black iron palings. Brick pylons, or sometimes cast-concrete lions, would flank the drive, barricaded by an intricate scrolled gate, beyond which the modest house crouched in abjection. Rolling through this neighborhood with its *Children-At-Play* speed limit, I passed one small flat-roofed place about which an improbable farm had developed, with the usual chickens and goats, but also what looked, in my peripheral vision, like a water buffalo. Two emus high-stepped along the fence, glaring and snaking their necks. From his ambush in the ditch by the house, a little bat-eared dog exploded, to harry me in a frenzy of barking until the road bent and I lost him.

The Malkins' house was a brick split-level, built into a rise in the land. As I approached, it seemed to levitate above a cloud of leggy azalea bushes and human detritus. I had heard the term *yard art* before, and it was apt here. The entire property was a study in the art of entropy. In addition to Howard's collection of cars-in-progress, there were overturned bicycles in great quantity. I saw mismatched skates, a plastic wading pool brimming with rain and algae, any number of water guns and swimming-pool floats, naked dolls, shoes, a clay-stained pair of boy's underpants, a concrete statue of Our Lady of Grace a little off-kilter among the roots of a tree. What wasn't contained in that yard? *Yard* was the American word, which I had learnt to use just as I'd learnt to say *trailer*. The Malkins' outdoor environment hardly constituted a *garden*. As I clambered from my car, a cat came hurrying from the carport to mew and purr round my ankles: a normal cat with hair and eyes. Carrying my basket, I advanced to the door.

Admitted by a heavy, shaggy teenaged boy in a Star Wars t-shirt, I found Janet lying not in bed, but on a cracked leatherette sofa in a little back den off the kitchen. Seeing her, I thought of Lucy. If Lucy looked like a young Janet, then the current Janet was a vision of what Lucy might become. Janet had the same dark curls, but uncombed and threaded with silver. Much childbearing had left her body slack and shapeless, though that might have been the effect of the clothes she habitually wore, large loose t-shirts and baggy drawstring trousers. In such an outfit she lay regally on the sofa. Her t-shirt, I noticed, proclaimed the theme of a Vacation Bible School I remembered from several summers ago, when it seemed that every Protestant church in Annesdale was putting on the same program. *Jesus Down Under*, the t-shirt said, above the image of a cartoon kangaroo clutching a large black Bible in its paw. Janet's pregnant belly strained at the kangaroo graphic, making it appear pregnant as well.

"You found us." The gladness in her voice made me ashamed all over again. She began to struggle up from the sofa. Then, as if remembering orders, she lay back down. "All right, all right, I'm being a good girl," she announced to no one in particular. "I *told* Howie to tell you to come see me."

"And here I am." *At last,* I did not add. I proffered the basket. "I cooked a chicken at the weekend, you see, and—"

"Dominic!" Janet raised her voice. The boy in the Star Wars shirt reappeared in the kitchen doorway. Lucy had told me that there were loud Malkins and quiet Malkins; this boy must have been one of the quiet ones.

"Miss Kirsty has brought us some dinner," his mother said, falling into the children's habit of naming me. "Take that basket and put what's in it in the fridge." Silently the boy did as he was told.

All the available chairs, as far as I could see, were covered with washing in various stages of being folded. Selecting an ottoman to perch upon, I tried not to peer about me, either with interest or with a critical eye. A couple of the older girls were drifting in and out, arguing with each other, sometimes picking items out of the jumble of washing and carrying them away, sometimes not. Through the picture window above the couch where Janet lay, I could see a wooded back garden and in it, Henry grappling with a rake. It was still early in the season, and not many leaves had fallen yet, but with the rake, its handle projecting above his shoulder, Henry pawed at what there was.

"Look at Henry being helpful," I said.

Janet didn't raise herself to look. Perhaps she didn't need to. Mothers are said to have eyes in the backs of their heads, and it might very well be true.

"Henry is the good child right now," she told me. "You know they take turns. Everyone's horrible, except the one kid whose job it is to restore your faith in humanity. Today, that's Henry."

I cast about for something to say next and was horrified to hear myself ask, "How many are there, actually?"

But Janet only laughed. "Isn't that always the question? Here come the Malkins! All the way from New Jersey! Are there twenty of them? A million? How many?" She ran a hand over her taut belly and did not venture an exact number.

"My goodness." I noted with disgust how prim and old-ladyish I sounded.

Janet appeared not to notice. "Every one of them's a gift," she responded. If she said it somewhat automatically by now, who was I to blame her?

For a long time I sat listening to Janet talk. About what? I don't remember much of it now. My gaze rested on the brick fireplace, black and cavernous on this too-warm day. Its empty blackness seemed to darken the entire room. On the mantel above, a confusion of holy statues crowded, an entire Communion of Saints. The children's Confirmation saints, Janet told me.

"Plus, whenever I see anything Catholic in a thrift store, I rescue it. Here, take this." From somewhere about her on the sofa, she produced a small plastic image of the Infant of

Prague and thrust it into my hand. "Please. I don't have a good place for him. They multiply. Howie says I can't keep them all."

I accepted this gift and held it in my lap as Janet continued to talk. I entertained no devotion to the Infant of Prague. I could imagine what Mother Sain might have said on my bringing home such a thing. But now that I had it, I was responsible for it. If I set it down, there in the chaos of the Malkins' house, I might forget it, and it would be lost or broken. I was not superstitious. I had not been brought up in one of those Catholic homes full of statues; Granny Astrid wouldn't have had it, any more than Mother Sain would have done, or Ranse. Left on my own, I had not thought to rush out and buy any. I had no pious attachment to such objects, and I had hardly known anyone, in all my life, who had. Still, this one might have been blessed. Now it was mine to dispose of in some suitably reverent manner.

"That's a lovely Immaculate Heart you have," I remarked, for something else to say. Actually this painting above the empty fireplace put me in mind of the one in Auntie Lass's bedsit: Our Lady looking up virtuously yet coyly, as if a sword were not at that moment piercing her heart. She wore more or less the expression the nuns had exhorted us to put on when young men chatted us up, for example in the train.

"Oh, *Margaret* did that," Janet said. But which one was Margaret?

All over the house, people were doing things. Boys were thundering up and down the hall, shooting foam-rubber bullets at each other out of foam-rubber guns. There were girls in the dining room making crafts with glitter and feathers and hot glue. Beads crunched underfoot and rolled away beneath the furniture. Outside, and visible through the same picture window, the upper end of the driveway was strewn with car parts.

"Aren't those children helping you at all?" I roused myself to ask. Lucy, I thought. Where was Lucy, what was she so occupied with, that she couldn't run the household a little more?

Janet sighed. "They try. But they have *school.* And *jobs.* And *boyfriends.* They start to do some helpful thing, but then life calls them: *Come away! Come away!* And they say, *Okay, be right there.* You know how it is."

I did not know how it was, but I nodded anyway. Outside, the afternoon drew down, blue and meditative. Behind the house, Henry continued to feint at the leaves. In another part of the house, laughter broke out, sharp and staccato as bursts of gunfire. One of the older boys wandered through the den in black trousers, black dress shirt, and sock feet, a tie draped over his arm. "Where are my shoes, Ma?"

"For crying out loud, Moshe, how should I know where your shoes are?" said Janet. "I've been lying right here all day. Where did you leave them?"

"If I knew where I'd left them, I wouldn't be looking for them." Moshe stalked out.

"Work," said Janet, her voice carrying through the house. "It's like trying to get them out the door for school. It's just like *kindergarten,*" she ended in a shout.

"Yeah, yeah," said Moshe from somewhere else. A moment later a door slammed, and a car coughed to life in the driveway.

I rose from the ottoman. "I believe I've got him blocked in. I should be going anyway."

"Too late," said Janet prophetically. "He's already driven through the front yard." Beneath her t-shirt, an unseen person shifted and resettled. "But look, if you really have to go, just promise me you'll come back."

I promised, though not too heartily. I had found the

afternoon wearing. Having now visited the sick, I felt that I *had* visited the sick, conclusively. Visiting the sick had taken it right out of me. On my way out, carrying my Infant of Prague, I touched, as I had been told that Jews did, the tarnished silver mezuzah that hung on the outer frame of the front door. *Hear, O Israel, the Lord is your God, the Lord is One.* My zeal for his house was feeble at best; I wanted to make my small apology.

In a spirit of escape, I drove home. At the approach of Michaelmas, five o'clock was waning light, rosy clarity in the western sky, crickets holding their one thin unison note. When I put the car window down, the wind fanning the roadside grasses touched my cheek with coolness. After the Malkins' house, the quietness of the world pressed itself upon me, and I was grateful for it. As I climbed from my car in my own driveway, I realized that I'd been hunching my shoulders inside my cardigan, as if to ward off something. My neck ached with tension. For a moment I stood beneath the first faint stars, willing my body to unclench. Then I went inside to set my Infant on the mantel and feed my hairless cat.

* * *

When a week later the kitten still wasn't dead, I looked out Dr. Morrow, the veterinarian, in the parish directory. To my surprise, he seemed to know at once who I was. He promised to call in the next evening, after the day's rounds. "Got a bunch of goats to castrate," he told me.

Setting the kitten on the kitchen table, he palpated its abdomen with thin, probing fingers. "It *looks* chipper."

"You think it might live, then?"

"It's lived this long. It might as well keep on." He spoke

with polite disinterest.

"But why hasn't it got any hair?" I asked.

Dr. Morrow ran a finger over the bare wrinkled skin. "It' nothing you're going to catch. You can rest easy."

"That's good." I had caught myself scratching at imaginary itches.

"Otherwise?" he said. "There are actually hairless cat breeds."

"People breed them bald?" I looked, appalled, at the little creature on the table. "On purpose?"

"The more improbable an animal is, the more valuable it becomes. You wouldn't believe what people pay for naked things. Didn't know what a treasure you had, did you?" He laughed. Gathering his instruments, he settled his old felt hat on his head. "See you in church."

4

Sumac flamed along the roadsides. The maples yellowed. Sometimes at night I still heard the skittering noises of mice, but though I set the glue traps out with liturgical regularity, I caught nothing more. Meanwhile, the kitten continued not to die. He was a good kitten, dutiful in his use of the litter box. When I set him in it, he dabbled his little hole and squatted over it, naked tail upright and quivering. In the daytime, when the weather was warm, I took him outside, onto the screened front porch. Amused, I watched him bumble up and down in the sunshine within this safe enclosure, tapping his nose to the floorboards as a blind man might tap his cane. Beneath his dusty blue hide, a layer of flesh now clothed his ribs and spine. Though the skin between the desert-fox ears remained as furrowed as a plowed field, the rest of his wrinkles were starting to smooth away. He would never not look strange, even alarming, but at least he no longer appeared a starveling. He lurched a bit when he walked, but all kittens were lurchy. This one, I told myself, wasn't doing too badly.

As the autumn wore on, I tended the kitten, kept my house, cleaned the rectory, and went to church. There, on Sundays, I saw Howard and the children. The sight of them tagged me with a niggling guilt, like a slow leak whose source I couldn't trace. I began cooking whole chickens more frequently. I made quantities of soup, then hunted down my mother-in-law's chicken-and-dumplings recipe: her best company meal, though we'd so rarely entertained any company besides ourselves. On Sundays I took the thermal containers from the fridge, to hand off to Howard as he herded his children into the van after Mass. Before, I had cooked out of boredom. Or, more accurately, I had cooked meals for myself as an assertion that I existed, as surely as Ranse had existed, and was as much worth feeding as he had been. I had not believed it, and I had not wanted to eat what I cooked. Now I felt driven by something outside myself, a demand on my time and attention. I resented it, rather. Still, I did it.

Janet remained at home, apparently lying down. *Bed rest,* the family kept saying, those talismanic words which I hoped meant something. I asked after her regularly, of course, and was regularly told that she was fine, never better. Taking up my rosary dutifully to pray for her, I gave myself permission not to worry. I felt that in Janet's position, I should find someone else's worry an intolerable burden. Did people not prefer to be left alone?

Monday after Monday, the rectory continued not to need cleaning. I cleaned it anyway. The vacant refrigerator gleamed, sterile as a laboratory, whenever I opened it. I'd no idea what had become of my jar of chicken soup; it had vanished utterly, while Father Schuyler went on seeming to live on air. In church, contemplating him at the altar, I noted his famished aspect. Surely someone ought to worry about him, though something about him didn't invite worry. As soon as the Mass was ended, and he had processed out, he evaporated into the sacristy with a click of the lock.

"Is he shy or what?" I heard one lady say to another as we filtered out to the car park after a daily Mass. "Do they not teach them in that seminary how to talk to people?"

Her friend replied, "Next thing you know, he'll be turning his back on us. You watch."

It seemed to me that Father already turned his back on us at every opportunity.

Nevertheless, I knew what she meant. He had begun insisting that the Mass parts be sung in Latin, to complicated chant tones, and had marshalled the choir to teach them, not very authoritatively, to a grudging congregation on Sunday mornings before the Mass began. I could see that *ad orientem* might well be the next step. And what of it? Like other church ladies my age, I had spent my childhood staring at the back of the priest's head—Father Goudie's bald spot, Father Burke's tousled pillow hair—and studying the intricacies of his embroidered chasuble, as he faced God and lifted the Host for us to adore with him. We were all, as I have said, in love with Father Burke. His chasubles as well as his hair were things of beauty. It was just as well, really, that he turned his back. We did not want Father Burke to look at *us*. If he had, we might all have died on the spot.

* * *

The October days looked caught in amber. Amber was the color of the land as it rose and fell beneath the high, dry sky. At night the moon rounded and rode above the soft edge of the trees, breathing its calm blue light. The world at this time of the year felt enormous, tall and wide and empty. The kitten was company; still, I began to realize, I was lonely. How was it possible?

I began to notice anew my old favorite photograph of Ranse, which I kept on my bureau. It was only a head shot, done for work when Ranse was in his mid-forties, but I liked it. As if with new eyes, I saw him, solemn in dark suit and tie. I saw his silvering hair, his eyes smiling. At that time in our life together, he was always leaving: out of the door in the dark early mornings for the long drive to Charlotte. He was no longer the boy of the train, but a man with a briefcase who would return late, wrung out by the day. He would collapse into a chair at the kitchen table and wait for me to set his reheated supper before him. Often he would not have eaten lunch, and though he looked well enough, I worried about him. As always, he carried insulin about with him and injected himself without a thought, as he'd done in the days when he asked for sweet tea in pubs: the rush of sugar, then the magic jab, which made me cringe and look away. Always he ate what he wanted, or else he did not eat at all. Asked what he lived on, he might well have said, *Sweet tea and insulin.* Already I had begun to worry that this was not a diet conducive to longevity. When I looked at the photograph, all those worries returned to me, too late. So did regret. *I know I'm not handsome,* he had told me on the train. Had I ever, in all the intervening years, bothered to correct him? As I looked at him, that man on his way somewhere else was unbearably handsome. Even in the midst of my worry, I hadn't thought it possible that I could ache for him. Now I did.

Perhaps it was only the approach of All Saints and All Souls that made me so broody over the dead. I considered how far they were from me, how far I would have to go to get to them, assuming they were there to be got to. It wasn't only the sheer length of life, unrolling drearily before me, no end in sight. I was old, but not nearly old enough. Death might find me at any time, of course, but the chances of its doing so just now seemed unlikely. I was all too robust. When the leaves fell round my house, I went out and raked them. When the kitten was sick on the linoleum, I wiped it up. When another mouse floundered into a glue trap, I disposed of it and remembered to hang onto the tongs. Nothing I encountered was too much for me.

Also, I went to confession regularly. I did not fear damnation, except in the moments when it came to me that in dwelling so much on death I was ungrateful for my life. Even then, it wasn't the thought of hell that filled me with dread: at least, not a hell of fire or ice. What I did fear, I began to realize, was loneliness, the very thing I'd told Ranse that I craved. I had cultivated, as I've said, a positive appetite for the absence of human company. But now it occurred to me that I might lie craving in my grave. In the watches of the night, sometimes, I was afraid.

In this spirit, I brought out from the cupboard many family photographs. I had taken them down so that Wylie could paint the walls, and had never, in all this time, hung them back in their places. Until now, I hadn't thought to miss them. I'm not certain that I did miss them, even then, not exactly. I did not return them to the walls. But for several nights running, I took them out and looked at them.

Not surprisingly, most of them were pictures of Sains: Ranse's parents and grandparents, innumerable images of Ranse, the only child. I had a few photographs of my own, of course, though while Ranse's mother lived, I'd had no place to put them. Ranse and I had occupied his boyhood room upstairs, beneath the eaves, and the rest of the house was hers. After she died, we'd moved downstairs into the master bedroom, but the house had remained emphatically hers. When I'd ventured to suggest that we might buy ourselves a new mattress, Ranse had said, "This one Mama bought's less than ten years old." So we slept on it. I hadn't actually expected otherwise; you might say I'd lost the habit.

After so many years I'd lost, too, the habit of having my own familiar faces around me. I'd kept them in my bureau drawer, beneath my socks and underthings, until that came to seem a normal and appropriate arrangement. When we moved downstairs to Mother Sain's room, I merely transferred them from the upstairs bureau to the rather grander marble-topped walnut one which had belonged to her. Now I brought these out as well.

I set the photographs, as many as I could, on the mantel, so that the family, both sides, appeared to flank the Infant of Prague. In the midst of them, in his crown and his molded red plastic robe, he displayed the orb of the world in one hand, raised the other in blessing. Remembering the clutter of statues on the Malkins' mantel, I smiled. I would not have chosen the Infant of Prague for myself. But there he stood, sweet-faced, the little King of Heaven with some of his more questionable throng. I vowed myself to pray for them all through November, the coming month of departed souls. Naturally the Infant brought Janet to my mind. But Howard had intimated again and again that she was all right. Hadn't he? Of course I prayed for her.

My personal communion numbered more dead, of whom I had no photographs. I prayed for Dermott, of course. Did the other girls pray for him? It was Auntie Lass who'd sent me the newspaper clipping of his obituary, at the top of which she had written, in her large, precise teacher's hand, *Your old tutor, I believe.* In any case, Dermott's was not a flattering obituary. In the accompanying photograph, he looked old indeed, with a pathetic, bewildered look. I wondered when the photograph had been taken, and why the newspaper had included it, though under the circumstances, an image of the beautiful man I remembered would not have done the situation justice. That Dermott would have crinkled his eyes at us all, the succession of girls who stayed for a quiet drink in his rooms. Instead, the obituary insinuated his decline and fall, in a way that might have led us to triumph, assuming we were all still alive, and unscathed enough to experience a sense of victory.

But I felt no triumph. I had long since binned the clipping.

I regretted that I possessed no image of Sister Bede, or of my college's Senior Tutor. Her face recurred in my mind from time to time, broad and ruddy, her thick figure comfortable in its tweeds. She had been a classicist, but her real gift, I suspect, lay in her vocation as a sort of secular Mother Superior. There had been a time when I was ill; shortly after that, I went down from the university without taking my degree. The Senior Tutor, in her dealings with me, was both full of exhortation and unfailingly kind. She had not wanted to see my time wasted, or my life. I had done good work, I had promise, and I should stay where I was. But when I said that I was finished, she didn't berate me. She said only that I should think of the college always as my home. I would forever be part of them. For years I'd received post from the college, news and glossy fundraising circulars, so I suppose that what she'd said was true enough. I'd no idea what she had believed in, beyond the college, or if she believed in anything larger at all. But she had practiced mercy, and I hoped that in her case God would reciprocate.

* * *

Among the new houses along my road, Halloween lights began to glimmer. Once upon a time, I had thought the American practice at Christmastime, of stringing electric lights everywhere, an exercise in unbridled extravagance. Who in my village at home would have done such a thing? Electricity was expensive and possibly dangerous; remember Mrs. Moodie, who worried about our telly. It seemed to me, too, that this phenomenon began earlier and earlier every year. The lights came on in October, not at Thanksgiving, and were orange. In the brief blue twilights their strands shone out like a second sunset.

Ranse loved Halloween. He liked to bring home pumpkins from the produce stands and carve them. Though he had to be up early, he would spend half the night with his penknife, carving some intricate scene into the pumpkin's thick rind. One year it was the Great Fire of London. Another year it was Theseus wrestling the Minotaur, copied from a photograph of a Greek vase in a book I hadn't realized we owned.

"Don't talk to me," he would grunt as he worked—Ranse, who always begged me to talk to him. When the carving was finished, the candle lit, he would come and wake me. At three in the morning, we would stand in the front yard and admire together how the picture he'd made flared on the darkness.

At Halloween we kept a bowl of sweets at the ready, beside the front door, though nobody came. In those days we lived in greater isolation, surrounded by fields and woods. No children knocked at the door, and in the end Ranse ate up the sweets himself. It was no good saying, "Mind your blood sugar." Even his own mother never said that. He was her only child, and she indulged him. If he wanted to eat the entire bowl of Hershey's Kisses and turn down his supper, that was his privilege, she said.

Frequently in the early days of our marriage she took me aside. Men didn't like henpecking women, she told me. I had better watch myself. I had thought that caring what Ranse ate meant that I cared about Ranse; that was why I *made a wark about it*, as my father would have said. But surely she knew better than I did? If she didn't know better, she certainly loved Ranse better, or so I thought. Meekly I held my tongue. I might have blamed Mother Sain, I suppose, when eventually Ranse lost his sight. I might have blamed her when we thought he would lose a leg. I might have blamed her when, instead, deep under anesthesia, he lost his life. But by the time all those things happened, she was long dead herself, beyond blame, awaiting Ranse with eagerness at the eternal banquet table. I couldn't begrudge her. I couldn't believe otherwise. Besides, I too had let him eat up the chocolates.

In any event, someone had to be the child. This is how it often happens, I believe, when couples have no children of their own. Mrs. Moodie across the way, the same Mrs. Moodie who worried so over our telly, used to harangue her husband so that we could hear as we sat at our own kitchen table. *Andrew? Andrew! did you no take your pill?* Granny Astrid, Mrs. Moodie's greatest friend, used to say, "When she goes to bury him, she'll be shouting down the hole, *Andrew! You dinna take your pill!*" Even my mother smiled at that.

But this is how it goes, in my experience. We, too, had no children. From the beginning I had been honest with Ranse: there would be no children. He didn't want to believe me, but it was true. I had been ill. Something had gone wrong. Still, for a long time, he had hoped. I might have been wrong. As a Christian, too, he was open to the possibility, even the probability, of a miracle. But as the years passed and no miracle occurred, he ate up the chocolates I bought and said no more. And I did nothing to stop him.

* * *

Dermott's handmade wingtips were dark and buttery as the best chocolate. Carelessly in his chair he crossed his legs; the lamplight shone in the richness of those shoes. He read my essay; I studied those shoes, the most beautiful shoes in all creation. As his pencil moved over what I had written, my gaze shifted from his shoes to my own white vinyl boots, zipped up the inside of my calves, the latest thing. Clumping across the rain-polished court in those boots, I had felt grown up, a scholar and a sophisticate. Now, as I sat watching him read, the feeling fizzled to nothing. When he moved his hand in the lamplight, its magnified shadow fell over me. With his silver-threaded dark hair that fell onto his forehead, his long languid body, his white fingers, he might have been another Father Burke, laicized, worldly, more manicured, with better shoes. If Father Burke had looked at me, in all my pre-adolescent awkwardness, I would have dropped dead. When Dermott looked at me, I did drop dead.

He sat at the desk beneath the window. The bitter autumn pressed close outside. I sat where he had directed me to sit, in the dull-green Morris chair, whose arms I clutched in my nervousness until my hands were numb. Dermott was reading my essay, turning the pages, smiling to himself. My heart thudded. Was he laughing at me? What would he say? At last he cast down the page he was reading.

"You're a clever girl. You must know already that this is all a bit *credulous*." His eyes crinkled.

I cast about in my mind for some answer, something not stupid or childish or superstitious or *folkloric*, for God's sake. Already Dermott laughed at my accent as something quaint. If I had been older or braver, I might have asked what he meant by *credulous*. This was not a word Sister Bede had ever used. In her class, between explications of the poems, she had evoked for us the cat-and-mouse game of Southwell's secret priesthood, the hides he climbed in and out of, the hair's-breadth escapes, the hawking terms he sweated to remember. As much as the poems thrilled her, and us, it was the bold words at the gibbet that stirred us, the mental spectacle of the bowels steaming as they were unreeled from the warm and quivering body. Sister Bede did not laugh at these things. She never intimated that our poet had wasted his life, that he might have done anything else but what was asked of him. Was this what it meant to be *credulous?*

"I mean to say," Dermott went on, "you don't believe all that, surely? Southwell and all those silly Jesuits? The *Old Faith*? Not seriously, my darling girl?"

Sister Bede would have laughed at Dermott. Silly man, she would have said. Moreover, she would have prayed for him. Sitting there in the silence, with the ticking of the rain, the electric fire glowing with all its bars on, I did not think of Sister Bede at all. I did not think to pray. Dermott had called me his *darling girl,* and that was what I needed, of all things. If I didn't feel utterly happy, it was only my own stupidity that got in the way.

Dermott was watching me. "Tell me truly, my lovely. I shall be so disappointed. I thought we'd a meeting of minds here. You *don't* believe all that?"

All about us, his books lined the walls. They stood in stacks on the floor and breathed out their musty yellow scent. If I wanted to take my degree, I should have to stuff my head with what was in those books. There would be no room for anything else. I should have to stuff my head with them if I wanted Dermott. Or if not Dermott, then someone like Dermott. But why not Dermott? After all, he wasn't Father Burke. He belonged to another world entirely: *the* world. Somehow, if I were to make my real mind, that mind Dermott said I'd the makings of, I must reckon with these books. I must let Dermott help me make it.

He was watching me. The books were waiting.

"Is it time for a drink?" he said at last. The cut crystal gleamed in the lamplight. Handed a glass, I breathed the peaty scent it held.

I do not know that my mind was made, that night or any other time during the twilit weeks of that one fleeting autumn. Something was made between us, I will tell you that, something transitory and irrevocable all at once. Our Lord was not wrong when he spoke of *one flesh.* He did not speak of a meeting of minds. The mind is a vaporous thing. It passes through the minds it meets and continues on its way. But the body . . .

Of course the time came when, on arriving for our appointments, I found other people with Dermott in his rooms. Our meetings had become not one-to-one tutorials, but seminars. He read aloud to us, lectured a bit, encouraged us to speak. There was another girl who turned up for these sessions, a girl I hadn't seen before: tall, white-faced, Irish. Once, as the group was breaking up, I saw Dermott draw her aside. "Do write something for me and bring it round," I heard him murmur. "We'll have a little talk." It was exactly what he had said to me, weeks before. The light from the window shone on her straight black hair, turning it almost blue.

I went to see Dermott once, uninvited. Only once. It was the sort of thing a girl in a relationship might do, I thought: pop round and surprise the man she'd been sleeping with.

He hadn't looked pleased. He had not invited me in. He had simply stood in the staircase doorway, the light of his rooms behind him. His voice had sounded harried.

"Did you have an appointment?" he'd said. "Was there something you particularly wanted to ask?"

I had gained weight lately. Tired and sick with work, I hardly looked my best. Even in the dim stairwell, I caught Dermott's appraising glance.

"A particular question that absolutely can't wait? Because—" He looked past me, as if he expected someone else at any moment.

"No," I said. "Sorry. Never mind."

The door closed. The stairway went dark. I stumbled back down the stairs in my stupid heeled boots. Back in the light of day, I saw I'd laddered my newest nylons. It was that, I told myself, that made me cry.

* * *

The last Saturday in October, when I went to confession as usual, I was startled to find not Father Schuyler behind the screen, but the Bishop. Though it had been thirty years, I recognized his voice at once. Long ago, he had been our pastor, in his first parish assignment. A soft-voiced, gentle, self-deprecating man, he had seemed as shocked as anyone else to find himself created Bishop. But as far as I could tell, he was a good Bishop. He visited his parishes; he spoke with his priests. And now here he was, crouched in our closet of reconciliation, listening to me as once again I retailed my dreary little sins of commission and omission.

On the Sunday morning, he was there to concelebrate. I expected that he would preach, but instead, Father Schuyler rose to the ambo as usual. All about me, I could feel the congregation shift and resettle itself in resignation. A sheaf of papers shook in Father's hands. He didn't look well. As he launched into his homily, someone behind me whispered, "Didn't I tell you people were complaining?"

This homily was a mild one by Father's standards: no demons, no exhortations to extremes of penance. Unusually, he focused on the psalm, which was one of my private favorites. *When the Lord brought back the captives from Zion, we were like men dreaming.* He preached on the mercy of God, which human beings can hardly bring themselves to believe in. He preached briefly, his voice unsteady. When he sat down, his face looked paler than ever.

Afterwards, instead of escaping into the sacristy, he stood at the Bishop's elbow and shook people's hands. Ordinarily I ducked out through the side door without greeting the pastor, assuming that the pastor was there to be greeted. Today, instead, I waited in the queue. In my turn, I let the Bishop take my hand in his cool, dry one.

"It's good to have you here," I told him, and I meant it. My heart did warm nostalgically to the sight of him.

"Ah, yes, Mrs.—"

"Mrs. Sain, your Excellency," I said. "It has been a long time."

He smiled, but his smile had become the practiced smile of the Bishop, who greets many people and remembers none of them. Oh, well. It had been a long time. I shook Father Schuyler's hand; he looked catatonic. I wondered whether he had known in advance that the Bishop was coming.

* * *

It had been the Bishop, all those years ago, a new pastor in his first parish, who heard the first confession I'd made since leaving school. The last time I'd gone had been sixth form: all of us queued against the back wall of the chapel, because that was what we did on Saturday afternoons. Later, knocking about on my own in a university town, released from the sisters and the measured rounds of school life, I sometimes thought of going to confession. Somehow I never quite got round to it. I had lost the knack for self-examination. As for contrition, if

I'd let myself feel it, I'd have had to stop doing any number of things I did not want to stop doing and start doing things I felt no inclination to do. As I did with the terse, dutiful letters my mother wrote me once a week, thin and dry in my pigeonhole in the porter's lodge, I pushed aside my sins, unopened and unread. I knew what the envelopes contained. The news was always the same. *Later*, I said.

Though I hadn't meant it when I said it, I did one day arrive at *later*. I'd been married some years by then, settled in Annesdale, in the house with Ranse and Mother Sain. I'd been there long enough that my married life had ceased to seem alien to me. My former life felt like something dreamt, not lived. I had learnt to operate the hoover, drive the car, do the shopping and the cooking. My native accent, already somewhat homogenized by my time at university, had begun to take on the flat vowels of the North Carolina Piedmont. I would always be an outsider, but by the time *later* came round, I'd grown used to it all. *The new normal,* I've heard people say, and so it was.

As a rule, on Sundays, Ranse drove his mother to worship at Spake's Fork Baptist Church, a white cinderblock edifice with a graveled car park, a steeple like a dunce cap, and a window-unit air conditioner in what might have been a small, square stained-glass transom above the front doors. Because Ranse expected it, I accompanied them. Sunday after Sunday, I sat with them in the damp rattling breath of the air conditioner, listening to the swish of Bible pages as people turned them, following the sermon. I was depressed by the whitewashed plainness of the interior, with its raised dais at the front, the American flag in its stand to the preacher's right hand when he stood in his black gown behind the unadorned pine lectern that served as a pulpit, the Ten Commandments posted on the wall above the choir, who sat in blue-satin ranks behind the pulpit and gazed on us with stoicism when not engaged in singing. All of it both did and did not remind me of the chapels I had known in my youth. It both did and did not resemble what I knew of the breadth of the Christian religion. I had cast off that religion like an old coat—cast it off, or mislaid it. Wherever I'd left it, it wasn't here.

Mother Sain fretted for my own sake as well as for Ranse's, and that of any children we might have. Like Ranse, knowing even less about my past than he did, she too lived in anticipation of a miracle. Should that miracle occur—which of course it did not—she worried that I would set it a poor example. But I do her an injustice. In her way, she practiced charity towards me. When I caught her looking at me, her eyes were not hostile, but troubled. Sometimes out of the blue she would say to me, "It's such a *comfort* to have Jesus as your personal Savior." Or she would ask, "Do you ever think about getting saved?" Once I overheard her confiding to Ranse, "I just *wish* she'd go on and be born again."

"Now, Mama," I heard him say. "Don't fuss. One way or another she'll come around."

I have come to believe that we pray not only without ceasing, but without meaning to. Mother Sain would not have thought that she was praying when she said those words, but I believe that she must have been. Eventually her prayer was answered, though not in the way she would have chosen. As she saw it, I had never been a Christian of any description. My baptism, imposed on me in my unconscious infancy, could not have been a real baptism, a baptism of faith, born of a single moment of decision for Christ. How could it have been, when I didn't remember anything about it? How could other people have made those promises without my conscious consent? To her, my childhood Catholicism was a paganism from which she longed to see me definitively delivered. If I no longer bothered to practice that paganism, to her my lapse represented the setting of my feet on the road to eternal salvation. Naturally she also desired some solid assurance that Ranse and any children of ours would be spared the fiery pit of incense, Latin mutterings, and bingo.

But, well. Ranse had said that I would come round one way or another, and so I did. At the time, we had been married nearly ten years. Mother Sain had begun to slip into dementia, but was not yet so far gone that she couldn't play bridge with her friends. Many of them were slipping, too; I can only imagine how repetitive the conversations became, or how eccentric the strategies at cards. That March day, I'd dropped her at the home of a Mrs. Abernethy, a leading Annesdale matron. Thanking her maid—rest eternal, light perpetual—I fled the fragrant house with its shiny blue satin upholsteries and triple-layered drapes. Shoulders tensed, I drove out of the neighborhood, beneath the laced bare branches of the old oaks, and turned west out of town on the rural highway. I had time to kill, and I meant to kill it, though my plans for its execution remained hazy in my mind.

I knew that Annesdale had a Catholic church, just as I knew that it had a municipal airport and a Knights of Pythias lodge. Nondescript as it was, set back from the road on its plot of meadowland, I had never paid the church any mind. Like the airport and the Knights of Pythias, it was nothing to do with me. Yes, I had been infatuated with Father Burke. Yes, Sister Bede had been good to me. Yes, yes, I might say to myself, those were the days. Those were the days, and like everything else I'd loved, they had gone from me. There was only that ugly building, alien in its ugliness, which lurked in grasses at the edge of my view as I drove past it, going to town or coming home again.

That day, however, as I drove the highway, driving simply

to drive, with no destination in mind, my eye fell on the large crucifix, recently erected beside the road. On the blocky concrete cross, stained cardboard-box brown, an incongruously delicate white corpus levitated in the shifting spring sunshine. Impulsively I checked my speed and turned down the drive. Why I did so I couldn't tell you even now. I couldn't even call it *holy chance.* It was an impulse in the truest sense of that word: unpremeditated, instinctual, compulsive. It was demanded of me; therefore, I did it.

Nobody seemed to be about. It would all be locked up, I told myself. Nevertheless, I got out of my car. To my surprise, the door yielded to my yanking. I went inside, into a smell of waxed linoleum. The empty church, with its plain walls and its raised dais at the front, might have been Spake's Fork Baptist Church, save for the postcard-sized Stations of the Cross round the walls, the modest altar draped in purple. Of course. It was Lent. I thought I had cast off the measuring of liturgical time. Still, there it was, waiting to readmit me to its seasons. That day, I did nothing but sit in the quiet. I felt an intruder. I felt I'd returned to a house I'd sold, whose current owner might happen upon me making myself at home. But like Janet, in that quiet, I looked at the tabernacle. What was in the tabernacle looked at me. For a long time we looked at each other. When I got up to leave, I knew what I would do next.

On my way out, I noted the sign in the narthex that listed confession times. A first confession after years away is bound to be memorable, at least to the penitent. Naturally, I had much to say, many more sins of commission, and not a few of omission. There was much I had done, much I had not done, for years and years, and I was weary of carrying it all with me. People speak of weeping in the confessional, but I never have, and I didn't then. I felt too tired for weeping, and too cold in my soul. I simply told it all.

When I was finished, the young priest said in his gentle voice, "Remember this: those things are in the past. Whatever else happens, you are not that person anymore. Do you understand?"

"Yes, Father," I said. I went out, leaving my sins behind me. I prayed my penance, and I went home. Next day, while Ranse read the funny papers, I went to Mass and received the Body and Blood of God. All these years later, here I was again, repeating the cycle: born again, born again, born again. It was what Mother Sain had wished for me, after all. She did not consider, nor did I know, having never given birth, how long it can take or what hard work it is.

* * *

The queue to shake the Bishop's hand had been long. And of course, everyone had to shake hands twice, first with the Bishop, then more awkwardly with Father Schuyler. As I emerged from the church door and made for my car, I was surprised to find Howard Malkin still shepherding his children into their big dented van. "Get in, now. Hannah, get in. Help Henry with his booster seat. Has anybody seen Lucy? Is she still in there talking? Talking, talking, always talking —"

"I'm right here, Dad," said Lucy from the depths of the van.

"All right, all right. Isaac, you climb in the very back, now, and be my scout. You tell me if anybody's behind me." He handed another of his daughters into the van. Then, seeing me, he waved. "I try to park so I can drive straight out," he said. "The whole rear end of this van is one giant blind spot. If I have to reverse, I station somebody to make sure the coast is clear." Slamming the door on the last of his children, he added, "Janet says come see her. She wonders where you've been."

"Indeed I shall." I spoke with more conviction than I'd mustered last time, but also with a pang of remorse. What was it I had been telling myself? I imagined Janet, waiting on her cracked sofa, *wanting* to be intruded upon, and I was ashamed. I should have something to confess, next time I went.

Hearing my step in the kitchen, the kitten set up a loud cry from his box by the cooker. Scooping him up, setting him on his litter, I said to myself, *Here am I with my ugly baby.* The empty eyes stared up at me as if they saw me. By now he knew who I was, and he generally had a good idea *where* I was. Upon completing his task, he turned round and smelt what he had done, then scraped litter over his productions with an expert paw, exactly as if he could see what he was doing. Then, sniffing his way forward, he crept to the edge of the litter box and stepped off. He smacked the floor face first and emitted a startled squeak.

"There, you." I moved to set him on his feet again, but he was faster than I was. Sniffing, he came to me and bumped his nose along my shoe and up my ankle. I poured him a little kitten chow. He followed the crinkle of the bag, the rattle of the food, mewing strenuously. As he ate, he continued to talk. "Mewf," he said, chewing. "Mowf."

While I stood at the kitchen window eating my sandwich, he skittered about the floor, batting at nothing, leaping and pouncing. Once he ran into the table leg. He fell back with a cry, shaking his head. Then he was off again, sidling, levitating, playing like any kitten.

In spite of myself, I smiled to see him. As if he heard my smile as a call, he came to me.

"Mow," he said, and sharpened his claws on my trouser cuff.

* * *

On Monday the weather turned. The sky hung cloud-heavy over my house. The last black-eyed Susans had gone to seed, and the beds along the front porch were full of their dark knobs. Crows were calling back and forth in flat, sardonic voices and striding with upright purpose across my front-yard grass.

To my surprise, when I arrived to do the Monday cleaning, I found Father Schuyler at home. He sat beneath the picture window at the secretary's desk, with its crucifix and unlit candles. He was studying some papers spread before him. Remembering Father Trotter and the bottles in the typewriter compartment, I wondered whether Father Schuyler ever drank. He might have wanted a drink after the weekend I imagined he'd had.

"Writing your homily, Father?" I said a little lamely.

He glanced up in annoyance. Then his expression softened. "I wish. I'd rather write homilies than notes for the parish council meeting. Which is what I'm doing right now, unfortunately."

"Did you have a good visit with the Bishop?" It was something to say, though perhaps not precisely the right thing to say.

"A good visit?" He laughed in a strangled way. "I guess you could call it a good visit. It was very revelatory."

"Yes," I said, "I can see how it might have been. If you're busy, Father, I can come back another time —"

He laid down the page he had been holding. "No, no, that's all right. I have some noise-canceling headphones here. Make all the racket you want."

I occupied myself with cleaning. As always, the house

looked untouched. When I had finished, I went to take my leave of Father and, once he'd removed the noise-canceling headphones and could understand me without lip-reading, I ventured to remark that it looked as though nobody lived there at all.

"Do you not eat, Father?" I said. "People have noticed that you've lost weight."

He sighed. "People have noticed a lot of things. As was explained to me at length this past weekend."

"Are you happy at all, Father? In the parish, that is. I mean—" I put my hand to my lips as if I meant, too late, to press the words back in.

But Father only smiled at me, a little sadly. "No, never mind. I know what people think. I know how it all looks. I'm not really good with people, you know."

Yes, I thought. If there was one thing we did know, it was that Father wasn't good with people.

"I don't mind preaching. That I can do just fine. I can deal with two hundred faces. Just not one at a time, asking me questions and expecting me to answer."

I gazed at him in wonder.

"I know," he said. "I know what you're thinking. I have been to therapy. I was the kind of kid parents worry about. But you know, by the time I entered the process for ordination, I was fine. Not an extrovert, but perfectly functional. I could deal." Again the strangled laugh. "I think my formators thought I'd end up in Rome, getting a Ph.D. They didn't quite envision this parish, or me in it. But they also didn't seem to worry about me too much."

"That's hopeful," I said.

"It was. For a long time I felt great. In the seminary . . . but now . . ." He sighed and drummed his fingers on the desk.

"This reminds me," I said after a moment's thought, "of the Ignatian Spiritual Exercises."

"Ah." Another faint smile. "You know the Spiritual Exercises?"

"A little. At least, the bit that sticks in my head is what Saint Ignatius says about all the things that come to us in our lives. Our vocations, but also all our difficulties."

"They're sent to us to help us get to heaven," said Father. "Yes. I often meditate on that. I never meant to go into parish ministry. I thought I'd be a monk. A Carmelite. All that silence sounded like heaven on earth to me."

Yes, I could certainly see that it would.

"I didn't last three months. I went in, and I was ecstatically happy. I felt closer to God there than I've ever felt in my life, before or since. I'd look out the window to the churchyard, where every monk knows he's going to end up sooner or later, and the sight filled me with the most enormous sense of peace and well-being. Then one day my superior called me in, told me I didn't have a vocation, and sent me home."

"That must have been a blow," I said.

He winced at the memory. "Yes. My childhood parish had given me a big emotional send-off, so to turn up again after three months—you can imagine the humiliation. Hometown Boy Achieves Monk Fail."

He blinked hard. For a moment his face clenched like a fist. His bleak expression made me want to stroke his head, but I restrained myself.

After a moment he continued, steadying his voice. "So then I didn't know what to do with myself. I had to get out of the house, make some money. My parents made that clear. I wasn't going to sit in my room reconstructing the contemplative life I'd left. You'll always be a Carmelite, my superior said. Not like that, you won't, said my dad." His voice trailed away.

After a moment I prompted him. "What did you do, then, Father?"

"I waited tables. And I was fine. I hated it, but I did it. It felt meaningless, and then of course I'm an introvert. It was kind of excruciating, night after night. But I could make myself go through the motions." He threw me a glance. "Then I entered the process for the priesthood. I never really expected that to work out. I'd failed at being a monk. Why should I succeed at being a seminarian? But I did. I was an exemplary seminarian. I was unbelievably good at being a seminarian. After that I was a not-bad parochial vicar. Now here I am."

"And?"

"And the Bishop has had a stern word with me. In fact, over the weekend, he had many stern words." Father rested his elbows on the desk and rubbed his eyes. "And I promised I'd do better. If I can't do this—the parish thing, in this parish—he doesn't know what he'll do with me. I —" He looked up, and his anxious eyes caught mine. "I don't know, either. What am I going to do?"

I felt that at this juncture, possibly, another stern word was indicated. "For starters, Father, I suggest that you eat more. You're no good to anybody if you waste away."

"The Desert Fathers attained holiness through extensive fasting." His tone had regained its austerity. This was more familiar ground.

"They attained holiness on the tops of bloody pillars," I said. "They sat up there and did a spot of devil-wrestling. And then people brought them food. Which they ate, like sensible men." I glared at him. Really, once I let myself, I found I could be angry with him. Or if not angry, exactly, out of patience. "You don't live on the top of a pillar, Father. You're in a parish. With people."

He rewarded me with a less pallid smile. "You're one to talk."

"What? What's that supposed to mean?" I snatched up

my handbag and made as if to go.

Father laughed outright. "Write these words on your heart, my daughter," he said, and raised his hand in blessing.

* * *

Which words, exactly, I should write on my heart, I did not know. Did Father think that I needed, myself, an efficacious little spot of devil-wrestling? *I'll show him,* I said. That afternoon, after some prayer and some girding of loins, I presented myself again at the Malkins' door. I was surprised again, after ringing the bell for some minutes, that it was Janet who answered.

"Aren't you supposed to be horizontal?" I asked her.

"Nobody else listens for the door."

The house was quiet. On my way in, I had seen the two biggest boys peering beneath the bonnet of a dented car, but otherwise the children had vanished. Janet led me back to the den, festooned as before with a week's worth of washing.

She lowered herself with some difficulty onto the sofa. "The girls are in the basement doing some craft thing. Lucy told the little ones that they could use hot glue and watch *Yours, Mine, and Ours.*"

Indeed, from somewhere below I could hear the blare of a television, periodic outbursts of laughter.

Janet was counting on her fingers. "Isaac's supposed to be doing math homework. He got in trouble at school last week. Apparently he's done no homework since the second week of September, so now it's all detention all the time. And Henry's somewhere. He tucks himself away. But he'll turn up." She laughed.

My face must have marveled at her nonchalance. Like most childless people, I could not imagine misplacing a child, let alone laughing about it.

Janet said, "Lately he's been doing this thing where he gets out of bed in the middle of the night and roams around. He's not sleepwalking, he claims. He's totally awake. When we ask him what's going on, he just says, *I have been NIGHT EXPLORING*. Like, oh, okay, NIGHT EXPLORING. That explains everything, kid."

More explosions of laughter from the basement, then a little girls' voice rose in lamentation. "Margaret, why did you use up all the glitter before it was my turn?"

"We've been finding him in some weird places in the morning." Janet kept talking as always, unruffled by the commotion. "Last week he woke up in the fireplace. Another time he was out in the bushes. Fast asleep, and mad as hell when we woke him up, like somebody had put a spell on him."

She spoke with animation, but the skin beneath her sea-glass eyes looked smudged with charcoal. "Are you all right?" I asked her.

"Eh." She waved a hand. "I'm tired. And tired of doing nothing. It makes me tired to lie here. But they're still worried about the placenta. They say it's too low or too loose or something. I still get these little bits of bleeding. I don't know how lying here is going to change anything, but doctors like to think you're doing something. So here I lie, until they tell me I can get up. I'm staying put, I promise you, I really am."

"Aren't those children helping you at all?" I had asked last time; I couldn't help asking again. I couldn't help how censorious I undoubtedly sounded, and I waited for Janet to take umbrage.

But she only laughed again. "Oh, yeah. Super helpful. And now we have a boyfriend on the scene. He's Lucy's, and he works at the Bi-Lo, and I keep getting his name wrong. It's one of those *-ayden* names that every other person has anymore. *Brayden, Cayden, Grayden, Hayden, Jayden, Zayden.* Something like that. I just mumble so only the *-ayden* part comes out. He seems to be here for dinner every night, regardless. Lucy," she called, as Lucy emerged from the kitchen. "Is he here now? What's his name?"

Lucy advanced into the den with a bag of popcorn in her hand. "It's *Kane*, Mom, like *Citizen Kane*, but thanks for playing. He's downstairs right now gluing eyes on a plate for my Halloween costume. Hi, Miss Kirsty." She proffered the popcorn. I accepted some, though I didn't want it, and then had to chew it, a mouthful of styrofoam.

"That's my job," said Janet. "What's he doing making your Halloween costume?"

"It must be love," sang Lucy, to a tune of her own devising. "What's for dinner?"

I had gone digging in my deep-freeze before I came. "I brought you two pans of chicken casserole," I told Janet now. "My mother-in-law's famous bridge-party recipe. Frozen solid at the moment, so you can eat them tonight or save them for later. It's really just chicken and rice, something everybody likes, I hope. Perhaps one of the children would bring the pans in from the car?"

Lucy, whom I had been almost disliking, flashed me the smile that must have won young Kane's heart. Even I, crusty as I was, could see how he would have melted. "I'll get them, Miss Kirsty. I am helping, really I am. I've been making supper a lot. And Hannah and Margaret and Clare. Even Miriam and Naomi can make box mac and cheese if they have to. But Mom usually decides what we're having. She holds the reins. Right, Mom?"

"I'm queen of this house, and don't you forget it," said

Janet. Dancing from the room, Lucy paused to kiss the top of her mother's head.

I sat with Janet until dusk began to fall. Setting out, I'd meant only to stop in for a moment with my food offering, then beg off to go to confession: Father had instituted a time every weekday afternoon. Since my exchange with Howard the day before, I'd felt burdened. Now that I was with Janet, however, it seemed to me that whatever reparation I needed to make for my sins, this small work of mercy might suffice. Truly, though, the longer I sat, the less like a reparation it all felt. It was pleasant to sit in the midst of that chaos which bothered nobody, apparently, but me. It wasn't my chaos, there was nothing I could do about it, and after a while, when nobody else seemed to mind it, I stopped minding as well. I was pleased when Howard came in with grease smeared down the front of his t-shirt and—having stopped to wash his hands—touched my shoulder to ask me how I was. I sat comfortably among the family's washing while the girls paraded their half-finished Halloween costumes before Janet and me. They were all dressing as their names, which is to say as saints or Hebrews, with many drapes and veils and little props to indicate who they were. Isaac dragged in with his maths book and won parole for the evening.

Outside, darkness was falling. "Dominic," Janet called in the direction of the kitchen. "Is there wine? Bring Miss Kirsty a glass of wine!"

Dominic, barefoot, big and shambling like his father, with black curls falling into his eyes, brought me red wine in a half-pint jam jar. I drank it and felt merry and confidential with Janet, who drank seltzer water from a can. She told me many things about herself, too many for me to retail here. It gave me a feeling of intimacy to be told so much. Whom had I ever known to be so trusting? Only Ranse.

Going out, touching the mezuzah as I went, I met Henry in the shadowy front garden, creeping on hands and knees among the leggy azaleas.

"I am a cat," he called to me. "I am stalking, stalking, stalking the birds. But." He stood up out of the azaleas like a girl bursting from a cake. "I am only stalking. Not killing."

"That's good," I said. "You should come and meet my cat sometime. You could teach him a thing or two about stalking."

"I could teach him swimming," said Henry.

"Oh, yes? The lessons are going well?"

"I can go like this now." He made a flailing motion with his arms.

"I see. Well done. Keep up the good work," I said.

He regarded me severely, as I had seen him look at Lucy. "I intend to."

Driving home in the dark, I passed the turning for Wylie Springfield's trailer neighborhood. Darkness veiled the rutted side road, the gray tangle of kudzu vines, the neat little patches of lawn round each trailer. Through the blinds drawn down over the small windows, lights shone dimly. As I coasted past, looking down into the ravine, one trailer's door opened, and a human shadow extended itself briefly across the yellowing grass. The door snapped shut again; the shadow vanished. I drove on.

I hadn't seen Wylie since the Sunday he'd brought me the kitten. This struck me as strange. Though he had never been quite a daily presence in my life, still I'd long fancied I felt him near me, hovering and attentive, even when he didn't ring my doorbell. I liked that feeling. It must be, I thought, what having a grown son would be like. You didn't want him under foot all the time. You didn't want him living in your basement, eating up your food, watching telly till all hours. People did have sons who grew up and moved away, but not too far. I had heard women remark that the bulb in their ceiling light had burned out, and that they'd have to ring their son to come and change it. Presumably the son would do so. Perhaps he would stay to supper. He might bring his own children to visit while he changed the bulb, replaced the toilet seat, put up the Christmas tree, all the innumerable things that an aging woman can do perfectly well herself, as I have had reason to know. It's not necessarily that you can't do those things. But if there's someone who'll come and do them for you, to repay the debt of his own life to the creditor who gave it to him, then why would you do those things, and rob that person of his opportunity? Of course, with Wylie, it wasn't quite like that. But when a week went by, then two, then three, and I didn't see him, what I missed was that almost feeling.

5

In the afternoons the sun shone, warming the screened porch. In that light and warmth, I let the kitten out for his constitutional. As I sat on the swing with my book, he tore up and down the porch, neatly missing chair and table legs in his flight. I watched him in fascination. Already he was long-legged, though his ears remained oversized, like a gargoyle's. He might have been a living gargoyle, in fact, made of liquid stone. Batlike he navigated, hurtling about, though I knew that if I scraped a chair back or moved my leg, he'd run into it. I had seen him miscalculate, fly into the kitchen table leg like a bird hitting a window, and fall back with a cry of pain and rage. When this happened, he would shake his sightless head, smell about him to take his bearings, then be off again. His capacity for memorizing his surroundings impressed me. Once or twice I'd thought of scrambling the furniture, just to see how long it took him to recalibrate the map in his head. I thought he might consider this a game. But then again, it seemed cruel. I'd left things where they stood. When he tired of exploring the porch, he came to me and with his little excruciating claws, climbed my trouser leg to settle himself on my lap. His eyeless face wore a look of satisfaction. I stroked his spine with one finger and felt him vibrate.

I bought a large bag of Halloween sweets. Now that I did have neighbors, I had to be ready for them to come knocking. One year I'd forgotten trick-or-treat and had awakened on

All Saints Day to festoons of toilet paper in all my trees. Have I mentioned that I do not love children? Experimentally, I sampled one of the little chocolate bars, which of course, being American, was not simply chocolate, but consisted of layers: chocolate, nougat, caramel, and some variety of crushed nut. I couldn't finish it. It was with no sense of sacrifice on my part that I twisted up the open end of the bag and stashed it all away in the deep freezer.

The night before Halloween, I dreamt of Ranse. Who can say where these things come from, or why? I have never believed in dreams as prophetic, sent by God. At most, I think, they are the subconscious mind's way of trying to work something out, some problem it isn't even aware of, perhaps, in its conscious state. Often, since Ranse died, I had dreamt of him. He came to me so vividly, in strange places and situations, that when I woke I invariably reached out to touch him before remembering that he had gone.

I had had this particular dream recurrently. In it, I was walking beside the river. Rain peppered my face. I felt it. I could see it puckering the river's skin. I could smell the dream-river, taste the cold on my lips. And though I refused to look at Ranse, who walked beside me along the towpath, I could feel him. I could more than feel him. His wet down-filled jacket had a smell. His clean skin had a smell. An energy seemed to radiate from him, magnetically warm. I felt my shoulder brush his as we looked at the river, side by side. Even through the thickness of my coat, I could feel some current move between us. Before us, the brown river swirled and eddied, carrying sticks and leaves and bits of rubbish in great whorls downstream to the weir.

Ranse touched my arm. "What's that in the water?"

The water was full of things. I looked where he pointed.

"That's a baby," said Ranse.

I saw it. Whirled on the current, tossed among branches and sweet papers and empty IPA cans, a small human form came floating, face down. Its arms and legs wavered whitely on the dark water.

Ranse was shrugging off his jacket; I caught it before it could fall to the ground. "I'm going in," he said.

"You can't." Struggling with the jacket, I reached for him. For reasons I could never explain outside the dream, it was crucial, the most crucial thing of all, that I not drop Ranse's jacket on the wet towpath. The jacket was heavy and wanted to slither from my hands; I wrestled with it as with a living thing. "You'll freeze," I said.

But he was unbuttoning his shirt. "I can't leave a baby in that water."

I looked again more closely. The object in the water came on, naked and pale, swirled this way and that as the currents buffeted it. "It's only a doll," I said.

"Looks real to me." He was unlacing his shoes. My hands were occupied with his jacket, heavier and heavier every minute.

"No, it's only a doll. A real baby would be—" What? Blue, I thought. Dead. Not inanimate, but dead. "It's a doll. Let it go."

All the while I was holding his jacket, weighted with rain and a will of its own. A sleeve would pull loose and dangle; frantically I gathered it up again, but then the other sleeve would fall. Meanwhile, the thing in the water bumped and turned and went past us. I watched it, too. Now—I thought —perhaps its whiteness was tinged with blue. As it passed, it seemed to twitch with sudden life.

"It does look real," I said. In that instant the jacket was gone from my arms, and Ranse stood beside me, clothed and shod.

"I guess you're right." I felt him sigh. The thing swept past us and away. Whatever it was, it was lost to us. We would never know any more about it.

In the darkness I awoke, confused. For a moment I'd no idea where I was. I might have been in my bed in college. I might have been at home, a child, listening to the wind and rain, the battering of the sea. Or I might have sprung into existence that minute, fully formed, an old woman in Annesdale with thick ankles and faded hair, slapped out of nothingness into life. As always, reflexively, I reached for Ranse. Then I remembered.

As I lay counting my own heartbeats, the other scene came to me, the one I knew I hadn't dreamt: one scene, or a series of them, all the same, like a recurring dream. A handful of weeks, that was all it had been, but even as I lived them, they had felt like a dream, with a dream's telescoping time. A handful of weeks, an eternity. So often, in that dreamlike waking life, I had stepped from those college rooms to walk beside the river, clearing my head. Now, having walked beside the river, I returned in the waking dream of memory to that familiar room: the dull-green Morris chair, the books, the rain, the electric fire drying the air, the row of sharpened pencils on the table. I sat with my knees cocked up, tugging my skirt down, contemplating the ladder in my nylons. Dermott was reading what I had written. In the dim room, the waning daylight struck cold fire in his hair, where silver strands showed among the dark.

He cast down the page he had been holding and crinkled his eyes at me. "You're a clever girl. This is quite good. But it's still awfully *credulous*, don't you think?"

"Oh, well." Unthinking, I picked at the laddered place on my leg.

He was looking at me with fondness and laughter. "You

don't believe it all, surely? A clever girl like you? Southwell and those dreary old Jesuits? Poor things, they took it all so seriously, whether they were *actually* spies for P. Two or not. That's the fascinating bit, don't you think? *Were* they spies and traitors?"

I floundered for some intelligible response. "Oh, well, perhaps, in a sense?"

"In a *sense*." His voice mocked me affectionately. "Dear child. That's one way to put it. But surely, my lovely, we've all learnt something from the passage of time. You can't sit here, on this side of the Enlightenment, and have the same sort of mind as they did. Can you?"

I ran my finger over the ladder in my nylons, feeling the sudden roughness.

"You've such a beautiful mind, darling. But it's got to grow up, hasn't it?"

"Yes," I said. "I suppose you're right."

"Quite right. I knew you were cleverer than all that."

For a moment he watched me. All about us, on the walls and on the floor, the books held their yellow breath.

"So truly," he said at last. "Tell me you don't believe all this you've written me. Not *seriously*, my darling girl."

I laughed and picked at the widening hole in my nylons. "Oh, no. I mean, one doesn't. That is, I went to convent school. Nuns." I laughed again. "It is only a draft, you know."

"Of course it is. It's there to be rewritten. You *are* going to work hard at rewriting, darling?"

"Yes. Yes, naturally. Of course I am." *Darling.* I laughed again. My voice was an alien noise in the quiet room. "I'll go home straightway and rewrite it. The whole bloody thing."

Dermott's eyes still crinkled, though now he did not look at me. His long fingers straightened the page he had just set down. *Enough of that,* the gesture said. He aligned the row of pencils on the desk beside my essay. When the straightness of it all satisfied him, he turned to me.

"Oh, don't go just yet. After all that, don't you think you deserve a drink?" As if he didn't notice what he did, he reached with one white finger and touched the rent I'd made in my nylons.

"Yes." Relief washed over me, or some similar sensation. "Yes, thank you. A drink would be divine."

* * *

After many brilliant days, All Hallows Eve dawned murky and wet. Through the dank morning fog, the Halloween lights on the neighboring houses made a sullen pinkish glow. I put on a heavier cardigan and kept the kitten inside. Not for the first time, I wondered how I was going to maintain him through the winter. Confining him to the house was the obvious solution, but even so, the house was drafty. If I wanted a cardigan, then surely a naked cat needed something between his bare skin and the air. Could you buy a jumper for a cat? And even if you could, would you succeed in putting him into it? How would you keep it on him? Even without eyes, this cat was clever. I'd seen him work a bit of lint from beneath the sofa, using his paws like hands. He was persistent, too, and frequently climbed me as if I were a tree. All my clothing had begun to develop a bouclé look from constant snagging by his claws. Watching him go up and down the stairs, I thought, *They shall need no light from lamps or the sun*. He was a very biblical creature, after all. On the other hand, when he climbed me and rode about the house on my shoulder, I felt like a witch with my leathery little familiar. Anyone seeing us would have mistaken us for—yes, that.

From its darkling start, the day continued *dreich*: chilly and bleak. At intervals rain blew up and jeweled all the windows. I went about the house doing little jobs of autumn cleaning, but I felt strangely tired and left most of them unfinished. I would begin to tidy out a kitchen drawer, then realize that I'd been standing for five minutes with a potato peeler in my hand and no idea why I'd picked it up or what I'd meant to do with it. A tickle had begun in my throat. Taking my sweets from the freezer where I'd hidden them, I hoped that my Halloween visitors would be early and few.

At five o'clock, coughing into my elbow, telling myself I'd only got allergies, I went to the Vigil Mass for All Saints. Father Schuyler, pale in his bright gold chasuble, processed in gales of incense on the heels of many altar boys, who went forward frowning in concentration, pressing their white-gloved hands together. My head was beginning to ache. We sang "For All the Saints" imperfectly, the organist seeming perplexed, as she was every year, by the timing, the choir rushing in before the downbeat. In the tinny light, Father's forehead shone with anxiety. His homily's theme: penance as the path to sainthood for us all. At last it was over, and I went home.

By now the tickle in my throat had become a raw spot. I could feel its outline, red and sharp, every time I swallowed. Although I still told myself it was only allergies, such as I often experienced in the autumn, I was beginning not to believe myself. As I stood at the kitchen window, drinking a mug of chicken broth while the kitten climbed my leg, the doorbell rang.

Though I had my bowl of sweets at the ready, I responded with some deliberation. Pulling off the kitten like a burr, I thrust him into my bedroom and shut the door. It wasn't only children abroad at Halloween. In his university days, Ranse had known a fraternity of men who liked to serve up vodka punch in a bowl chilled by a floating block of ice with a guinea pig frozen into it. There were people who found this sort of thing amusing, and Halloween seemed a likely time for them to be abroad. The kitten mewed and put his paws imploringly through the crack beneath the bedroom door, but I hardened my heart. He could bloody well stay where he was.

A car idled before the house in the dusk. On the screened porch stood a young couple with a baby in a pushchair. The baby, fast asleep, wore a pillowy pumpkin costume and a little orange beanie trimmed with green leaf and stem. The mother and father, who might have been as old as twenty, were dressed as zombies, with blood on their plaid flannel shirts, their faces made up to suggest putrefaction. At least, I assumed that the girl was the baby's mother, the boy its father. Really though, you never know, and perhaps it is better not to assume.

"Hello," I said scratchily.

They held up their pillowcases. "Trick or treat."

"Is this for him or for you?" I nodded at the sleeping baby.

"Aw." The girl smiled a brown smile. "He don't eat candy yet, he's too little. Can I have one of them Three Musketeer?"

Oh, well, I thought, and dropped a handful of chocolates into each pillowcase. They thanked me and went away.

This first group were followed by a straggle of similar groups. Each group included two or three adults, who might or might not have been related to each other, accompanied by children who might or might not have been related to each other or to any of the adults. Handing out sweets, I began to consider how people used each other as costumes, or props, or accessories. Did the adults accessorize themselves with children for the nocturnal adventure of Halloween, or did the children fit themselves out with whatever adults happened to be on hand? It was hard to say. Perhaps the convenience was mutual. In any case, there were many zombies. I congratulated numerous decaying five-year-olds for having reached my door before complete decomposition set in. Even the adults looked perplexed when I said things like that. Possibly, from their perspective, decay was the normal mode of existence, and I was the one who hadn't got the message.

I greeted also many little knots of teenagers, some in costume and some not, all bearing pillowcases or plastic grocery bags, which they raised in supplication. Two young men, memorably, wore aluminum-foil helmets and carried between them a sign that read, *Wake Up, Sheeple!*

"And what are you?" I asked them as I doled out the sweets.

"A conspiracy theory," they responded cheerfully, and went their way like the rest.

My throat felt more and more raw. My head had begun to pound. Between callers, I sat in the front room with a cup of tea and tried to read. The winter before, as a concession to age and frailty, I had bought an electric heater made in the image of a cast-iron wood-burning stove, with legs and a little glass door that swung open to reveal controls. By means of these you could switch on a blower, an incandescent bulb, and a revolving loop of cellophane printed with flame patterns in red and orange. When the heater was on, the flame patterns flowed up and around and back again, illuminated by the bulb, while heat purred from some aperture in the unit's underside. I had set it in the living-room fireplace, where I could no longer build a real wood fire, even if I'd had the energy to do such a thing. Years ago Ranse had had the chimney sealed, to keep the central heating from flying up it into the sky, the squirrels from falling down it into our house. My faux woodstove drank up an alarming amount of electricity, at least as much as the central heating had done in the old days, and all autumn I had been loath to switch it on, but now without qualm I did. The very sight of it, with its illusion of fire, was comforting somehow. I sat close to it, so that the warmth radiated over my feet and legs. Even so, I was cold and longed for my bed.

The trick-or-treaters had tapered away, and I was just considering turning out the lights, when the bell rang again. Laying my book aside, heaving myself with reluctance from my chair, I opened the door to Wylie, his neighbor Maricruz, and, reclined in his wheelchair, her son Miguel. I remembered again Wylie's account of Maricruz's wanderings in the desert and the baby's *yellow jaundice.* Then I wondered how they'd got the boy in his heavy chair up my front steps.

"Hello, stranger," I croaked.

Wylie looked sheepish. "Yeah. Did that cat go and die on you?"

"No, no," I said. "He's in good form."

"Do you love him yet?" Wylie grinned.

"I'm used to him. But where have you been? Was it something I said?"

Wylie's face reddened. "Aw. I been busy, I guess. Helping Maricruz. You know Maricruz." He indicated her, there at his side. Shyly we waved to each other.

"She don't speak a whole lot of English," Wylie said. "Good thing when you're in the construction business, you learn some Spanish. It's like you can't help it. So we can talk pretty good." As if to demonstrate, he turned to her and spoke in what seemed to be fluent, if oddly accented, Spanish. She replied even more rapidly, gesturing towards me. Miguel, curled in his chair, followed their conversation with his eyes. I wondered how much he was able to know.

"She says I can go on and tell you," said Wylie. "I reckon you might call us a *unit.*"

"Come again?"

"You know. Together. A *thang*." As Wylie spoke these words, I felt I could see the light radiating from him. Happiness, I thought, was a photo-emanant thing—if such a term existed, and I hadn't simply made it up on the spot.

"Well. Congratulations to the both of you," I said. I studied in my mind how to ask the next question that occurred to me, which was *Do you have plans?* Of course, this question only meant more questions that I couldn't very well ask, such as *Have you moved in together? What are the legal ramifications of your partnership?* And so on, all in the vein of none of my business.

Wylie seemed to intuit my thoughts. "I guess you'd call us engaged. I mean, Miss Kirsty, you know me. My intentions is one hundred percent—no, *two hundred*—two hundred *percent* honorable. But you know. Like they say. It's complicated." His gaze came to rest on the boy in his wheelchair. "I just figure, you know, a boy needs some man in his life. And she don't know where his daddy is, or if he's alive, or nothing like that. And it's not like they ever got married, you know, like in church. But you know. I mean." He looked hard into my eyes. "She's a good woman, I promise you that. She stays in her trailer. I stay in mine. No funny business. You know me, Miss Kirsty. Like I keep telling Father Schuyler, I'm a religious man."

"So you are," I said, smiling.

Maricruz had been watching Wylie as he talked. Doubtless she understood more than she could say. She worked at the produce stand, I knew, but what could she express in my own language, other than prices, pounds, pecks, bushels, please and thank you? A person could get by on few words, but how much more went on in the mind, pacing and pacing, looking for a way out and finding none? Surely it was a hard life in many ways, I thought, but that might be the hardest thing of all.

Now Maricruz spoke to Wylie again, gesturing to me.

Wylie cleared his throat. "She wants me to tell you she heard about this factory job. You know, shift work, pays good, but hard if you got a kid. Some cousin of hers or something in Georgia, big plant that's hiring. If I go with her, she can take that job, she says."

"I see." I hoped I sounded cheerful. "That's exciting news."

"She ain't a hundred percent decided yet."

"No, of course not. One wants to take one's time over a large decision," I said stiffly.

"Or there's her mama back home. She keeps, you know, wanting Maricruz to come back. She ain't never seen Miguelito all these years. You know how it is. Getting old and all."

I both did and did not know how it was. I made some murmur of assent.

"Or seems like, I don't know, Montana or someplace. That could be good. Out there you can kind of do what you want, you know what I mean? Big open space. I like that idea. But she ain't a hundred percent decided on anything. I guess I ain't a hundred percent decided either. But wherever she goes, I reckon I aim to go with her."

Maricruz had bent over Miguel, murmuring. Now she straightened. I saw her glance at Wylie. Something in that glance made my neck prickle. Had she understood him? Did she understand him? Did he understand her? A sudden uncertainty set me on edge.

"You must do what's best, of course," I said.

"Yeah." He took off his cap, smoothed his hair, put the cap back on. "Miss Kirsty, do you got any candy bars in there that don't have nuts? Miguelito, he can't have nuts."

I proffered my bowl. "I have several different ones in there, but I can never remember what's what. Why don't you look and choose?"

Together Wylie and Maricruz bent to look. The porch light shone on his blond hair, on the amber streaks painted into hers. When she had dropped a selection into the plastic shopping bag that drooped from the handlebars of the wheelchair, Maricruz smiled at me, nodded, and made a chopping motion with her hand.

"She says we'll cut them up, and he can eat them. Just so he don't choke."

Maricruz stroked Miguel's hair, gelled and spiked like any other boy's. His fisted hand jerked up as a baby's might do, all unwilled. "*Gracias*," she said. "Thank you."

"Trick or treat, Miss Kirsty." Wylie took hold of the chair on one side, Maricruz took the other, and together, with seeming ease, they hoisted it, and Miguel enthroned, down the steps. "Going for another little ride, Miguelito," I heard Wylie say as they crossed the yard to the street, where Maricruz's old silver van waited. As he slid back the side door, he turned again and shouted, "I'm gone come see how that kitty's getting along."

"You do that," I called back. But already the van door had slammed. The engine roared. A little dolefully, I went back into the house.

My headache by this time had assumed the quality of a sound, though whether it was a high-pitched sound like the whine of a mosquito, or a low-pitched sound like the rumble of the house falling in on me, I couldn't tell. In the kitchen I took two ibuprofen and stood propping myself at the sink, my eyes shut. Just as I was deciding, truly, to turn the lights off and go to my bed, the bell rang again.

"Trick or treat," said the Malkins.

At least, it was a fair contingent of Malkins. Janet, I was gratified to see, was not among them. As always, Howard lurked in the background, his black hoodie drawn up against the cold. The two oldest boys, Moshe and Dominic, were missing—at work, I presumed—but I counted the little boys, Isaac and Henry, and what looked like all the girls. From Lucy down, they were dressed as their names, saints or Hebrews in alternation. I recognized Miriam by the baby doll she carried in a basket, but it was fortunate that they had made signs for themselves, or I might have mistaken Naomi for Hannah for Clare, dressed as they all were in identical brown ponchos with mantillas draped over their heads. Margaret wore a tartan sash, however. Lucy, not unpredictably, carried a plate onto which two large, red-veined eyeballs had been glued—by the boyfriend, as I recalled. Closer inspection revealed these eyeballs to be candles.

"Goodness," I said. "Those are disgusting."

Lucy brandished her plate at me. "I know, right? I found them at the dollar store. I wanted to have them on the table at dinner, but Mom said no."

"A sensible lady, your mother," I said. Then, though my head thudded, I bent to speak to Henry. "That's a lovely crown you've got."

"Yes. Saint Henry was an emperor. He wanted to be a monk, but nobody would let him, so he had to go on being the king."

Through my banging headache, I smiled. "You should tell Father Schuyler about him sometime."

Again Henry fixed me with his severe look. "I *have* told Father Schuyler."

Over the children, who had taken the bowl from my hands and were doling out the remains of the sweets, Howard caught my eye. "Saint Henry is the patron saint of the childless. I thought that was pretty funny."

"How is Janet?" I asked him.

"Still hanging in there. Still the worry about the placenta.

Still the bedrest."

"How much longer has she got to do that?"

Howard shrugged. "However long they say. The baby's not due till December, I don't think. Sometimes we're not really sure about due dates." Noticing the children, who still scrabbled among the chocolates, he broke off. "Hey, Isaac, no. Hey. Don't take the last one. Stop it, you guys—"

"Don't worry," I said. "I was just going to turn the lights off. I'm happy to be rid of the lot."

"Well." Howard made as if to gather his children beneath his wing. "Janet says hi, anyway. She really wanted to come out tonight. She loves Halloween. She kept trying to convince me that if she kept the front seat reclined, that would count as bed rest."

"I hope you told her nothing doing."

"Pretty much. I told her to leave the front lights off, just not hand out candy at all this year. It's killing her, I tell you, not even getting to answer the door." He peered at me through the mist. "Do you have any idea how hard it is to keep that woman on her back?"

Only Howard, I thought, could say such a thing and imply no bawdy subtext. Only Howard or Ranse: men like children, in the real and good way that men could be like children and still be men.

"It's a full time job." One of the older girls was laughing through a mouthful of chocolate. "We keep telling Dad we don't need to go to school."

"Yeah, yeah," said Howard. "Like first thing in the morning. We made our special trip to see Miss Kirsty, but now it's time to go home." He reached through the children to lay an empathic hand on my arm. "Are you okay? I hope you don't mind my saying so, but you look a little pale."

I felt more than a little pale, but all I said was, "I'm all right. Just tired. Maybe a bit of a cold coming on." I shut the door on all the evening's reunions—Happy Halloween to me—and switched off the front-porch light.

* * *

In the night I awoke with the conviction that what I had was something more than a bit of a cold. I was alone. Though the kitten had protested when I shut him in the pantry cupboard, his mewing had subsided, and the house was silent. No mice rustled in the walls. I'd neglected to set out my glue traps; just as well. I couldn't have coped with a mouse. For a while I lay awake in the starless dark. Then I lost myself again in something that was not quite sleep.

Next day I knew I was ill. It was only flu, I suppose, but it was the sort of flu that doctors warn you about when they exhort you to get your jab every autumn. I'd been putting mine off. Served me right, I thought, though this flu, if that was what it was, seemed potent enough to override any cocktail of dead virus cells. It was the sort of flu that might make you begin to understand what the nineteen-eighteen pandemic was all about. My father, though still unborn himself, had lost two brothers and an infant sister in that pandemic. Granny Astrid never spoke of them, nobody did, but my mother had shown me the stones in the village churchyard.

It was after that, my mother said, that Granny began to worship in the boatwright's house. In those days it was the house and church of Magnus's father, old Thomas Wilson, but the religion was the same, minimalist yet full of chilly rigors. It was as if, in Granny's universe, two Gods coexisted: the God of the Church of Scotland, who ate children for breakfast, and the God of the front-room chapel, who exacted a weekly tax of psalm-singing in return for whatever the other God had let you keep. Of course my mother didn't say all that, but it was what I understood. Neither of those Gods, as far as I could tell, had anything to do with the God in the gleaming gold tabernacle, whom we visited at Lerwick. *Olaf, Sigurd, Sunniva*, the children were called. They might have been fictional characters, invented for a story nobody ever got round to telling.

The waters closed so completely over people. They had swallowed, in succession, everyone I had ever come close to loving: my father, my grandmother, my mother, my aunt, my husband. They had closed over Dermott, though as far as he had been concerned, the waters might have closed over me first. But he had gone, and here I stayed. People sank, the surface smoothed over; still you were left with their rippling reflections, glancing at you whenever light struck the water. As a child I'd assumed that Granny Astrid had not loved her lost children. She had not seemed to love anyone, until my father died and she gave up wanting to live. Later I realized how little I had ever understood or wanted to understand. If the reflections pained you, you looked away from the water. And if you were an island, surrounded on all sides? Still you tried to look away.

* * *

I can remember only one other time when I was so ill that I thought I would rather die than go on feeling the way I felt. If I could have risen from my body and run away, I would have done so. I would not have looked back. No Lot's wife, I. Now, waking in the small hours of All Saints, I felt that way again. It was my head, mostly. But it was also my elbows, my knees, my hips. My skin felt inside-out; the brush of the sheets against my bare arms hurt me. All my chest cavity was raw inside. My mouth had gone dry. What did the psalm say? *My tongue cleaves to the roof of my mouth? I gaze heavenward?* Through a red haze I heard the kitten crying. Somehow I must have got myself out of bed and to the kitchen, dragged down the bag of kitten chow, and poured it into and all round his bowl. Next thing I knew, I was in bed again, and he had climbed up to join me, denting my pillow with his body as he settled in. His dry, warm, rumpled side hummed against my neck.

Afterwards, I was never certain how many days I was ill. There were days. I remember the sun through the window pressing on my eyes. I buried my head in the bedclothes to escape it. There were nights. I woke, thirsty, with a gong banging in my head, and longed for someone to bring me water. When I was awake enough to think, the peril of my position was borne in upon me. I could see how people died in their houses and weren't found for days, weeks, months. Eventually, perhaps, one of my distant, recent, anonymous neighbors in the subdivisions might notice, driving past, the drifts of post piled up on the porch. How long after that would it be before someone thought to force the door? And then, what they'd find—I shuddered. Though I'd lived long alone, I had never thought of myself as desolate. Now I did, and the thought made me weep weak tears into my pillow. I might have welcomed death, but not this way. I didn't mind dying; I minded dying alone and unprepared. No, scratch that. I minded dying alone. Full stop.

I have said that I was, once before, so ill that death seemed preferable to life. Then, as now, I had been alone. That is, there were people about me always: in college, at lectures, in seminar groups, in the street. I was caught up in a constant press of people. But they were strangers. Even my friends were strangers. It was my good fortune, or my hard luck, that that year dresses with empire waists were in fashion. If I had gained weight round the middle, nobody noticed. Or if they did notice, they didn't know me well enough to ask questions. I didn't ask myself any questions, either. I told myself there was nothing to ask questions about. I was simply gaining weight round the middle and should perhaps not drink so much beer. If I felt tired—*fair laid by,* as the Shetlanders say—it was only the winter. I had passed Christmas at home with my mother, and that had not been restful. Holidays at home so seldom are, for anyone. If the emotions are exhausted, I reasoned with myself, then naturally the body feels it.

What I felt was not like sadness or pain. It was simply a kind of weight I dragged with me, to meals in hall, to the library, to supervisions. Dermott had ceased even to pretend interest in what I was writing. I could be as credulous as I wanted; it was nothing to him. I could have said precisely how many weeks it had been since he'd said anything more to me than *yes, yes, that's fine.* But I did not want to think how many weeks it had been. I did not want to add them up. I did not want them to add up to the burden I lugged everywhere beneath my heart. I had simply gathered my papers at the end of each brief, detached tutorial and gone away.

Then, inexplicably, I developed a fever. My head hurt. My body hurt. Worse, and bizarrely, a smell began to follow me about. Today I can describe it only by saying that if those Halloween zombies had been interested in verisimilitude, that vague, pervasive scent of decay would be the perfume they'd wear. At the time I thought it was only a sort of olfactory hallucination I was having, a delusive manifestation of my exhaustion and despair. I'd no idea that others could smell it, too. I felt too ill to realize that people were avoiding me, standing away in the post-office queue, hastening past me with caught breath in the stairwell. Only when I'd collapsed in the library and awakened in hospital did I confront the whole truth.

Well, really, I suppose I'd known it all the time. How could it not have been self-evident? What I'd been carrying had been a thing of substance, not emotion. In the weeks since Dermott had stopped wanting me, I had not been simply depressed. There had been something alive. It had been human and mortal. All those weeks, it had been growing. Then it had died. Perversely, my body, so drainingly laden with it, had not wanted to be rid of it. In a poetry lecture I'd been to once, the lecturer had made much of the fact that *womb*—aurally, visually, perfectly as a mirror—rhymes with *tomb*. In hospital I was at leisure to reflect on that lecture and that rhyme. If I hadn't felt so rotten, I might have taken pleasure in it.

While I was in hospital, the Senior Tutor came to see me. She was my only visitor. In her tweeds, with her goodhearted, honest, plain face, she sat beside my bed.

"I rang your mother, you know." As she spoke, she stroked a leather glove in her lap as if it were a pet. "Is she—pardon my asking, dear—but is she quite all right?"

"Sorry?" I was still drugged and dazed; otherwise I'd have known exactly what she meant.

"Well, I don't know how to put it. I told her you were quite seriously ill, and that perhaps she might make arrangements to come—a guest room in college, you know, and meals, that sort of thing. But she was rather—"

By now I had gathered my wits a little. "Yes," I said, "I can imagine." And I could. But how to explain it to the Senior Tutor? All those years ago, after my father's death, my mother had not taken me from the convent school after all. Instead, in that moment of decision, she had resigned herself—I could see it now—to my never coming home again. I would not return to take up the postmistress's job. I would not move back into my room at the top of the house, looking over our salt-battered garden. I would be a separate person, with my own existence. This was, to her, another death. I would never belong to her, and so she had renounced me. It had always been Auntie Lass, not my mother, who met me at the ferry from Aberdeen and was glad to see me. It was Auntie Lass who walked me down the quay to meet the fisherman who'd been arranged to bring me across the sound. On the other side, nobody met me at all.

"Get slick home," the man would say, and I would heave up my valise—later, the valise became a rucksack—and stagger up the stony street to my door, on which I would have to pound for some moments.

Mrs. Moodie, who must have been a hundred and two by then, might put her face to her front window. If she was feeling especially acidic, she might open her door.

"*Kinda weety wye*," she might say, meaning that it rained. She rolled her pale eye at me, the island's changeling.

All my mother ever said, when at last she emerged from the dimness, was, "Well. It's you, then."

I must have looked disconsolate. Awkwardly the Senior Tutor patted my arm. "When you come out, dear, we must have a chat."

"Yes," I lied. Then, meaning it, "Thank you."

I never went to have the chat. Instead, unexpectedly, just as I was regaining my old strength, my mother died. As I had done at Christmas, I made the long journey north by train and ferry. Auntie Lass met me at Lerwick, and together we went to the crematorium, where a jolly lady cleric in a pink alb, her stole printed with children's hands in yellow, blue, and red tempera paint, presided over some sort of service. I don't know what denomination she could have been: not Catholic, of course. The Church of England wouldn't ordain women for another two decades, though I was hazily aware of Anglican deaconesses. She might have been one of the infants'-school teachers in fancy dress for all I knew. I heard none of the little eulogy she delivered, only Auntie Lass saying piously, as the casket slid away through the little door into the furnace, "What your mother would have wanted." I suppose she would have been privy to this knowledge. For years and years, since my father died, I had not known my mother to want anything at all. I found myself wondering, half-relevantly, whether Auntie still had her painting of the Immaculate Heart hung over the mantel in the bedsit where she still lived. She didn't invite me back to her room after, but took me to a tea shop, where we sat until it was time for me to go. I had still my mother's house to sort out. She had left the house to Auntie Lass, not to me, but I was to go now and claim whatever I wanted from it.

Half-conscious, I let myself be handed over again to the prearranged fisherman and his boat. When the keel scraped on the stony beach at home, I went up the street and knocked, as I had been directed to do, at old Mrs. Moodie's door. Mrs. Moodie had died at last, but her great-niece Norma, with whom I had been at the village school, was living there with her husband.

When Norma opened the door, I saw the child on her hip. Another weighed heavily in her womb and stretched the waistband of her skirt. "I'll just get it," she said, shutting the door, leaving me to wait in the needling rain. When, after some minutes, she opened the door again, it was only to extend a white hand dangling a shiny new-cut key to my mother's front door. I hadn't recalled ever seeing a key to that door. I had never known it to be locked. Before I could say anything, Norma had shut her own door again. Well, we had never been friends.

The lock on my mother's door was new, like the key, and stiff. I had to struggle with it for some minutes before at last it turned, the door giving way with a sigh, the shut-up, unheated house exhaling its tomblike breath. She had died in the post office, at the end of a working day; it was when she didn't open up next morning that someone found the door unbolted, and her inside. Her heart, Auntie Lass had said, tapping her own breast. "*Hairt*, love." There, still, was her final cup of tea, half-drunk on the drainboard, the milk curdling. Her refrigerator was empty. The cupboards contained some random tins of soup. I swept the curled dead spiders from the windowsills and went through all the drawers, marveling at how little my mother had possessed, and nothing of beauty.

I found and packed the set of plaster Nativity figures I remembered from childhood. Granny Astrid had muttered about them with my father: *Statues. Popish idolatry. As for that.* The rest of the house I left for Auntie to dispose of. Auntie Lass had professed amazement, even a measure of embarrassment, at the arrangements my mother had made. By all rights the house should have come to me. I was glad that it had not, though I could not convince Auntie that having it off my hands was an unqualified relief. In all our conversations about it, she sounded flustered and breathless, changing the subject at the first opportunity. *My sister's left me a wee bonny house*, I imagined her telling her Lerwick friends, as one might speak of contracting a terminal disease. *I suppose I must go and live in it.* Live in it she did, for the rest of her life, cheerfully enough if the Christmas cards she sent were any indication. When she died, I received a solicitor's letter containing a check for two hundred pounds and the news that the *wee bonny house* had gone to a distant Aberdeen relative, who had cleared it out, sold it, and divided the proceeds among an extended family of heirs. All over again, I was relieved to have slipped that bond.

Nothing material, at any rate, could moor me to the past.

By the time I returned from my mother's funeral, I had not done any academic work in weeks. I did nothing to remedy that neglect, but instead went walking alone for long hours by the river in the cold. I might have tried to wake myself from the terrible dream I'd been having, but that seemed too much effort. The waking, the walking, the flow of the river: all of it was simply more dream. In that dream I had met Ranse. Now here I was in my bed, an ocean away, alone and ill, while a naked kitten slept in the curve of my neck.

* * *

The bedside telephone rang.

"Kirsty?" a man's voice said.

I licked my dry lips. "Who's that?" My voice was the rasp of a gate swinging shut. Or open.

"It's—" The voice hesitated, as if it weren't certain itself who it was. "It's Father. Father Schuyler. I'm sorry to bother you, but I was wondering, did you come to clean yesterday?"

Yesterday? What day was it?

"I really should have called sooner, but I wasn't sure—" Again he hesitated. "It's just that I'd left a glass in the sink, and when I came home in the afternoon, it was still there. That didn't seem like you. I should have realized—" His voice cracked with contrition and concern. "If you don't mind my saying so, you sound terrible."

"I think I must have got flu," I said. "The last thing I remember is Halloween."

"*Halloween?*" Again his voice cracked. "Has anyone been to see you? Checked on you, I mean?" He seemed to stumble over the terminology for that particular work of mercy, the visiting of the sick.

"Well, no, Father, but really—" I was going to say, *Really, I'm all right*, when it occurred to me that I wasn't all right at all.

"Is there anything you need?"

"Oh, no, Father," I began again automatically. Then I began to tally how many days it must have been since I'd last eaten. Once or twice, in my red fog, I had groped my way into the kitchen, made and forced down a cup of tea. I wasn't hungry now, as it happened, only aware of emptiness.

"Soup?" said Father. "I can't make soup, but cans? And orange juice? My mother always gave me orange juice when I was sick."

The laboriousness with which he brought out these thoughts made me smile, though even smiling hurt. "That's lovely, Father," I said, "but really—" Mercifully for me, I suppose, the dial tone cut short my feeble protests.

I was falling asleep again when the doorbell rang. I stumbled out of bed, waking the kitten, who remarked, "Mowp," in drowsy annoyance. Holding to the wall—the house tilted alarmingly—I groped my way to the door. Through the sidelight I could see Father Schuyler, a shadow in greatcoat and cassock, saturno pulled over his forehead.

I opened the door. "Hello, Father," I said, and fainted.

* * *

After that there was a confusion of voices, sirens, lights flashing palely in the sunshine. Hands lifted me. Then I was in hospital. When I woke again, there was daylight: the same day, or a different day? I didn't know. The window was bright with sun. Above my head, too, hung a bag of light. A tube of light ran down to my left hand, and my hand and arm felt cold, as if the wintry day were flowing from the bag down the tube and into my body. It was a different cold, somehow, from the chills that had come with the fever: a clean cold, like morning. Though I'd done nothing for days but lie in bed, I was exhausted and sweaty. The fever had broken. I felt broken, but I was myself again.

I lay back against the pillows. This empty feeling, too, I remembered. That other time, I had lain back against a much flatter pillow, in an iron bed with curtains drawn round, on a ward with many beds. I had remembered, as I remembered now, with striking clarity, that moment in Dermott's room, his laughing question that wasn't a question. *You don't believe all this, surely.* My answer had been less answer than assent. It was right, I understood, that I should be punished. But what was the punishment? To conceive, or to lose what I'd conceived? Which was the sentence, which the commutation? Even now, so many years later, I couldn't have said. It all seemed tangled up together, damnation and grace, so that hindsight, which is said to bring such clarity, still made a jumble of it. If there was a pattern, I could see no sense in it. Still, here I was. That was something, I supposed.

A thought struck me, and I fumbled for the call button at my bedside. A squat maroon-haired woman in purple scrubs appeared beside my bed.

"What you need, sweet thing?"

"My cat," I croaked. "Is anyone seeing to my cat?"

"Honey, I don't know a thing about your kittycat, but somebody'll look out for it. Somebody sure was looking out for you."

"How long have I been here?" I asked.

She pecked at the tablet device she carried. "Looks like

you came in Tuesday morning."

"What day is it now?"

"Today is—" With her free hand, she consulted the sport watch she wore. "Today is Thursday. You must of had that old flu something bad," she added, intent again on her tablet.

"It certainly felt that way," I told her.

"We don't usually see it like this until after Christmas. January, February. That's when you get folks dying. Of course, *you* didn't die, honey," she added, as if I might mistake my state of being. "You're getting some good fluids in you. Are you hungry?"

I considered. Was I hungry? Yes, I was hungry. I was not only not dead, but actually alive. Alive and hungry.

"Well, let me go see what you can have. It might have to be something soft, like Jello. But princess, I *promise* I will bring you something."

Princess. Relaxing onto my pillows, I smiled at the ghost of Mother Sain. Somewhere in the bright morning air, I imagined that she nodded to me, her mouth an inscrutable line.

* * *

Her grudging acceptance could count, I supposed, as an approximation of love. She used every morning to make breakfast for us, mountains of breakfast: scrambled eggs, stiff twigs of bacon, slabs of fried livermush, for which I never developed a taste. Ranse disappointed her by tossing down his coffee and bolting from the table. The drive to work was long, and, as a newly married man, he was often tired in the morning. He slept later than he meant to. In the mornings, then, his mother was left alone with me. When I professed not to have an appetite, she looked knowing. If I'd produced the child she clearly expected, she would have taken me to her heart without question, though I did wear my hair untidily and decline her sweet iced tea.

Of course I didn't produce the child, then or ever. More than once I overheard my mother-in-law asking Ranse why on earth he had married me. Her meaning was clear: what, other than pregnancy, could possibly have made me attractive to him? She had put me down as a bad girl, which naturally was not wrong. I was a bad girl; I knew so myself. But I wasn't bad in the way she thought. That is, I hadn't been bad with Ranse. On the other hand, I couldn't say that I'd been good to him. That he'd wanted to marry me was as much a mystery to me as it was to Mother Sain. It was so inexplicable and undeserved as to constitute the action of grace, which must have been why I'd said yes.

And if the whole project wasn't a success, it wasn't exactly a failure, either. It was nice enough. Ranse loved me. Mother Sain and I arrived at our truce. I cleaned her house for her. I learnt to drive, so that I could do the shopping and take her to her many doctors' appointments, or to play bridge with her friends. As the bridge mornings disintegrated and the appointments increased, it fell to me to devise little treats for her. "You must be hungry after all those jabs," I would tell her as I buckled her seatbelt round her in the hospital car park. "Shall we stop at City Lunch on our way home?"

"I could do with me some livermush," she would say, gazing flatly at a row of pink crape myrtles along the car park's landscaped perimeter.

By that time she had long since stopped looking pointedly at my middle. She had instead become a child. I was the one who could cajole her into her clothes, into the car and the indignity of the seatbelt. I was the one who could induce her to eat. She had forgotten my name; worse, she had forgotten Ranse's. He could only stand by in despair, watching me spoon in porridge and wipe her whiskered chin. "Mama?" he would say. "Mama?" But she shut her eyes and turned her face away, gripping my hand in her own bony claw. The nursing staff, meanwhile, clustered round her, calling her Annaluree and doll baby, names she would not have answered to, even if she had understood that they were addressed to her.

* * *

Roaming among these thoughts, I must have fallen asleep again. Next thing I knew, the purple nurse was bending over me with a dish of shivering emerald Jello. I was hungry and ate it. As I set down my spoon, Father Schuyler put his head in at the door.

"Kirsty. Ah. You look—better."

"Yes, thank you, Father." I set the empty dish on the bed table. "I feel better."

"I have to ask you something," he said.

"Yes, Father?"

"There's a thing in your house. What is it?"

"Thing?"

"An animal of some kind. It looks blind."

"Oh." I felt a jolt of alarm. "That's my cat. Is he all right? Has anyone seen to him?"

"That's a *cat*?" He advanced into the room now, turning his saturno nervously in his hands like a steering wheel.

"Yes," I said. "He's a bit eccentric."

Father sat down in the leatherette armchair beside the bed. "I'll say. Where in the world did you get a thing like that?"

"Wylie Springfield brought him to me. For a mouser, you know."

"A mouser." Father eyed me doubtfully. "Well, I didn't know what it was, but it seemed tame, and I thought you must have it on purpose, so I've been feeding it."

"Thank you, Father." Limp with relief, for I had been worrying, I settled myself more comfortably.

"Oh, well, it's nothing." He looked abashed.

"It's not nothing," I said. "And if you don't mind my saying so, all of this is the sort of thing you find difficult. I know that."

He shifted uneasily in his chair. "All the more graces, I guess. Lucky me."

"No, lucky me," I told him. "I never quite realized until now—"

"It is not good for the man to be alone," he murmured.

"Well, if by *man* the Lord meant old ladies, then no, it is not good. It was a bit frightening, lying there thinking I might die in my bed and nobody would know for days or weeks."

"Surely not weeks," said Father. "I missed you when you didn't come to clean."

And rang straight away the next day, I thought but did not say. Though it was true, he didn't deserve my cruelty. Well: the truth, which was cruel. I thought to spare him that.

Again he shifted in his chair, with a creaking and farting of faux leather. I had the feeling that he was waiting for me to open a spiritual conversation, to pose some theological question that had been boiling dry at the back of my mind. Alas, I had no such question. Father and I regarded each other in mutual embarrassment.

"Is anyone else in hospital at the moment?" I asked to break the silence. "Are you making your appointed rounds today?"

"No, no, just you. I mean, there are the usual shut-ins.

There's one lady who slams the door in my face every time I try to bring her Communion. Phyllis Somebody. You wouldn't know anything about her, would you?"

I shook my head. There were so few people I knew, really. Perhaps if I'd seen her at Mass, ten or twenty years ago, I'd have recognized her. But as a name? Phyllis Somebody? No.

"Well, she seems loony as a bat," he said. "It's a little disconcerting."

"You might ask the church secretary about her," I said, before remembering that the church secretary was twenty-two years old and spoke chiefly Spanish. It was entirely probable that, in the days when this Phyllis was in her right mind, attending Holy Mass, and known to people, the church secretary hadn't yet taken up residence in this country. Possibly she hadn't been born.

"Yes, I could ask Daniela." Father's tone was uncertain. Obviously he was thinking the same things that I was. He sat a moment longer with his saturno on his knees. Then abruptly he said, "Would you like to pray before I go?"

What could I say? "Yes, Father, of course, thank you." I bent my head and he murmured a hasty sequence: Our Father, Hail Mary, Glory Be. Above me he made the sign of the cross and was gone.

* * *

I was some days in hospital. Once home, I lay about like the sea at low tide. Every few days, as a penance, I thought, Father Schuyler came to see me. More than once he reassured me that he was able to clean his own house for the present, and that I should feel no great compulsion to rise from my convalescent couch on his account. He also brought me things from the supermarket: more orange juice, a brand of tea I didn't particularly care for, and a great quantity of soup in tins. For all of this I thanked him gravely.

"I'm trying," he said.

I told him that I was happy to be practiced upon, and to keep up the good work.

Otherwise I saw no one. I slept much, read without registering a word, and looked out of the windows at the landscape, brown and gray and auburn at the onset of winter. I turned on my little fireplace heater, and the kitten came and lay before it, purring with satisfaction. When he grew bored with the heater, he leapt onto the sofa beside me, burrowing into the blanket I'd spread over my knees. From the mantel my assembled dead looked down at us, the little crowned Christ Child in their midst.

6

Thanksgiving came and went, not much celebrated by me. I had never understood it, this American holiday dedicated to eating. I had never understood Mother Sain's determination to roast both a turkey and a ham, to make both mashed potatoes and mashed yams topped with marshmallows, and to bake four kinds of pie, all for three people. I had never understood Ranse's unquestioning expectation that, when his mother became incapable of this abundance, I would tie on her apron and follow her blueprint. Mind you, while Ranse lived, I had done my best, though I had drawn the line at sweet-potato casserole with exploded marshmallows on top. It was a relief not to bother anymore, not to spend Advent eating up the remains to make room for the Christmas feast.

Now the neighbors' white holiday lights shone starrily through the clear, cold nights. Inflatable snowmen stood about on the patchy yellow lawns, where illuminated reindeer also grazed. When at last I felt well enough to go to Mass, I found the Spanish-speaking congregation practicing, as they did every year, the dance they performed in the car park between Masses on the Sunday closest to the feast of Our Lady of Guadalupe. When I came for confession on Saturdays and Mass on Wednesday evenings, I could hear the drum booming from the parish hall, two long beats, three short. On the day, the dancers would be wearing feathers on their heads, at their wrists, at their ankles. From the parish-hall door they would dance out, crouching, turning, smiling as they circled past each other. Boom, boom, boom-boom-boom.

"Do they have to do this?" Father said. "It seems pagan."

We were standing by the front door of the church. The drum echoed from the hall. Outside, the evening was drawing down, cold and faintly patterned with stars.

"Think of it as a conversion dance, Father," I said. "*The old things have passed away; behold, new things have come.* That's what it means to them."

"Yes. Yes. That is a good way to think of it, you're right." He sounded relieved not to have to override his better impulses. The Bishop must still have been very much on his mind. For my own part, I remembered the Bishop—our young pastor, all those years ago—wearing a sombrero, clapping out of rhythm with the drum, as the pioneer generation of dancers in this parish dipped and circled across the car park.

"You should have known my Granny, Father," I said. "She slept with a knife on Christmas Eve, to frighten away the trows."

"Trows?"

"Fairies. Afraid of iron, you see. They'd be abroad at Yuletide, and up to their mischief."

Father laughed uncertainly. "You're making that up."

"I am not, Father." I smiled at his incredulity. "I merely speak of people who remember a darker world." I suppose that means all of us, I thought, but by then the conversation was puttering out. Father had turned away, bracing himself, to greet the dancers as their practice ended.

"*Hola,*" I heard him say in his flat Midwestern accent. "*Como estas?* Everything okay? Yes? Hi, how are you? *Hola, hola . . .*"

In previous years I had seen Maricruz dancing with the others, her arms outstretched like a hawk's wings riding the wind. Even before I'd known her name, the look of exaltation on her face as she danced had been enough to draw my attention. It was the only time I'd ever seen her detached from Miguel in his chair. Now, though, as the practice ended and people began to straggle out into the night, talking and laughing, I didn't glimpse her among them. This too drew my attention, for a moment, at any rate. Then my thoughts turned to other things.

I was making my supper, so ordinary that there is no need to describe it, while the kitten, now in the leggy stage of feline adolescence, cavorted about the kitchen. Since I'd come home from hospital, I hadn't bothered setting out the glue traps again. But that night, after I'd eaten, I moved the refrigerator and cooker with some difficulty, to survey with near-despair the little piles of black pellets secreted behind them.

"Damn." I should have to recommence putting the traps out. "When," I demanded of the kitten, "are you going to start doing me a good turn for a change?"

"Merp," he said, and fixed his claws in my trouser leg.

I did the washing up, then sat down in the living room with my book. My determination to complete my interrupted learning had paled somewhat in the aftermath of illness. Let the day be sufficient unto the day, I thought. Still, it was Southwell who lay on the little table beside my rocking chair, so when I had switched on the heater, I took him up again. Turning this time not to Mary Magdalen and her tears, but to "The Triumphs Over Death," I read:

If it be a blessing for the virtuous to mourn, it is a reward of the same to be comforted; and he that pronounced the one, promised the other. I doubt not but that Spirit, whose nature is Love, and whose name Comforter, as he knows the cause of your grief, so hath he salved it with supplies of grace, pouring into your wound no less oil of mercy, than wine of justice; yet since courtesy oweth compassion as a duty to the afflicted, and Nature hath ingrafted a desire to find it, I thought good to show you, by proof, that you carry not your cares alone, though the load that lieth on others can little lighten your burthen.

Ah, those burthens, I thought. That *burthen* of grief, particularly, was a tricky one. People came to you to help you bear it—if they knew about it. If, like me, you were not much of a talker, then you were rather on your own. And if your grief was complicated by regret, chiefly the regret that you were not sadder than you were, because you had not loved very adequately what you had lost—what then? You couldn't very well say to your friends, assuming you had any: *My grief is not so heavy, and that is my burthen, so help me carry it, please.* Then, lashings of the wine of justice were precisely what your wound cried out for. Your wound, which liked to drink alone.

I stopped reading and gazed for a long time at the heater's revolving cellophane flames. The kitten, prowling in, smelt his way across the floor and climbed into my lap. Stroking him, I felt the ruched-velvet skin along his sides, the wrinkles between his ears. He purred emphatically and flexed his claws. A miraculous creature, this, I thought. He was the trick played on old evolution, the organism with its survival mechanisms bred out of it, which yet survived. Self-insufficient, it had to make itself necessary in some way to its host organism, or else be a parasite. Just how this particular organism made himself necessary to me I couldn't say. Perhaps he was a parasite, bleeding me dry. Certainly he had not yet done that for which I had acquired him. In my house, the mice still gnawed and defecated, and here he sat thrumming on my knee, complacent as if he had earned his place there.

That night, I dreamed again that I walked by the river. As always, the sun leaked wanly through white cloud. The water bulged, brown and turgid, between its wet banks. Swirl, swirl went the currents, stippled with rain. Ranse stood beside me.

Though I couldn't see his face, I smelled the fusty wet down of his jacket.

"What's that?" He pointed at the water. The white thing with its splayed arms and legs came eddying towards us, dead and alive all at once, animated by the water that had drowned it.

"It's nothing," I said. "Nothing. Let it go."

In my sleep I heard, though I thought I dreamt it, a great wind out of the west, bending the trees, tearing off the last clinging leaves, scouring my roof. All night it breathed, till the stars were breathed away, new clouds blown in.

* * *

I awoke in the morning before it was light. Rain was falling outside. The kitten purred by my shoulder, and on the whole I felt disinclined to rise and dress. Just as the idea formed itself, of staying in bed for once, the phone began to ring. Huddled beneath my blankets, I listened to it. Doubtless it was the county alert system, telephoning to issue a dense-fog advisory. They didn't quite ring to tell you it was raining, but they did like to interrupt you, day and night, to point out weather conditions you'd already seen with your own eyes. Duly noted, I thought. The ringing stopped. Then it started again. The county alert system left voice messages; it didn't ring right back. Grumbling, still half-asleep, I put my hand out of the bedclothes and groped about on the nightstand.

By the time I put my hand on the receiver, the ringing had stopped again, but only for a second. When the phone rang for a third time, I snatched it up in some annoyance.

There was a silence on the other end.

"Hello?" I repeated sharply.

For answer I heard a little startled gasp.

"Who's that?" I said.

"I'm sorry, Miss Kirsty. It's Lucy. Lucy Malkin. I didn't even think about the time."

"What time *is* it?"

"I don't actually know." She was panting as if she'd been running. "I've been up all night, and I've kind of lost track of things."

"What's wrong, Lucy?" Something was wrong, clearly, for her to be calling me like this.

"Well, we have, I guess, a situation?"

"A situation? What sort of situation?"

Her voice came in dry jerks, as if someone were shaking her by the shoulders. "Like—an—emergency?—I guess?"

I thought of Janet, horizontal on her sofa. "Is your mother all right, Lucy?"

"No," said Lucy in her strange dry voice. "I mean, yes. I mean, no. I mean, it's not Mom." She gasped again. "It's Henry."

Little by little, I got the story out of her. It came to me with fragments of remembered detail: Henry among the azaleas. Henry flailing his arms, saying, "I can go like this." Henry and his *night exploring.* The children's wading pool, forgotten in the yard, full of algae-slimed rainwater.

"We were all still up," said Lucy. "We were watching these old Marx Brothers movies Dad likes. I don't actually think they're that funny, but anyway. And suddenly nobody knew where Henry was."

They'd gone out looking, laughing, calling Henry's name in the dark, putting their heads in all his strange hiding places. It was Howard who had found him. I shook my head, trying not to see. Something white in the green-black water. Face down. *Unresponsive*, a long word for a person as small as Henry. And the wrong word. If ever a person were responsive, Henry was.

"We don't know how it happened. It wasn't that much water. He was taking swimming lessons in water deeper than that. But in the dark—and it was cold—and maybe he hit his head. We don't know." Lucy was telling me all this in a voice like a water-swelled knot. "Dad got him out. At first there wasn't any heartbeat. And then there was. Moshe did CPR, because he knows how, he had to do a class one time. I was calling 911—"

The ambulance had come. Janet and Howard had followed it to hospital.

"I mean, you know, he has a heartbeat." She spoke lightly, but her voice was tight and hard.

"Where there's life there's hope," I heard myself say fatuously.

"Well, I mean, yeah." On this terrain, Lucy sounded more like herself. "Obviously. They're still at the hospital. Mom and Dad. They made the rest of us stay home. Mom calls with reports. He's holding his own, I guess? That's what she said, you know, just now. *Holding his own.* And she wanted me to call you."

"It's kind of you to tell me, Lucy," I said. "I suppose you've rung Father Schuyler already?"

A silence. "Mom and Dad probably didn't think. You know how they are."

Yes, I did know. "Well, someone should ring him now."

"I don't know." Another silence. "I hate to bother him."

"That man is paid to be bothered," I said. As Lucy did not answer, I added, "Would you like for me to phone?"

"Yeah," she breathed. "Yeah, please. Thank you."

I caught Father—so he told me—as he was beginning the

Office of Readings in his chapel. "I really shouldn't leave my cell phone on during prayers. It's a terrible habit."

"I'm glad you did," I said. I was standing in the kitchen now, listening to my kettle come to a boil, stretching the cord of the old wall phone so that I could reach it to make my tea. "You must go to the Malkins in hospital. At once. It's an emergency."

"What? Who?"

I wanted to shriek with exasperation. Instead I tried to explain what Lucy had told me.

"When you say *emergency*–"

Again I tried to make him understand what I had heard. As I hadn't got my own mind round it, it was difficult to put into words.

"But what do I do?" he said.

I wanted, just then, to reach through the telephone and shake him until his teeth fell out. "It's very simple, Father. Get into your car. Drive to the hospital. At the information desk, ask for them. *Malkin*. The patient would be *Henry* Malkin. *Henry*."

"Henry," Father repeated.

"They'd have come through Emergency. And Father, I should go prepared to anoint somebody, if I were you."

He said nothing..

"Father?" I said. "Are you there?"

"I'm here." His voice was faint.

"Well, don't be. *Go*." I slammed the receiver into its cradle with such force that the cradle broke free of the wall, and the whole contraption clattered to the kitchen floor in a confusion of wires. Somewhere in the afterlife, my father the berserker had set down his teacup.

I dressed, not considering what garments I put on or what it was I meant to do when I was clothed. I felt not in my right mind at all. Yet I must do something. I flipped through the parish directory, picked up the phone from the kitchen floor—mercifully I hadn't killed the dial tone—and rang Lucy back.

An hour later I was standing in the Malkins' kitchen, with its knotty-pine cabinets, its balding linoleum, its counters oversprawled with dishes. I was waiting for cinnamon buns, sticky dough prised from a cardboard cylinder, to heat in the oven.

"That's what you want for breakfast?" I'd said to Lucy.

"I can't think of anything else. Everybody likes cinnamon rolls. The can kind, I mean, not like from a bakery. Even Henry will eat cinnamon rolls —" On the phone she had gone quiet.

I had driven to the Bi-Lo, which opened early, and found the cardboard-cylinder cinnamon buns. The store brand, Lucy had said. Those were the ones they liked. Now the house smelt of cinnamon. *Shop buns,* Granny Astrid would have said, but the fragrance was comforting.

As I was taking the tray from the oven, the other little boy—*Isaac,* I told myself—wandered into the kitchen. "Oh, wow," he said, "we get *cinnamon rolls?* You guys," he shouted to the rest of the house. "*Cinnamon rolls!*"

I busied myself squeezing the thick icing over the fat baked spirals. In my own childhood, in addition to shop tarts, we'd had shop scones that made the inside of your mouth feel coated with talcum powder. We had thought them a great treat; heaven knows what was in them.

The front door banged. Janet appeared in the kitchen doorway. Her face made my heart contract. She'd grown ancient overnight: ancient in the sense of stone, where the weather's worn away the grass and soil and everything else, stripping the hill naked where it's most exposed.

She said, "I knew you'd be here." Before I could step away, she had put her arms round me. Though I was hardly fragile, I feared I might buckle beneath her desperate weight. The hard knot of her stomach pressed against me.

"I'm sorry," I said. "I'm sorry." What else could I say? *Sorry*, that paltry word, stretches so thin over so many broken things. I knew without asking what it was I was sorry for. Still I hoped that I was wrong.

"I know." Janet laid her head on my shoulder: a bony shoulder, not comforting. "God, I'm so tired. We were there all night. Howie's still there. He says you don't leave them alone, ever. He says you're supposed to sit with candles, but I don't know—"

"Oh, Janet," I said.

With some awkwardness, for I was still holding the plastic icing pouch, I patted her back. Children had come pouring into the kitchen and stood round waiting, as I realized, for permission to eat.

Janet put me from her. "Wait!" she commanded. "Wait for Father to bless the food."

"He's here?"

"He drove me home." She put her hand on my arm, as if to keep me within reach. "Thank you. You called him. I should have thought to, but I just—"

Hearing her voice tremble, I pressed her to keep talking. The prospect of Janet's tears terrified me.

She wiped her eyes with the heel of her hand. "Yeah, well, so. We were up in, you know, intensive care. There we were, and there was Henry, and they had him hooked up to a billion things already, and we just didn't know, you know. He looked so awful. They get all—waterlogged, I guess. But we thought he could wake up. You know, somebody's breathing, and you can see their heart squiggling up and down on the stupid monitor. You think that means something."

"Yes," I said.

"So Father came just—well, just as—I mean, he was in time."

"Oh, God, Janet," I said. How was it that I had known, but still hoped?

She put her hand on my arm. Her fingers tightened so that they left marks after. "No, no. It was good. I mean, no. It was horrible, the worst. I can't tell you how horrible it was. I can't even feel how horrible it was. Like my brain will not do that right now. But it was beautiful, too. I don't know. I can't explain. I tried to say something to Howie—about, you know, how something, you know, like that, could be beautiful—but he just looked at me like I'd lost my mind." She sighed and leaned on me harder. "Maybe I have. I don't even know anymore."

"Go and lie down," I told her. "Someone will bring you something to eat." Might there possibly be something to eat in the house besides cinnamon rolls, something of greater substance? I had my doubts. I remembered thinking that in a crisis, the Malkins would make a bonfire and roast marshmallows. Now it seemed to me that they would do this only because there was nothing else.

As Janet thumped away, Father Schuyler looked in at the kitchen. As always, he wore a cassock, this one crisper and newer than his day-out cassock but buttoned crookedly up the front. He was unshaven. In one hand he carried a prayer book, also crisp and new. In the other, still, as if he'd driven from the hospital without realizing that he was holding it, the little black leatherette sick-call satchel. He looked like a sleepwalker startled awake, dazed and hollow-eyed.

"Come and bless these cinnamon rolls, Father," I said.

Afterwards, we stood together in the dark front hallway.

"Oh," he breathed. He continued to clutch the satchel. It trembled in his hand. "I've never seen anything like that."

"It was bad, Father?"

"I've seen people die." He shook his head as if to clear it. "And dead bodies. But this was my first child."

I pushed some thoughts away. "How is Howard?"

"Well, he was very upset." That was an understatement, surely, but I held my tongue. Father continued, "I was able to reassure him—I think—but he didn't want the Sacrament."

No, I supposed he didn't. I wondered, too, just how much Father had been able to reassure him, what Christian hope might mean to Howard. Possibly it meant nothing at all. I remembered them that day in the narthex: Howard, patting Henry's head, surprised to find a little boy under his patting hand. Henry and his marveling eyes. Now, I thought, both of those people were gone. One of them remained in this life, but the little boy and the man who had been father to that little boy: both gone forever among the shadows of *Sheol*.

"They were trying to send him home," Father said. "Or at least make him leave, so that they could have the body taken away. But he says that Jews don't leave a body unattended until it's in the ground. I don't suppose there's a rabbi in Annesdale?"

"Not that I've ever heard, Father." Howard was likely the only Jew within a thirty-mile radius. There were rabbis in Charlotte, but they would be strangers. Or would they be? The rites surrounding the dead, those of one's own faith, were in themselves an intimacy. You didn't have to know the person performing them. At a time like this, the person was hardly the point. You wanted the proper words said, and in them you found yourself at home.

I remembered, again, my mother's funeral, arranged by Auntie Lass. "What your mother wanted," she had told me at the Lerwick crematorium, seeing me gape at the lady cleric in her pink alb. I had to grant that Auntie Lass knew my mother's wishes better than I did. But there were no proper words. There was no homecoming then, not for me, only a jolly empty eulogy, then a clutch of helium balloons which Auntie Lass and I were instructed to release outside and watch drift away inland, buffeted by the sea winds. I suppose we were meant to think of the soul, but the balloons, as the winds battered them down into the waves, were all too sadly inanimate, and the fish and birds that tried to eat them no doubt died.

Father Schuyler was still talking. "I told the doctors—" Clutching his prayer book, he rubbed his forearm across his eyes. "I forget what I told them. I might not have been completely diplomatic. But they're letting him stay, and he can go with the body when they take it to the morgue. He can stay there, too, as long as he wants. That's all arranged."

The body. It. We looked at each other.

* * *

Annesdale was, and is, a two-funeral-home town. The Sains had dealt always with Garnett Funeral Home: Baptist-owned and constructed on the model of the First Baptist Church, in red brick with white columns across the front and a modest steeple. The chapel inside was all frosted blue carpeting and yellow oak, with dais and lectern and, as well, a sort of room off to the side where a soloist could warble out "There is a Fountain Filled With Blood," or "In the Garden," invisible to the congregated mourners. Here I had accompanied Mother Sain to many sendings-off, while she was still in a fit state to remember those friends who predeceased her. In due course, naturally, I had attended her own services there. Ranse, too, had been buried from Garnett's, by his own wish, as set down in writing. He'd been afraid I would have requiems said over him, and incense swung, in the Catholic Church, when it was too late for him to have any say-so.

By the time he died, his lifelong congregation, Spake's Fork Baptist Church, had dwindled away to nothing. For some years we had gone halfheartedly to the First Baptist Church, until his health worsened, and then we went nowhere. Ranse had not especially liked the minister at First Baptist; we had never spoken to the man face to face. When I came to need one, I knew no preacher of that denomination whom I was willing to call for Ranse's committal to the earth. Not entirely in a spirit of having the last word, I summoned Father Trotter. I chose as well not to comply with Ranse's wish to be buried in his Masonic apron, for which I hope he will not reproach me in the hereafter. It was my prudential judgment that our mutual hopes of a happier hereafter were contingent on my burning the Masonic apron in the back garden and having him dressed in his best charcoal suit, with one of Wylie's rosaries in his breast pocket, under the handkerchief. "You'll thank me," I told him, before they put the lid down.

Though I had, as a matter of duty, attended many funerals in the parish—in the Church's view, to bury the dead, if not quite literally, constitutes yet another work of mercy—I had not heretofore been acquainted with the other funeral home, Blanco's. It sat, a squat gray cinderblock building, by the railway line on the eastern fringes of Annesdale, where the town began to dissolve into countryside. I had passed it on my way to and from the Malkins', but I had hardly registered that it was there.

This afternoon, it was visibly a mob scene. Though I had been punctual, even early, already the queue snaked out of the door and round the side of the building in the cold windy sunshine. I recognized members of the CCW and the altar guild. Numerous people in jeans and plaid shirts murmured to each other in Spanish as they waited. I saw Dr. Morrow, the veterinarian. There were children everywhere, and a huddle of young people wearing Bi-Lo supermarket uniforms, who were weeping on each other's shoulders. Had they known Henry, I wondered. How well did they know Lucy? Or was it simply that when you are young, it's delicious to feel a little sad?

Nodding to people I knew by sight, I took my place in the queue. I clutched my coat about me, for the weather had decided to turn cold, and shuffled forward, bit by bit, with everyone else. A woman I recognized from the parish came down the queue, whispering to each person in turn that she was taking donations to help the family, to defray the funeral costs. I rummaged in my handbag and handed her a twenty-dollar bill.

At last I was inside the building. Here, in a blast of central heating, the queue moved down a narrow corridor, past the black sign on its metal post, *Malkin Family* spelt out in white stick-on letters. I had been to wakes before where people had stood about in clusters, chatting, hailing each other in a carnival spirit. This visitation, by contrast, was deadly silent, except for the rise and fall of voices in an inner room. In front of me, a tiny white-haired lady had taken out her rosary and begun to pray in Spanish. Automatically I fished in my handbag for mine. But after a moment I realized that it wasn't the rosary they were saying.

Howard was chanting in a language that rolled from him like water. He recited a line in that language, fluid and—to my uncomprehending ear—wordless. Then he echoed it in English. "May His great Name grow exalted and sanctified."

I heard Janet's voice, toneless. "Amen." Half a beat behind her, the children said, "Amen."

"In the world that He created as He willed."

The lady in front of me, leaning on a rubber-tipped aluminum cane, prayed aloud with the Malkins in a thin, penetrating voice. "*Santa Maria, Madre de Dios, ruega por nostrotos peccadores, ahora y en la hora de nuestro muerte. Amen.*" She intoned her amen perfectly in time with theirs.

We shuffled forward again. I could hear Howard praying, on and on, but beneath the current of his voice, I could also hear Janet talking to people.

"Thank you," she was saying. "Thank you for coming. Amen. Thank you. Thank you. Amen."

At last I reached the inner room. Entering from the shadowy corridor was like entering some sacred space, the courts of the Lord, quivering with candlelight. Every surface—every end table, every console, every window ledge in the ersatz parlor—was crowded with candles, exhaling a potent hot smell of beeswax. A fire hazard, surely, I thought. The room was jammed with people, chiefly Malkins. I could see the children, from Lucy down to Isaac, backed against the far wall, their faces stricken, each of them wearing, pinned to the breast, a black ribbon. On two folding chairs in their midst, side by side, as on thrones, sat Janet and Howard. Howard held a prayer book with a carved leather cover, a beautiful thing.

The queue moved forward.

"Blessed is He," Howard chanted, in a prophetic voice entirely unlike his own. "Beyond any blessing and song."

The queue moved forward.

All the years of my life, what I have dreaded about visitations and wakes is the open casket. Always it's there, whether the deceased is Irish or Costa Rican or a former Pentecostal snake handler. Always you arrive at it, as at the central exhibit in a museum, and must kneel on the prie-dieu before that leaden stillness and say some prayer for the repose of that soul, the consolation of those who mourn. Always, in that moment, my mind went blank. I couldn't remember the simplest Hail Mary. Always I knelt with my eyes tight shut and my mind going *yawp yawp* at God.

There was no open casket here, thank God. Later I learned that in Jewish custom, to look upon the dead is to mock them. You don't eat or drink in their presence, or sing, or listen to music, or talk in an ordinary way; to do any of these things is to remind the dead of what they've lost. So little Henry lay modestly hidden beneath his white pall. The prie-dieu was there, though, and when my turn came, I knelt. Even with my eyes shut, I could feel the smallness of the box, the smallness of the body inside it. *Yawp, you bastard*, said my mind to God.

"May there be abundant peace from Heaven," Howard chanted. "And life upon us and upon all Israel."

I stood before Howard and touched his shoulder, an awkward gesture. He glanced up, then back at his book. "Now say: Amen."

"Amen," said Janet beside him.

I stood before her and looked down at her. Her white dress strained across her pregnant belly. "I'm sorry," I said inadequately, again.

She didn't glance up at the sound of my voice. Even so, I could see the smudges beneath her eyes. I wondered whether she had slept at all. Had the doctors cleared her to get up from bed rest? I suspected that she had ceased to care. Possibly she had forgotten the weight she carried, what it was. She should be at home, I thought severely. So should Howard, and so should the rest of them. Henry should be there in their midst. Should be, should be. A stupid word, *should*.

"Thank you for coming," Janet said dully. Then I was shuffled along, and she was thanking the person behind me for coming.

When at last I reached the door, and escape lay before me, Lucy caught me up. "We're going to sit shiva," she said.

"What does that mean?"

Her sea-glass eyes widened. "It's a Jewish thing, I guess?

We start tomorrow, after—after we come home again, you know, after, like, the Mass and everything. You come over and sit with us and pray, I guess, and it goes on for like days. I've never seen anyone do it, but Dad says we have to."

"I'll come," I told her, and moved on.

7

Driving home through the remnants of the brilliant afternoon, I passed the turn-off to Wylie's trailer neighborhood. Impulsively, at the next road, I turned round and went back, my car jouncing and scraping down the rutted drive.

There were the trailers, their modest cluster hemmed by scrub woods, roped with winter-dead kudzu vines. In all my years in Annesdale, I'd never quite got used to living in a place with vegetation like that. Ranse used to say that you could stand still and watch it grow. Even in dormancy it had the forbidding quality of something biding its time. It had eaten the woods; given half a moment it would eat the trailers as well. Still, the people kept their immaculate little plots of yellow Bermuda grass. Their winter gardens stood furrowed and ready, some with great lush heads of cabbage among the dead tomato vines, still grayly twined on their stakes. I thought of Father Schuyler's Latin signs, and though my heart lay heavy within me, I could not help smiling.

Unlike other similar enclaves I had passed in the countryside, this one communicated an air not of deprivation or decay, but merely of sparseness. Here there were no rusted schoolbuses set down for use as storage sheds, no odds and ends of metal strewn about, no piles of broken chairs and window-unit air conditioners half covered with tarpaulins, no Confederate flag staked in the center as a kind of gravitational pole. This little community, if you could call it that, had the feel of a place whose people expected to leave it. But beside the steps of a trailer, a galvanized pail stood bursting with yellow pansies, the color so fresh and sharp in all that grayness that it hurt my eyes to look at it.

Of course I'd no idea which trailer was Wylie's, or where to ask after him. As I hesitated, a door opened, and a woman appeared, squat and dark, wearing a gigantic purple t-shirt over black leggings. Her feet were bare, and she carried a baby, who sat upright in her arms and studied me with serious eyes.

"Hello?" she called. "Can I help?"

Thank God for people who spoke English. I was grateful that I myself had learned to speak it, to make plain what I wanted to say. "Wylie Springfield? I'm looking for Wylie Springfield. Do you know him?"

"Gone," she said.

"Sorry?"

"His house is there." She pointed. "Nobody home."

I thanked her. Turning to where she had pointed, I ascended the two wooden steps and knocked at the metal door. The sound reverberated inside. At the window, the thin plastic blinds were pulled down and shut. I knocked again. "Wylie?"

No answer.

I turned back to say something to the woman with the baby, but she had disappeared. I couldn't tell, anymore, from which trailer she had emerged. For all I knew, she might have been assumed into heaven while I stood there knocking at Wylie's door. I wondered which trailer had belonged to Maricruz and Miguel – or, if not belonged to, then which one had held them for a time. I wondered whether, if I knocked and asked, anyone would tell me. Then I wondered why I wanted to know.

In the middle of the night I awoke from troubled sleep. It was the graveyard hour, as they say, dark and silent. The kitten slept tranquilly on my pillow. Looking at him in the darkness, I wondered what boundary existed between sleeping and waking, when one had no eyes to close and open again to the light. I ran a finger down the curve of his little bare backbone; he murmured and stirred but did not rouse.

I on the other hand was wide awake. I got out of bed and went to the window. The cold night was plush-blue, spiked with stars. I hoped that someone had given Janet something to make her sleep. Howard, I knew, would keep watch with Henry till the morning, Henry whose body would sleep till the world ended, in that vast glittering night. Even now, Ranse was sleeping in the Mount Olive Cemetery on Highway 172. His father and mother slept near him. My father and mother, Granny and Auntie Lass slept in the great night that reached halfway round the world—slept, that is, if a million flakes of ash can be said to sleep. Sister Bede slept in her narrow grave in the nuns' burial ground. Somewhere, the Senior Tutor. And Dermott, of course: everyone I'd loved not enough in this life, or too much.

Why, you might ask, should I persist in counting Dermott among my dead? Why this bondage to that memory? In the dark, looking out at the stars, I asked myself that question now. It was all so long ago, so brief and meaningless. Why, after a decades-long marriage to a far better man, did I keep turning over that affair in my mind in this stupid way? On the one hand, it seemed to me a spiritual prison where I paced endlessly, longing for freedom. On the other hand, there had been, in spite of everything, something true and lasting: true, and therefore inescapable. He had been father to my child. Never mind that neither of us had wanted to know it. That day when I'd gone to see him, what would I have said? Could I have told him then what I wouldn't tell myself? When he opened the door and looked at me, had he guessed?

If he had not shut the door on me again, what would have been the outcome? Not a marriage, surely. Not any of the silly things I'd dreamed. It would, most likely, have been something worse. In the cold, shadowy stairwell, raising my hand to knock at his door, I had known more than I cared to admit. I'd felt the desertion of my illusions. He didn't want me; he would not have dreamed of wanting a child. In time, anyway, of its own accord, the child would go the way of my illusions. All of it: there and gone like a candle blown out, yet its smoke was the shape of the rest of my life. Sleeping in the vastness of the night—this was as close as I would come to speculating about his eternal fate—Dermott had been father to my child. Though I might yet be free of him, that was the one inescapable fact.

* * *

After the cold spell, the next day opened damp and warm, as December days can do without warning in Annesdale. When I stepped outside, a green wind met me. It touched my faded hair, unruly as it still was, no matter how I cut or combed it, into wildness. A mad old lady I must have looked, my hair a fat cloud, my most recent black frock—bought for Ranse—too tight across my backside. A mad old lady everyone must have thought me, stalking into church on my unaccustomed heels, clutching my rosary. In the narthex I stopped to sign the guest book. My handwriting, my own name, looked spiky and strange, the signature of a madwoman. I took my seat in a pew near the back.

I had been present at many funerals, and this was another one. In the course of all my burial or crematory experiences—my father, Granny Astrid, my mother, Mother Sain,

Ranse—with their various acknowledgments of our Creator's role in these inevitabilities, I had perfected, almost without trying, a level of composure that was more like being encased in plaster than anything else. I had begun with my father's death to practice this composure. If I had wept, if I had betrayed anything other than a sturdy iron loyalty, my mother would have broken down completely, perhaps permanently, and Granny Astrid would have been ashamed of me. That Granny Astrid had followed my father so quickly out of the world, that my mother had broken down despite my resolutions: none of that made any difference to me. Perhaps all along it was myself whom I was protecting from breakdown. At any rate, I would not fall to bits.

I did not fall to bits when Moshe and Dominic entered, bearing between them the veiled box so small a Christmas present might have come out of it. I did not fall to bits when Janet, Howard, and the rest of the children followed them, dressed all in white, black ribbons still pinned to their breasts. I clutched my own elbows so hard that later I'd be alarmed by the bruises my fingers left, but I did not fall to bits.

The Mass was any funeral Mass, the choir singing all the usual selections, thought to be consoling: "Lord of All Hopefulness," "I Heard the Voice of Jesus Say," "The King of Love My Shepherd Is." The soprano's vibrato was more pronounced than usual; when I glanced over at her, I saw that she was weeping as she sang. Well, I thought, she had children. I had seen them, three little girls. Naturally she would imagine. Anyone would. Even I might imagine. But I did not fall to bits.

"Henry was buried with Christ in baptism," Father intoned. Beneath the pale shaven dome of his head, his face looked drawn and ill. Even in the church's dull acoustics, his voice rose and reverberated with a life of its own, transcending his familiar body. But I did not fall to bits.

At last we emerged into the tumult of the day. Clouds were gusting over us. Beneath their dark bellies, the grass glowed unearthly green. What was the old proverb? *A green Christmas, a full churchyard.* Dr. Martin, the veterinarian, appeared beside me and took my arm. "Watch your step, now," he said. We got into our cars, flicked on our headlights, queued—so much queueing for death—and made our slow procession to the cemetery.

The American funeral, like the crem service familiar to me in my youth, operates according to its own death-obfuscating conventions. There, the waiting fire is a fact, but the doors close upon it. Here, the fact is the open grave. You are prevented, however, by design and forethought, from confronting that fact head-on. What is more, you expect to be prevented, and that expectation is a form of solace, or so it's conventionally presumed. You expect to encounter the hole in the ground only from an orchestrated distance. The funeral home erects a canopy over the spot and carpets the grass beneath with a superfluous layer of Astroturf, a comfortable lie beneath your feet. By the time you find your seat, the casket has been positioned above the open vault in such a manner that at no time does anyone, even the presiding cleric, catch sight of the dark void beneath it. Generally the casket remains poised on its hydraulic lift until after everyone has said their final goodbyes, drifted away. If you don't want to think of the deceased as buried, you don't have to, at least until much later, when you have composed yourself enough to return with flowers.

Janet and Howard had refused all orchestration. As I climbed from my car and fell in with the rest of the mourners, I glimpsed the two of them standing together in a corner of the cemetery near the woods, beneath the open sky: no canopy, no Astroturf, only an oblong, four-year-old-sized wound laid open in the red clay, like a vagina. Lucy's words returned to me—*She's having some vaginal bleeding*–but also the incredulity of the biblical Nicodemus, who had come by night seeking the Christ, to be told he must enter the womb a second time.

We stood round that hole. There was nowhere else to stand. As Father Schuyler read the prayers, I shut my eyes so that I wouldn't have to see what came next. There would be, today, no walking away from the still-life beneath the canopy: flower-draped casket, empty chairs. I heard the chunk of the spade, and despite myself, I looked. Howard, his face horribly set, was shoveling earth into the hole. *Clump*, it went hollowly on the lid of the box. Behind him, Janet and the children stood like a photographic backdrop, not alive, not moving. Janet's pregnant belly strained at her white dress. Her sea-glass eyes made two smudges in her ashen face. I prayed that she was not, just then, bleeding. *Clump*, went the clods of red earth.

At last it was finished. Nobody moved. Nobody spoke. Then, off to the side, someone else's little boy, dressed like a miniature banker in waistcoat and tie, bent, picked up a pine-cone, and flicked it at one of the soprano's daughters. With a shriek she leapt at him, and all in an instant, beneath the galloping sky, the world was all laughing, screeching, running children. The younger Malkin children, Naomi, Isaac, Miriam, broke free of the arms encircling them and ran wild with the rest.

Returning alone to my car, I paused at the Sain family plot. At Christmas, dutifully, like everyone else, I should bring poinsettias to Mr. Ransome and Mother Sain, tucked into their graves as into a double bed. I should bring one to Ranse as well, though he had never liked poinsettias. Flowers, he had believed, belonged to the springtime. I'm bringing you one anyway, I told him silently as I stood at his feet. He had no headstone, only a flat bronze plaque set into the yellow winter grass, with his name, his birth and death days. My name, too, was inscribed there, beside his, with my birthday and a hyphen. This was our true marriage bed, I thought. Ranse waited for me to come to him, to be tucked in, to lie in the dark without taking his hand. To the right of the hyphen would go, eventually, a day I passed every year, but would never recognize as my own.

* * *

Afterwards, the Malkins sat shiva. No, they had said to the church women, we don't want a reception. We don't want a lunch in the parish hall. We're going home, and people can come to us.

"But what are we supposed to do?" said one lady in a plaintive tone, clutching her friend's arm as they picked their way across the tufted cemetery grass. The wind plucked at their dark dresses and stood their short, permed hair, defiantly amber and flaxen, on end.

The friend patted her. "Go to their house. That's what they said. I guess we'll find out more when we get there."

What we did find, when we got there, was Malkins. In the small bare formal living room, always closed off, Lucy had told me, to preserve its status as the clean room, Howard perched on the piano bench. Flanked by pillows and children, Janet reclined on the sofa, her feet on the ottoman dragged from the back den. As Howard began to explain what was happening, her eyes rested on him as if she were seeing him for the first time and summing him up. With one absentminded hand, she stroked the mound of her stomach.

Howard was speaking. Again, as I watched him, he seemed

to become a person I had not known: the father not of a family, but of a nation. Though he looked hollow-eyed, his round face sagging like a tire gone flat, he sat upright on the piano bench. His voice was firm, even resonant. Always, before, he had lurked at the back of his flock of children, patting, imploring, borne along on their relentless current. Now, holding himself erect, he spoke for them all. Nobody else knew what to say.

"Jews sit shiva, see, for seven days after the burial. And this is about community. So, for example, we don't prepare meals during this time, but everybody's loaded us up with casseroles and things, so we're good there, thanks."

Somewhere in the crowd a child moaned, "Fried chicken. Please no more fried chicken." Several people tittered.

"So," said Howard, ignoring the interruption, "we're the family. Obviously. And we're going to pray together, like, the rosary, I guess?" Here he glanced at Janet, who met his gaze with sudden fierceness. "So, yes, I guess definitely we have to say the rosary, but we'll also pray the Kaddish, which is the Jewish prayer for the dead, as some of you might remember. Or maybe not. Anyway—" He stopped and twisted his hands together, as if to wring from himself what he wanted to say. "And so, for example, you don't have to ring the doorbell, just walk in. You don't have to know the prayers or anything. It's okay if you don't. I mean, I'm sure you don't, and that's all right. I'll read them. Otherwise, you know, if you just want to talk about, you know." He swallowed. "You know, to talk. About Henry. That would be appropriate to do."

Just then, it seemed that nobody wanted to talk about Henry. Janet sat stroking her belly, lost in meditation.

Behind me, the front door opened and shut. "What is it we're doing?" Father Schuyler murmured into my ear.

"Waiting," I told him, though I'd no idea for what.

After a time, the children began to fidget, then to bounce

up from where they were sitting and filter away to other parts of the house. Adults looked at their wristwatches and phone screens.

"Thank you for coming," said Howard to the room in general.

A lady I recognized as a fellow daily Mass-goer touched his shoulder in farewell. "It was a beautiful service."

"Well, I hated it." Howard rose abruptly, brushing the lady aside, and thudded away into the kitchen.

I too felt it was time to take my leave. Father Schuyler had slid past me to sit on the sofa; he was talking earnestly to Janet, who appeared not to see him. I looked about me, but there was nobody to receive my farewells. Straightening my handbag on my shoulder, I slipped from the house and started down the drive to the road, where I had parked. I passed the azaleas, evergreen, still leggy and unkept. No child crept among them now.

"Miss Kirsty!"

I turned and saw Lucy bounding after me, her white dress flying, her feet bare. She caught me up and, to my vast surprise and discomfort, clasped me in a muscular embrace.

"Thank you so much for being here," she panted. "You're coming again tomorrow, right?"

I hadn't planned to, of course. Despite what Howard had said, my instinct had been to give them privacy in their grief. Perhaps, though, this had been only the impulse of self-preservation. Perhaps it was my own privacy I cared for, not theirs.

"Yes, if you want me, of course I'll come again tomorrow," I heard myself say.

"Thank goodness."

"Why do you say that?" I asked her.

"I don't know. We just like you, that's all. You're different, like us."

What on earth did that mean? It seemed to me that to be different was to be like anybody. There was nothing so very remarkable in that. It was the human condition.

"Mom and Dad like you," Lucy continued. "*Henry* liked you. He didn't talk much to people outside the family. But he always wanted to talk to you."

I remembered the Lone Star tick. If I had known—if I had known what? That a tick, of all things, would be what existed between another person and myself? What would my knowing that have changed? I'd no idea.

"Mom says all our lives are an eyelash. Just like Henry's."

"I suppose she's right," I said. At the moment my own life seemed to be going on and on, fattening on wasted time.

"Well." Lucy shifted her weight from one foot to the other. Her legs had gone into gooseflesh, and I wondered what she had done with her shoes.

"I'll come again tomorrow." I patted her awkwardly to seal the promise and turned away.

In the evening I stood as usual at the kitchen window, eating unbuttered toast and watching the neighborhood Christmas lights scintillate beneath a low ceiling of cloud. I had been too exhausted to take the butter from the fridge, too numb to feel hungry. My jaws went up and down, open and shut, pulverizing each dry mouthful. *Thy weeping was for a man*, my Jesuit had written, addressing Mary Magdalen as she stood at the tomb. *And thy tears have obtained angels.* Well, I was no Magdalen. I had no tears. I of all people would be the last to obtain any angels.

* * *

The next day, Lucy met me at the door. "Help," she said.

She stood in the cold, disheveled, in a cotton summer dress that hadn't been ironed. Her bare feet were white on the concrete step.

"What's wrong?" I asked her.

"My Grandma Malkin is here. Did *you* know I had a Grandma Malkin? I didn't, until today. But Dad called her, and now she's here, and nobody knows what to do with her."

I let myself be led inside. In the living room I found, as yesterday, the sofa lined with fidgeting children. Janet and Howard, however, were not in evidence. Instead, beside the piano, a small birdlike woman with a cap of silver hair stood tapping her foot. She wore an exquisite black flowing pantsuit in some silky fabric that fit her like water. Tap tap, went her tiny foot in its spiky black heel. In the silence, energy radiated from her like heat from a woodstove.

"Um, Grandma?" said Lucy.

The woman turned sharply. "Which one are you, again?"

"I'm Lucy, Grandma. And this is our friend Miss Kirsty."

I stepped forward. "Kirsty Sain. From the parish. The church, you know." Two seconds in, and already I could hear myself beginning to babble.

She looked me up and down. "I see."

"You've come from New Jersey, then?" It was the only half-rational thing I could think to say.

"My son called me two days ago. A little last minute, if I was going to make it to a funeral. You understand we hadn't spoken in twenty years."

God help me. This was excruciating going.

"Yes, I had understood there to be some . . ." What was the word I wanted? *Estrangement*? *Fragmentation*? *Catastrophe*?

Howard's mother cast a roving glance about the room. Her eyes rested on the children, sitting in rigid silence on the sofa and on upright chairs along the walls. "Look, don't you people want to go play or something? You really don't have to sit here. Why don't you go someplace else and let the grownups talk?"

Like air from a balloon, tension rushed from the room, and with it the children. Mrs. Malkin caught at Lucy on her way out. "Make sure they don't bother your mother."

To me she said, "I made Janet lie down. Her killing herself won't bring that poor child back. I told Howard what I thought about this display, too. It's a little late to be rediscovering your supposed identity, I said, forcing your family through this whole show, to prove God knows what to God knows whom." Again she tapped her foot, and I felt her energy wash over me in waves.

"Where is Howard now?" I asked cautiously.

"He went out in that awful van."

Somehow I wasn't surprised.

"He said something about needing some space," his mother continued. "I don't blame him for that. This house would send anybody over the edge. But now here I am with all these kids, and I don't know what he thinks I'm supposed to do with them."

"Possibly he thinks you'd like to get to know them," I said a little too bluntly.

Mrs. Malkin moved to one of the chairs. "Sit down."

She sat down herself, upright as a dancer, her back not touching the back of the chair. "Do you want coffee? I understand there is some."

I did not want coffee.

Mrs. Malkin ran a hand over her shining hair. "This is all a shock, you understand. I really don't know how to respond."

"I imagine it is difficult," I said.

"My husband didn't want me to come. I mean, to call us, after all this time. They couldn't be bothered to tell us when the children were *born*."

"Sometimes, possibly—" I was treading with caution. What did I know? "Sometimes perhaps it takes a crisis—"

Mrs. Malkin raised a silky eyebrow. How on earth had that spare body produced a person the size of Howard?

"You don't think their whole life is a crisis?" she said.

I had no answer for this.

"We never liked Janet, you know. All through school, there she was, running after Howard, and we never liked her." Mrs. Malkin glanced again about the living room, which looked, to my eye, like a model of conscientious tidiness. The only sign that it belonged to the Malkins was a naked fashion doll thrust head-down between the sofa cushions, white legs protruding like those of Icarus in the famous painting.

"It wasn't that she wasn't Jewish," Howard's mother continued. "We're tolerant people. We don't—I mean, we're pretty laissez-faire. We keep kosher-*ish*, you know what I mean? No pork chops, that's a bridge too far, but I'll eat a cheeseburger. My mother would roll over, but that's the way it is. Anyway, our son Brian, Howard's older brother—" She paused, as if to judge whether Howard had ever said anything at all about his origins.

"Yes," I prompted her. "He's a doctor, I believe?"

"A retinal surgeon. Well." She tipped me another significant look. "Brian has, you know, a male partner. A very nice man. They've been together for many years now, with an apartment in the city and a house at the shore, a very nice house."

I waited for her to continue.

"Anyway, when, you know, when Brian told us about Piers—I mean, we knew that Piers lived with him, but I suppose it didn't occur to us—anyway, naturally this wasn't easy news to digest, especially for my husband. He tends to be a little rigid. And of course we had wanted grandchildren, and all that—" Again her voice trailed away.

"Things so seldom turn out the way you envision," I said helpfully, I hoped.

She sighed. "No. But Piers is a lovely man. We're fond of him, and he and Brian are very attentive. My husband is twenty years older than I am, you see, and he's become quite frail. So it's good to have Brian and Piers nearby. Piers isn't Jewish, either," she added. "More and more it just seems not to matter all that much."

We sat in silence for a moment.

"But we never liked Janet," Mrs. Malkin repeated. Her voice trembled. "She was a slutty, trashy girl going nowhere. And look what she's given my son. A slutty, trashy, nowhere life. But that's the way it is." She raised her hands, then let them fall into her lap. "What are you going to do?"

"She did give him children," I said. "Surely—"

"We've had no relationship with those children. We've been entirely cut off."

I thought of the Aberdeen grandparents I had never known—though whose fault was that? I couldn't have said. Nobody had ever told me anything about it. At any rate, I felt now that I was going to stop being careful. "I had understood that Janet and Howard felt cut off." By you, I did not have to say.

"Look." Mrs. Malkin's foot went tap-tap-tap. "I told you, we're tolerant people. We accepted Piers. We might not like the situation, but we can learn to appreciate the person.

Howard didn't give us a chance."

"I believe Janet felt rather the same way," I said.

Howard's mother might have lashed out at me then. Instead she shook loose some imaginary wrinkle in her black tunic. Then she smiled tautly. "We're doing this all backward, you know. Cutting into the scar tissue, and we don't even know each other's names. I mean, you told me, but I've forgotten it already. I'm Vivian."

I repeated my name. She thrust a tiny hand at me, and I clasped it, feeling that I might crush it in my own bony paw. We sat back and assessed each other in silence.

"You're not from around here," Vivian said at last. "Ireland?"

"Close enough." Again I recalled that Easter Vigil, when I'd stood beside Howard in the little crowd outside the church. *Do you miss your home*, he had asked me. In all my years in Annesdale, I could not remember ever having been asked before where I came from, let alone whether I missed it. I was in Annesdale; I simply *was* in Annesdale, as in the Promised Land. As far as Annesdale was concerned, no other place existed.

"And do you have children?" Vivian asked next.

"No," I said.

"Well." Her voice softened. "Maybe you haven't missed much. I'm feeling too old for all this right now."

Having no answer, I rose to go. Through the front window I spied Father Schuyler's car pulling into the toy-strewn driveway. "Here's the priest," I said.

Vivian put a hand to her forehead. "Oh, God. Really? Now?"

"I should warn you that he is a bit awkward with people."

"What's he doing in that line of work?" Vivian smiled again, less tautly. "I won't eat him, I promise."

Lucy with her boyfriend, tall and shadowy, emerged from the kitchen with a plate of little triangle-cut sandwiches, which she proffered. "Something to eat, Miss Kirsty?"

She looked so sad and hopeful that I took two, though I wasn't hungry. As I stood eating them hurriedly by the door, she passed on into the living room. I heard the murmur of her voice. I heard Vivian say, "Do you happen to have any that aren't ham?"

I might have gone back and extricated Lucy from her predicament. But really, it was none of my business. Perhaps over ham sandwiches, Vivian might begin working out some sort of relationship with her granddaughter. She didn't, of course, have to eat the sandwiches. That might have been another bridge too far.

On the doorstep I met Father Schuyler, saturno in hand. Touching the mezuzah, I said, "Howard's mother has come, Father."

He blinked. "I didn't know Howard *had* a mother."

"Oh, yes. She's in the living room with Lucy."

"But what do I do with her?"

"Let her do the talking." I left him steeling himself to knock at the door.

As I was getting into my car, I heard Janet call my name. Barefoot like Lucy, wearing a voluminous t-shirt and exercise trousers, bearing the weight of her unborn child like an afterthought, she came lumbering across the grass.

"Don't make me laugh," she said. "If I laugh, I have contractions and pee my pants."

I couldn't imagine what there might be to laugh at. "What are you doing out here?" I said.

"Sneaking. I went out the basement door, just for a minute. Oh, my God." She put her hand on my arm. "Thank you for coming. Howie didn't tell me he was calling her. He just sprang her on me."

"Well, she came. It seems a gesture."

"Yeah, I guess." Janet studied her white feet in the yellow winter grass. "But I know what she thinks about me. I know what she thinks about all of this. I mean, it's our life. It was fine. And now that it's falling apart, here she is to watch it fall apart. Child Protective Services got here the same time she did, if that tells you anything."

"Oh, Janet."

"Yep. They'd been here before, too. *And* at the hospital. Like my four-year-old is lying here brain-dead, and you want to ask me a bunch of stupid questions about my home life, thank you very much? They're gone now, and the kids are still here, so that's something. But yep. A whole nother dimension, because this wasn't enough fun already."

There were things I might have said, I suppose. Instead of saying them, I patted her shoulder with a tentative hand. "How are you? Are you all right?"

"No."

We stood there in the mild afternoon, the world greening around us as if it were springtime. I braced myself for Janet's tears, but after a pause she seemed to gather herself.

"Howie says he's leaving," she said.

"*Leaving?*" I felt my face fall open in astonishment. "What do you mean, *leaving*?"

"Me. He's leaving me. That's where he's gone right now, to look for a place."

"I don't believe it, Janet."

She shrugged. "He says he's been unhappy for a long time, but what the hell? Last weekend we were watching movies and eating popcorn and talking about baby names. He was happy enough then. We were *all* happy then."

The vision of them all, crowded together, eating popcorn

and laughing: it didn't bear thinking about. "*Does* the baby have a name? He or she?"

"Howie names them. He waits until they're born. We never find out what they are beforehand. That's his rule. It's always a state secret. But once he sees them, it's like an inspiration strikes him, and he just *knows.* I mean, sometimes he doesn't know right away. With a couple of them, the baptism has been the big unveiling. Margaret, I think. And maybe Naomi. It's the girls he gets hung up on. There are so many girls' names. I can make a list of suggestions, I'm allowed to talk about it, but he has to know *the* name, you know what I mean?" She sighed. "I can't really blame him. It's too hard to think about anything right now. I can't imagine caring about anything ever again."

"But you will," I heard myself say. Really, though, what did I know?

"Yeah." She sighed again. "Anyway, what are you gonna do about it?"

It was a rhetorical question, clearly, the same question Vivian had just put to me. *What are you going to do?* Janet didn't want an answer, any more than Vivian had.

"I will pray for you," I said. It was a paltry offering. I felt its paltriness. But it did strike me as the one possible thing to do. I patted her again, and she turned away to the house.

A warmish early dark was falling. The new houses along the road shimmered in their baths of white light. When I let myself into the house, the kitten, hungry, came running from wherever he had spent his afternoon, and mewed and stubbed his nose along the side of my foot. I fed him, then opened a tin of the soup Father Schuyler had brought me in my illness. It came to a boil in the saucepan; I regarded it with disgust. When was the last time I had cooked a proper meal, to maintain the charade that I considered myself worth feeding?

In the night I heard again the sound of rain and wind. The kitten had left his place on my pillow and gone off somewhere while I slept. I was alone. The dark about me felt infinite. It was the graveyard hour; worse, it was the hour of the soul's grave, the hour that made the psalmist cry, *My one companion is darkness.*

"Oh, God," I said aloud. All this time, I hadn't wept. All my life. Not for my father, not for my mother, not for my grandmother, my mother-in-law, my husband. Not for my child, known so slightly, loved so little, that I scarcely felt I deserved to weep for it. All that time, I had felt beyond tears.

"Oh, God. Oh, God," I said. I wanted to die. I wanted to be dead. I wanted to have died in my illness. Why hadn't I? It was so stupid, a child's dying, while I went on and on. "Oh, God. Oh, God." My body was rigid with the effort of grief. My jaw ached; my cheeks hurt; my bones felt sucked dry. "Oh, God. Oh, God," I kept saying. There was nobody to hear me. Even the kitten had abandoned me. Outside, the rain fell, the wind blew. In its own good time, the morning came.

8

For some days afterward, though the Malkins were a constant weight in my mind, I made myself scarce. However long Vivian meant to stay, whatever she meant to do while she was there, I felt that I was better out of the way. Feeling that I'd been long from home myself, I tried to put these problems aside, and to pick up the threads of my familiar life.

Halfheartedly I went about making my house fair, as the Advent carol says. Always I associated the purple, penitential seasons, Advent and Lent, with more than the usual housekeeping. I dusted the photographs in their frames, moved them onto tables and shelves, and wiped the mantel clean. As I swept the shining floors, the kitten skittering after my broom, I heard my footsteps echo in the stillness, and I thought of Wylie. Which of the jobs, if any, had materialized? Where had he gone, he and Maricruz and Miguel? Had they gone together? I remembered her glance and the prickle at the back of my neck. I hadn't known then what her glance meant; I didn't now. But any time I shut my eyes, I might see Maricruz at the wheel of her van, driving through some vast open landscape in the dark. Always, when I saw her, she was traveling at night. The wind moved over the silver van and was left behind. Did Wylie sit beside her in the passenger seat, unsleeping, keeping watch? Or did he follow her through the darkness alone, in his own truck, hoping to catch her up? Though I did not know the answer, I could see the set of his face, the doggedness of love.

Over everything the stars cast their handfuls of cold fire.

In the evenings I read my Jesuit. As always, his voice in my ear was Sister Bede's, luminous as a vision. *For in this weak unarméd wise/The gates of hell he will surprise.* The couplet rang in my head as I was falling asleep, and when I made my tea in the morning, as the sun shone blandly through the windows. The house was full of light, illuminating the dust I had been neglecting. Again I swept and wiped and cast it away. Outside, the weather continued springlike, and beneath the trees out back, already I could see the first green teeth of daffodils breaking through the damp earth.

I took the plastic Infant of Prague from the mantel and stood him on the dining-room sideboard. From a box in the linen cupboard I drew out the little plaster Christmas crib figures I had brought from my mother's house. With my books and photographs, these had formed the sum total of my own bits and bobs, boxed and sent by slow boat when I married. Now, as my mother had done in my childhood, I hid the Infant Christ away in a teacup in the kitchen, to await the day of His birth. On the mantel, above my ersatz woodstove, where the Infant had stood, I arranged Mary and Joseph, either side of the empty manger. They were chipped now with much handling. Mary's dark hair beneath her veil had a plaster-white patch right in front, as if she had aged on the road to Bethlehem, and her hair dye had begun to grow out. The lantern Joseph had brandished, all my early life, had long since broken off and been lost. Still, there they stood, waiting as always for the Incarnation to catch them up. They caught my eye every time I passed through that room, and again I thought of Janet and Howard. Remembering Vivian, I continued to keep my distance.

I had no child or grandchild, no soul to enchant but my own. In my widowhood I had ceased to bother with a tree or lights, stockings or a great dinner, any of the usual signposts of Christmas in a family. As always, alone, I would go soberly to Midnight Mass. When I came home again, I would bring out the Christ Child from His hiding place. With care I would lay Him in the chipped brown manger. I would light my candles, switch on my pretend fire. Perhaps the kitten would sit purring on my knee. *A beautiful sight, we're happy tonight*: a wrung-out old woman and her blind, bald cat. If I had been anthropomorphically inclined, I might have hung a stocking for the kitten. Instead I would give him tinned chicken for a treat. My own dinner I hardly planned for. What was the point in cooking for myself? I existed, all right; no need to go on proving it. Still, I had another whole chicken in the deep-freeze, which I might bestir myself to roast. Then I might make soup to feed me throughout Christmastide, if I could bestir myself to eat it. All this was more than feast enough for me. I felt glutted just thinking about it.

In his homily for the Vigil Mass of Gaudete Sunday, Father Schuyler stressed the theme of light in darkness, appropriate as it was dark already outside. He reminded the Saturday-night congregation that his vestment for the day—a new dark-magenta fiddleback chasuble in stiff, shiny damask—was not to be referred to as *pink*.

"Father does *not* wear Barbie clothes." With severity he peered out over the rims of a pair of tortoiseshell reading glasses, which I feared he had bought at the dollar store as a prop for the occasion. "The color for the third Sunday in Advent is *not*—I repeat, *not*—pink. It is *rose*."

Since the Bishop's visit, Father had, with a certain level of obviousness, been forcing himself to stand and greet his parishioners at the church door after the Mass. As I impelled myself to stand in that exit queue, I heard him quizzing people one by one as they shook his hand.

"What color am I wearing? I'll give you a hint. It's not pink."

"Oh, Father!" The woman who had accused him of turning his back on us was giggling like a girl with a crush. Though in fact we had had Mass *ad orientem* since the beginning of Advent, she might have been laughing at Father Trotter, springing bottles from the secretary's desk.

"We better watch out, Father," the woman said archly. "Next thing we know, you'll be giving us a test."

"Study hard," Father responded with effortful levity.

When my turn came, and we shook hands, he didn't let me go immediately. "Kirsty, have you spoken with the Malkins?"

"Well, Howard's mother is there, you see, Father, and I thought—"

"There are further complications." Leaning close to me, in a manner entirely inconsistent with what I knew of his personality, he lowered his voice. "Howard—though I advised him strenuously against such a step—has moved out of the house."

"Do you know where he's gone?" I asked in alarm. Though Janet had told me that Howard meant to leave her, I hadn't imagined that he would actually carry out this action. Howard had never struck me as having that much personal momentum. As long as nobody pushed him out of the house, I had felt certain that he wouldn't go.

"He's staying with some friend from his work, I understand. Somebody with a garage apartment or something."

"I see."

"And then there's the daughter."

The daughter? "Which one, Father?"

"The oldest. The one who comes to confession all the time." Father produced a tidy pad of facial tissue from his sleeve and patted at his damp forehead. "She turned up at the rectory the other night. Alone. I had to stand out in the rain to talk to her."

Lucy, naturally. I could imagine the scene. "Yes, of course, Father, standing outside was only proper."

"I can't possibly have girls turning up at the rectory."

"No, Father, of course not. But what did she want?"

"To tell me she needed to get married. I told her the thing to do was call the church office—in the daytime, during regular office hours—and make an appointment. We'll have to set up the usual Pre-Cana program, and they'll need to register for the diocesan retreat—"

"But whom is she marrying?" I said, though even as I said it, the shadowy form of the boyfriend, whose name was something ending in *-ayden*, or else not, rose in my mind. "And why now?"

"Times of crisis often result in other crises," Father said. "That's what they say, anyway. Maybe if you paid them a visit, you'd learn more. The girl—" He looked at me questioningly.

I supplied her name. "Lucy, Father."

"Lucy was a little incoherent the other night."

"Is she pregnant?"

He looked startled. "I didn't ask."

Again I felt like shaking him until his teeth fell out. "It would seem to me, begging your pardon, Father, that that would be something to find out."

"Well, she is a very devout young woman, so naturally I assumed—"

"Never assume, Father," I said, and went away thinking.

I thought as I ate my frugal supper and watched the kitten play. I thought as I cleaned my teeth and got into bed. In the morning, I resolved, I would go to them. I didn't know what I would do when I got there, but I would go.

I fell asleep thinking. Sometime in the small hours, the phone woke me.

Of course the phone is ringing, I said to myself in my sleep as I reached for it. *Hello, Lucy,* I nearly said, still asleep. But it wasn't Lucy.

It was Vivian Malkin who said, "I'm sorry to call at this hour."

Instantly I was awake. "Oh, no, no. Not at all." I wondered what hour it was.

"Janet asked me to, you see. We're waiting for the ambulance."

"Ambulance? What's wrong?" I asked stupidly, before it dawned on me.

"Baby time," said Vivian. "She's having regular contractions. But what she told me about the placenta worries me. You know I'm an obstetrician, right?"

"No," I said. "I'd no idea."

"I'm retired. But this is my stuff. I'm not just somebody's mother-in-law making a fuss. That's what I keep telling Janet. She says she spent the whole fall lying down, and I say, tough, sweetheart. That's basically been our conversation. This has not been a great situation." I could hear Vivian's fingers tapping a little tattoo on the back of the phone as she spoke.

"And you've called for an ambulance?" I said in alarm.

"I don't drive. And I don't want to wake the children. And really, despite all Janet's protests to the contrary, this is a high-risk scenario. We're talking a possible placental abruption. We need to get her there, stat."

Whatever *possible placental abruption* meant, exactly, it sounded serious. "Thank you for letting me know," I said.

Oddly, Vivian laughed. "Oh, no. I'm not just cluing you in. Janet wants you to come."

"Come?"

"To the hospital. She wants you with her."

Holding the phone, I fell back against my pillows. "With her? You mean—"

"Would it be too hard for you to be in the delivery room?" Vivian's sharp voice was suddenly gentle. "You said you didn't have children. I won't ask. But look, I hear the ambulance." Her tone became hurried. "She's probably having a c-section. If I had to guess, I'd say we show up, they take one look at her, and they put her right under. Crash, boom. She won't know who's there and who's not. If you could just wait in the waiting room—"

That much I could do. Ringing off, I swung my legs over the side of the bed and felt for my slippers.

At that hour, in the wide, empty, purple-carpeted hospital lobby, lit by one overpowering industrial-sized chandelier, the information desk was vacant. I had to track down a person in green scrubs, who told me where to go to find someone who might be able to find a Janet Malkin in the labyrinthine computer system of the small rural hospital. When I did find that person, a large weary-looking woman in—this time—lavender floral scrubs behind the emergency-room intake desk, I was directed to the labor-and-delivery waiting room, down yellow-lit corridors and round corners. In that windowless white room, laid out in rows of alternating blue and green plastic chairs, I sat in the cold pallor of the fluorescent light. Outside, as in a parallel universe, I knew that soon the dawn would break.

The only other person in the waiting room was a woman eating a thick hamburger over a Styrofoam takeaway container balanced on her knees. As she ate, the hamburger dripped a pinkish discharge of mingled ketchup and mayonnaise into the container. She glanced up at me over the hamburger as I sat down. I noted the sign informing me that, due to the onset of cold and flu season, no magazines would be made available in any hospital waiting room. I hadn't expected to catch up on Hollywood gossip while I waited, but since they'd pointed it out, I did experience, in spite of myself, a certain frisson of deprivation.

The woman with the hamburger chewed and swallowed. "What do you think? They gone love it or list it?"

"Sorry?"

She nodded at the television, the sound turned down, where a realtor was showing a couple the view of a backyard swimming pool through a set of French doors. "They're looking at all these new houses. But this lady's fixing up their'n. They can stay in it, all fixed up, or they can sell it and buy them a new one. I like that house there. The old one don't have a pool. You got somebody having a baby?"

"No," I said. She looked at me oddly. "I'm waiting to find out," I added, clarifying nothing.

"Well." She continued to eye me dubiously. "That's what this waiting room is *for*. I got my oldest girl in there right now, having her second. With the first one I tried to stay in the room with her, but she hollered and cut up and told me to go to hell, so this time I said fine, I'll carry you to the hospital, but I ain't fixing to stay with you. She ain't but nineteen. You can't hardly talk sense into somebody that age. I was just the same as she is. Told my own mama to go to hell."

The woman bit into her hamburger again with a look of inexplicable satisfaction. Together we watched the television, I in stupefaction, she in a spirit of fatalism.

"See? I told you they'd list it. They never like their own house as much. You can make it prettier all you want, but if it don't work, it don't work. You want coffee, honey? They got some out there in the lobby. I reckon it ain't cold yet."

In this way we passed an hour or so. Outside, I knew, the sky was silvering, then flushing rose, but I didn't see it. I wanted tea but drank the tepid coffee from the lobby instead. If something didn't happen soon, I began to think, I should have to go home again and see to my kitten. It was what I wanted to do: to be at home, in the warmth and quiet of my house, with my strange little familiar. I was getting witchy in my old age, I thought. Soon I should be muttering prophecies by the fireside and telling over all the dark ancient stories. In the meantime, I did not want to expend hours in the labor-and-delivery waiting room, watching home-improvement television with this woman whose nineteen-year-old daughter was having her second and telling them all to go to hell. But there we were.

While Ranse was having, in that same hospital, the operation from which he never awoke, I had sat in a similar room with a similar woman. It was winter then, too, though Christmas was past. Her boyfriend, the other woman told me, also had the sugar diabetes. Boyfriend: it had sounded such a young and bounding word, gratingly inappropriate on the lips of this woman who was, she informed me, *forty-three year old.* Her front teeth were out. Her colorless hair straggled down the sides of her colorless face like gravy over a biscuit of the American sort, such as Mother Sain had liked to bake for breakfast. This woman was in every way a human biscuit of the American sort.

Both our men were having their legs off, which was so horrible to me that I wanted to think of anything else, anything at all, but she was fixated.

"Did yours have a big old sore?" she kept asking me.

Yes, yes, mine had had a big old sore. I didn't want to think about it.

"My peepaw, he had his leg off."

I didn't want to hear about her peepaw and his leg. I did not want to hear that he had liked to show her what was left of it, when she was a *peerie lass.* Of course she didn't say *peerie lass.* She said *little girl.* It was impossible to me that this woman had ever been a child whose peepaw had enticed her to *come see my stump, doll baby.*

No, no, no, I thought. When the nurse put her head in, summoning me to confer with the surgeon, I leapt up in relief. Anything but the big old sore, anything but this woman and her peepaw and his stump. Even death, I had thought, which it was.

* * *

Eventually a nurse came to call the hamburger woman away. I was alone with the television, but only for a moment. Another nurse, this one in crimson scrubs, looked in and said, "Somebody here for Malkin?"

I found Janet in a narrow white room with the blinds drawn. In the railed bed she lay prone and deflated, tethered by IV lines, a blood-pressure cuff, and a fingertip oxygen sensor. Though she appeared no longer pregnant, I saw no sign of any baby. Vivian stood at the foot of the bed, studying the monitors that bleeped and blipped above Janet's head. I wondered where she had been while I had sat in the waiting room.

Janet blinked at me in sleepy confusion. Beneath the white blankets, her arms and legs were shaking. Her teeth chattered when she spoke. "I thought you'd be Howie."

"No," I said inadequately. We looked at each other.

"I had to go in the ambulance." She shook and shook, like a person freezing to death.

Vivian caught my look. "It's a very common post-partum reaction. The shaking, I mean. Not much fun, but it does go away on its own."

Dreamily Janet flicked her hand, and the oxygen monitor flew off. "I didn't want an ambulance. They're so expensive.

I thought Howie would drive me. But the ambulance came anyway, and here I am."

Leaning over the foot of the bed, Vivian picked the monitor out of the bedclothes and clamped it onto the finger her daughter-in-law held up obediently, like a child waiting for a sticking plaster.

"The baby was kind of gray," Janet said next. "That's what they tell me. They were trying to get her to cry."

"A girl?" I said.

"That's what they tell me."

"But she's all right?"

A nurse came bustling in. She looked at Vivian, who exuded a daunting professional energy. Vivian stepped aside to give her access to the bed.

"Sugar pie, let's see that blood pressure. Is one of these ladies your mama?"

As Janet looked at me, her mouth quirked in an odd, sad, tooth-rattling smile. "Yeah, why not?" she said. "Why not you?"

The nurse, inured to the strange things patients said as anesthesia wore off, went on calmly reading various monitors and tapping notes into the tablet device that she carried.

"Well," Janet said, "you could be."

I glanced at Vivian, who shrugged. *Have at it,* her look said.

"Hey, Mom, do me a favor? Go find my baby?"

"Follow the signs to the nursery," the nurse said, still intent on her charting.

"And then find Howie," said Janet. "I don't know where the hell he's gone. It's not like him. He's always here. Did he go with the baby? If he's with the baby, tell him to come here to me."

I followed the signs to the nursery, all bright lights behind a plexiglass wall, and asked for Malkin. There was, of course, no Howard. I had not expected there to be. Still, I experienced a pang of sorrow. Wherever Howard was, he had not gone with the baby. I could not send him down to Janet.

"Are you family, honey?" asked the nursery nurse at the half-door.

"A friend of the family."

"Well, my love, we can only admit somebody wearing a matching wristband, or else on our approved family list. Security reasons."

"I quite understand," I said. "But the mother can't get out of bed, and she's asked me to come and see that the baby's all right. Could you hold her up, perhaps? Then I can say I've seen her."

The nurse bent over a clear plastic bin at the end of a row of identical clear plastic bins. Then she turned back to me, smiling. In her arms I saw a tight little roll of striped hospital flannel, topped by a pink stocking toque. Between the toque and the blanket, a rumple of crimson skin.

"You made her cry, then," I observed.

"She was a tough cookie. We had to drop cold water right in her face. I hated to do it, but she had to get oxygenated somehow, and she was holding out on us. Ol' Baby Girl Malkin." She joggled the baby affectionately in her arms.

"And she's really all right? I understood that it was a high-risk delivery."

The nurse smiled again. "She's fine."

"Well, it's a relief. They said she was gray."

"They just come out that way sometimes. And then you have to work to pink them up. But she's perfect. Just a little old sack of stubborn sugar." The nurse jounced the baby again. "You go tell her mama not to worry."

* * *

The morning before Christmas Eve, Janet was to be discharged with the baby from hospital. Lucy and Moshe—furious, I had heard, at being allowed to sleep through the ambulance—were to take all the children in the big van to fetch them home. The whole process, I imagined, would occupy some hours, which was just as well. I might have felt compelled to go over, first thing. They might have expected me to. These expectations, so unfamiliar to me, could grow wearing, as I had discovered.

Meanwhile, it was a Monday. I'd my rectory-cleaning to do, fixed in my calendar, an immovable observance, for the good of my soul. What good did it do Father Schuyler? Over the course of the autumn I had had my doubts. Still, all Advent, as if it were my own house, I'd done my best to make the rectory fair. As always, it was a challenge to clean what was already spotless. Today, however, I noted a spillage of crumbs round the toaster. I leapt upon them with my damp cloth, then took up the toaster and shook it upside-down over the sink. More crumbs fell out. Washing them away down the drain, wiping behind the toaster, I felt filled with purpose, even power. Here at last was a battlefield I recognized. On it I might triumph.

In the dining room, I noted anew, with some amusement, the Advent wreath on the violet-clothed table. The wreath's three purple and one pink candle had been burned down improbably to the same height. It was no great stretch to imagine Father, in the long solitary evenings, timing the burning of candles scientifically, being chafed if one came out taller or shorter than the others. It was the sort of thing Ransc might have done, if I had ever lit Advent candles at home while he was alive. Of course I had not. An Advent wreath would have constituted one more thing beside the point. Ranse was perfectly capable of believing in God without all this unbiblical folderol, thank you very much. Still, I'd seen him carve jack-o-lanterns and light candles in the dark. What exactly had he thought he was doing? Perhaps I would never know. Or perhaps one day I wouldn't have to wonder: that was my great hope.

As I was untying my coverall, Father himself came banging in.

My heart jerked in my chest. "Goodness, Father. You startled me."

"Oh, that's right, it's Monday." He looked exhausted. His coat fell from his shoulders onto a kitchen chair. "You'd think I'd remember my own day off."

"Have you not been recreating, Father?"

He smiled at the word. "I've been out all night. Remember that lady who slammed the door on me? Phyllis? I've just been ushering her out of this life."

Reflexively I crossed myself, saying, in my mind, the proper formula for the dead: *rest eternal, light perpetual.*

"Well, bless," I said aloud, though as far as I could remember, I hadn't known Phyllis at all.

"There was a son who took care of her, which I gather means that he sat in a recliner and watched television. Jerry. He wasn't going to get up and let the priest in, that's for sure, at least until Mother decided to lie down and start dying. That brought him to his senses. I was able to hear her confession, and his, too. It had been forty years." He shook his head incredulously. "How do people do it?"

"I don't know," I said. It seemed to me a stroke of the most incredible grace that I had not gone the rest of my life without the sacraments.

As usual, Father stood nervously shuffling the post on the kitchen island. I had brought it in, many heavy, colored envelopes containing Christmas greetings and, perhaps, restaurant gift cards. Already a basket in the front entryway was half full of such gift cards, people's plastic good wishes, which I could not imagine the recipient's making use of.

Reading my thoughts, he held up the gift card that had just fallen from the envelope in his hand. "I'm giving these away like candy. Do you eat out? Do you want Chinese food?"

"I don't, Father, thank you." I forbore to remind him that I'd no one with whom to eat, in or out. The thought of sitting alone in a restaurant was a gloomy one. "Give it to somebody who'll use it," I was saying, when a thought struck me. "I'm going to the Malkins' from here. Would you like me to take some cards to them?"

"Perfect. Those children could load up in a car and go for Chinese. Though I've got to go out there sometime soon myself," he added. "I told Janet I'd come talk to her about baptizing the baby. I promised to see Lucy about this wedding, too, and it'll be easier for me to run her to ground while I'm there. She does keep assuring me there's no reason for haste. As it were."

He spoke with the sardonic tone of one who has seen it all, and again I smiled to myself. So young, he was, still. It was only his first Christmas: his first Christmas with us, at any rate. Age and experience, I hoped, would smooth that sharp edge of unearned wisdom away. I took up the gift cards he'd stacked on the counter and tucked them away in my handbag.

"And then," he continued with a rueful laugh, "the next thing she says, the very next thing, is *Couldn't we get married at Midnight Mass on Christmas?* No, I keep telling her, you could not. But she's very persistent." Father's gift-card tower wavered, but he stilled it with a touch. "We need to get that baby baptized. Under the circumstances, I'm very concerned that we nail down the details. That seems a lot more urgent than a wedding, but I foresee—"

"Difficulties?"

"Yes, difficulties. Exactly. But it would be nice to do it on the Feast of the Holy Family, don't you think? Maybe in the evening, after the Vigil Mass . . ." He went on ruminating for a while in this vein as I put on my coat and gathered my handbag.

"Has anyone spoken with Howard?" I said.

"I have. On the telephone. It wasn't a very productive conversation. I was wondering—" here he paused to study me. "That is, I wondered if you might say a word, Kirsty? To Howard, I mean."

"*Me*?" I set my handbag down again. "But what could I say?"

"I don't know. Ask the Holy Spirit to give you something to say. That's what I do."

Ah, I might have said, echoing his own sardonic tone. *Have we not seen that the Spirit sometimes chooses to leave us very much to our own devices?* But then, remembering something that I hadn't wanted to forget, I fished in my coat pocket. I brought out a wrapped parcel and set it on the kitchen island beside the stack of gift cards. "Happy Christmas, Father."

His eyebrows rose. "What's this?"

"Not a gift card," I told him, laughing.

"Do I open it now?" He picked up the little parcel and shook it experimentally.

"That depends. How much do you want to find under the tree come Christmas morning?"

"I wasn't planning to put up a tree," he said. "I'm going home after the Mass on Christmas morning. My mother always decorates to the nines. My dad says that this year she has a tree with lights for every window in the house, so I thought I could get away with not bothering."

My dad. Again I thought how young he was: somebody's boy. Well, they all were, weren't they? In his hands, though he didn't know it, this boy held the poems of another boy, my Jesuit: twenty-three at his ordination, twenty-five on his landing in England to begin the dangerous nine years of his mission. I had, of course, more than one volume of Southwell's poems at home; these had come in my box on the slow boat, long ago, and over time had been mixed in with the other books on the den shelves. This particular one, palm-sized, I had found pushed to the back of the shelf, behind two thick pictorial gardening books. Though I'd long forgotten its existence, rediscovering it transported me to a particular bright afternoon in the first week of my first term, when Dermott was only my supervisor, seen fleetingly, hardly met with. That day, I was in no hurry on my way to his rooms. Coming from my own college lodgings, dawdling down the narrow, cobbled St. Hilda's Lane, I'd stopped outside a secondhand bookshop to glance at the rack by the door. The little book, with its soft leather cover, *The Poetical Works of Robert Southwell* stamped in gold, beguiled me. Impulsively I'd bought it and carried it with me to my first supervision.

"Oh, yes, well, some people like him," Dermott had said carelessly.

And I had thought—well, never mind now what I'd thought. I was curious to know what Father Schuyler would make of my Jesuit. I had marked "The Burning Babe" for him with a rather irrelevant holy card I'd found in my bedside drawer: Saint Christopher, of all people. I'd no idea where it had come from, though as I reflected on it, perhaps it wasn't so irrelevant after all, this saint of dubious historicity bearing the Child, and the weight of all creation with Him, across the flood. One might draw some connection, I mused, though all I said aloud was, "Keep it till Christmas morning, then, Father. It's only Advent yet, after all."

"Yes, yes, of course." He weighed the parcel in his hand. "But now I'm impatient."

"Look upon this as an invitation to virtue." I put on my coat and hung my handbag over my shoulder.

"Oh, wait," said Father. "Before you go, there's something I have to show you. I've just discovered it. This house is full of surprises."

I followed him through to the living room. He stood before the secretary's desk. I noted the worn place in the refinished floor where he'd been scraping his chair in and out. On the desk sat a poinsettia in a pot so miniature that the spreading red bloom threatened to overbalance it. Father had propped it with a volume of the breviary.

"It's a lovely flower, Father."

"No, no, that's not what I wanted you to see. Look!" He bent, and in an instant I knew what was coming. He touched the door of the typewriter cabinet. Up sprang the platform, empty.

"Very clever," I said.

"I don't know what to do with it, but isn't it amazing?" I left him marveling.

* * *

At the Malkins', Vivian answered the door. "We meet again."

She stood aside to let me in. In my hand I bore a shiny pink gift bag with my present for the baby: yet another of my numerous volumes of Southwell. I'd turned it up, rummaging through the shelves, the same day I'd found Father's Christmas gift. This was a newer edition, someone's artistic pamphlet publication, A1-sized, done by an old letterpress on heavy handmade paper, with pen-and-ink illustrations. It was a beautiful, irreplaceable thing, though like the other, I'd bought it for a handful of silver off a market stall. It made an incongruous, perhaps even a hopeless gift for an infant. But, I had reasoned with myself, assuming it didn't get lost or destroyed in the intervening years, eventually she might grow into it. Perhaps the illustrations would attract her eye. In any event, it was something this child wouldn't already possess.

I set the bag down on a console table, curiously uncluttered, in the hallway. After the brightness of the day outside, the house lay dark and strangely empty. Passing the living room, I expected to see the light of a Christmas tree, and didn't. I suppose that even if Vivian had stayed away, nobody would have had the heart.

"Where are the children?" I asked her. "I've never known this place so quiet."

She smiled wryly. "In their rooms, I guess. Hiding from me. I've been putting them to work. Saturday was the Sabbath, and Sunday is supposed to be a day of rest for them, so they tell me, but all day Friday I stood over them until the laundry was put away, and the kitchen was cleaned up. Have you eaten lunch?"

"I haven't, actually." I let her lead me into the kitchen, which I hardly recognized for its cleanliness. In the light from the windows, I could see that Vivian had put off her silky black pantsuit and was wearing a crisply ironed pair of narrow blue jeans with what I am sure she thought of as a casual jumper, though the lavender knit was shot through with gleams of silver thread.

"I made Lucy take me to that supermarket where she works, so I could buy some actual groceries. People here were eating Cheez Doodles for supper the other night, until I busted them."

As she spoke she rummaged in the fridge, bright and wintry and gleaming with pyrex. She backed out with a lidded dish. "I made this macaroni and cheese, thinking it was something everybody would like. Turns out that unless it comes from a box and is orange, no child in this house will touch it. The cheese is real and not reconstituted from a powder. Would you like some? I'll just microwave it."

She busied herself, and we sat down with steaming plates at the kitchen table.

"There's wine, too," Vivian said, leaping up again. She was at least as old as I was; I admired her agility. "Don't you think some fortification is in order?"

"Oh, well, I'm driving, of course," I demurred, but she had already set out two glasses and poured.

Taking one, she raised it. "I don't drink much ordinarily, but there are times when it's welcome."

"I know what you mean." I raised my glass to her.

For a while we ate and drank in silence. After my morning's work, I was hungry. The macaroni with real cheese was better than either Mother Sain's Velveeta recipe or the almost cheeseless post-war macaroni that had been a staple of my mother's cooking.

"I've forgotten your name," Vivian said abruptly. "And where you're from. I'm going crazy trying to place your accent."

I smiled. After so many years in Annesdale, I was bound to sound eccentric, neither here nor there. In her late years Auntie Lass, during our rare telephone calls, used to claim that I sounded like the people on the American television show

Dynasty, which she and everyone else in the United Kingdom had watched with avidity.

"I've been in Annesdale my entire adult life," I told Vivian now. "But I come from the Shetland Islands, which nobody has heard of. They don't consider that the ponies or the sheepdogs come from somewhere."

Vivian's face brightened with interest. "But I know about the Shetlands. North of Scotland? I understand it's beautiful there. We used to travel, and I always wanted to go to there. Mostly because it was someplace I'd never been." She laughed. "My husband dislikes going places he's never been. So mostly we went to Paris and Florence. And now we don't go anywhere."

"You're the first person I've met on this side of the Atlantic to have any notion what or where Shetland is."

"This is a small place." Vivian shrugged. "What do you expect? Everybody in that supermarket looked like their parents were first cousins."

"I suppose that's the conventional view," I murmured. Ranse certainly had not been the bonfire of the table of affinities. Mother Sain had considered that the Sains were Annesdale aristocracy and above all that. I had not had it in me to inform her that *above all that* was precisely what the aristocracy, by definition, were not.

"Oh, I know, they're the salt of the earth, and they don't all have guns under their coats, and if you look hard enough, you can see the middle part in their eyebrows. We have people like that in New Jersey, too. Not our part of New Jersey so much, of course." She toyed with her macaroni. "I can't imagine what possessed Howard to want to live here to begin with."

"There was work for him," I said. "And the cost of living's reasonable." I sat a moment watching her turn her food over and over on her plate.

Without further preamble, she advanced the conversation she was clearly desperate to have. "Howard's moved out, you know. For the time being. Not far. More or less around the corner. A colleague of his has a guesthouse."

I smiled inwardly at this. "But he's all right?"

"I suppose that depends on your definition of *all right*." Vivian drank some wine. "He's not going to go throw himself in a river, if that's what you mean. Janet was convinced that that was exactly what he was going to do. There were hysterics. I had to ask her whether it had ever occurred to her that he might just have wanted another life."

Poor Janet. I berated myself for my earlier absence—though really, what could I have done for them? I'd hoped they'd all been mending their fences. Silly me.

"Look," Vivian said, "you're their friend. I know what you're probably thinking. It's not that I don't care what happens to Janet, or all those poor kids. They've just experienced a terrible, terrible thing. They loved that little boy, their brother, their son. There's not a person in this house who's not in pain. I have eyes. I can see. They don't have to tell me."

"Yes," I said.

"I did get rid of the Child Protective people at last. They seemed to find me plausible. With the Father."

"Good for you," I said, and meant it. Good for Father Schuyler, too.

"Between us we managed to tip the scale. It's tough, I know. Those people have to ask questions. Their whole job is not to believe in accidents." Again Vivian smoothed her perfect hair. "The kids didn't need that on top of everything else. It wouldn't achieve anything, to take them from their home. As much of a disaster as it is—"

"Yes," I said.

Vivian sighed. "I do want my son to do the right thing.

He got himself into this mess. He made more children than he can take care of, and now, when things are hard, he can't just walk away. It's his duty to make himself take care of them, even if that's asking the impossible. If he really decides to run away, I'll be ashamed of him. But he's my son, and he's in pain, too, and it's hard to stand by and watch that."

I felt suddenly tired of Howard. "Where is Janet?" I said.

"I sent her to bed with the baby. She keeps trying to get up, but for God's sake, she just had a c-section. Major abdominal surgery. She needs to walk around gently from time to time, not decide to rearrange the furniture."

"Would it help her to have some company? Or not?" I had finished my lunch. Now I rose with my dishes, my glass of wine still only half-drunk, and set them beside the sink.

"You can knock on her door and see. Through there." Vivian nodded in the direction of the den. "Just don't let her start lifting things heavier than her baby."

I went through the den, as alien in its tidiness as the kitchen had been, and down the dark hallway. From behind one closed door came girls' voices, raised in argument. Another door stood open, revealing a dim room walled with bunk beds, its floor a tangle of clothes and shoes. Clearly Vivian and her tidy-up operation had not yet penetrated to the children's bedrooms. A third door stood ajar, and I tapped at it.

Janet's voice called hoarsely from within. "Who is it?"

"It's Kirsty Sain," I called back. "I've come to say hello."

When Janet didn't reply, I gave the door a tentative push. The room was dark, curtains drawn against the bright day outside. As my eyes adjusted to the darkness, I saw Janet alone, save for the baby, propped against what looked like sofa cushions, on a large mattress on the floor. A duvet of some indeterminate color was spilled over her. The empty side—Howard's side—lay uncovered, a Howard-sized cavity in the mattress exposed beneath the thin fitted sheet. All around the mattress, the floor was littered with packets of nappies and wipes, cast-off clothing, and other litter. God forgive me, when I looked at Janet then, I remembered what Vivian had said about her —*slutty, trashy*—and I sympathized with Vivian.

I stepped into the room. "How are you?"

Janet shrugged.

"How's the baby?"

She shrugged again.

"Your mother-in-law's just given me a very nice lunch," I said. "Have you had anything to eat?"

Janet nodded to indicate a plate of half-eaten macaroni cheese on the floor beside her. "I'm not very hungry."

Coming further into the room, I looked about me for a place to sit down. There was none. I folded my arms. "Surely you must eat."

"I do eat," said Janet in some annoyance. "I just wish everybody would leave me the hell alone."

"Everybody is concerned for you. And wanting to care for you."

Through clenched teeth Janet said, "I have been just fine all this time. All these years. Where was *everybody* when Lucy was born? That's what I'd like to know."

I steeled myself for what I knew I must say. "Feeling perhaps as cast off by you as you felt cast off by them."

"That's not my fault."

"No, not entirely."

"Not my fault at all."

"As for that," I said.

In the half-darkness we glared at each other.

"Meanwhile," I added after a moment's silence. *You could be my mother*, she had said to me in hospital, or something like. Me, of all people. "It occurs to me that I have not done very well by you."

"What?"

"I was thinking of something you said to me. I should have been looking in on you more. I'm sorry."

"I said I was fine."

She didn't look fine: hair uncombed, the same bruised skin beneath her eyes. The smell of her unwashed body, and of sour milk, hung in the closed air about her. The baby, held apathetically to her breast, wore a nappie and nothing else.

"Have you spoken with Howard?" I was tired of Howard, but what else was there to talk about?

She looked up at me dully. "No, I have not spoken with Howard. I have no intention of speaking with Howard ever again."

"Even if he wanted to come back?"

"Why would he want to come back?" Janet's voice was brittle. "His mother is here to point out, every day, what a terrible life he's had with me. He'll end up going back to New Jersey with her, you wait and see."

"Go back to New Jersey and do what?" It was late in the day, it seemed to me, for Yale and law school.

"Who knows? Who cares?"

"And what will happen to you if he does that?"

She shrugged.

"Would you—" I hesitated. I was tired of Howard. I was tired of people thinking that I could talk to Howard, that there was anything I could say to change his mind. Still I said, "Would you like for me to see him?"

"See him? What do you mean?"

"If I spoke to him?"

"Speak to him if you want. I don't care."

I felt old suddenly, and tired. My legs ached. Why was there not a chair to sit in?

"I don't want to, especially," I told Janet. "I've a feeling it's none of my business at all. But I am fond of Howard, as well as you. Father Schuyler is anxious to baptize the baby," I added.

"Yeah." Again her tone was brittle, but her face softened. "He talked about God, you know. Henry. He would get these obsessions. Like that stupid tick thing. He couldn't get over how God would put a *star* on a tick's body. To him it was just like, there's God for you, doing another weird tiny totally random thing nobody would ever think about. He was always obsessed by these random things. And random people. The little guy." Her keening voice faded.

"I was very fond of Henry," I said inadequately. Surely I was one of those random people. "And I am fond of you. And—" I gestured at the baby. "Does she still not have a name?"

"Howard names them," Janet reminded me. "Only he's kind of forgotten about this one."

"I could talk to him about the baptism, if you like."

"Yeah, yeah." Janet sighed. "You do that. See where it gets you. Father Schuyler calls every day to talk to me about it. But what can I say? How can I plan anything? And however much Vivian is out there decontaminating my house, she's no help with baptisms."

"Have you asked her?"

"No." Janet's chin jutted like a defiant little child's. "No, I have not asked Vivian to help me plan a baptism."

"She might like to be asked," I said. "She might surprise you."

"I'm tired of being surprised. I'm truly completely freaking tired of surprises. But." She looked at me, and her expression changed. "Look. You're godmother. Okay? No excuses."

"*Me?*" It was what I'd said to Father as well. "What sort of godmother would I be?"

"A good one," Janet said. "I gave you that Infant of

Prague statue, right? I was thinking about that, and it seemed like a sign. We've had siblings be godparents before. Lucy was Henry's. I was thinking Moshe for godfather this time, and Hannah's old enough, but—well, like I said, it's like the Infant of Prague picked you."

"Did he?" It seemed a dubious sign to me.

Though whatever thoughts I was having, Janet kept talking. "I said okay to next Saturday. I mean, what the hell. We have to do it sometime, I guess."

"The Holy Family would be a lovely baptismal anniversary," I said stiltedly.

She fixed her imploring gaze on me. "You'd talk to Howie? Really?" Suddenly, it seemed, she did care.

"I can try," I told her, and thus committed myself to trying.

Again, as I was leaving, Lucy came running down the driveway, calling my name. With her she brought the boyfriend, or the fiancé, as I supposed I now must think of him, though I could not remember his name. All I recalled was Janet saying *-ayden* and being wrong.

"I didn't know you were here," Lucy panted, "or I'd have come out to see you."

"Hello." I tried not to stiffen as she flung her arms around me and clung. "How are you getting on? Are you hiding from your grandmother?"

Lucy made a face. "Not exactly. We're just spending a lot of time down in the basement. She says it's musty down there, so she stays upstairs. I've been helpful, don't worry," she added hastily. "We spent all day Friday cleaning practically the whole house."

"So I've seen. You did a very good job. Even my mother-in-law would approve." I smiled to myself, thinking of Mother Sain and the things she might have said about the Malkins. *Raised in a trailer park* was one phrase that came to mind.

Almost immediately, though, I thought of Wylie's neighborhood, everything flimsy and impermanent, yet immaculate. There had been much that Mother Sain didn't know.

Lucy shook herself free of me, as if I had been the one holding on. "Well, we're not total losers. We can clean up when we have to." Behind her, the boyfriend—a nice-looking boy, I saw now, black hair in a ponytail—granted me a stoic little nod.

"Also," said Lucy breathlessly, "we have news."

Of course I knew already. "Who's we?" I said.

"Kane and me." Lucy took his hand. "It's a secret. Nobody knows but you and Father Schuyler. We're engaged." Still clutching his hand, she waggled her free one at me. I saw the glitter of a tiny ring.

"Are you pregnant?" was, rather to my horror, the thing I could think to say.

Lucy flushed. "Miss Kirsty, what do you think I am?"

A lassie like the rest of us, I might have said. A human being. Surely Lucy remembered the story of her own origin: I might have said that. Instead I mumbled some words of apology. "Congratulations," I added lamely.

I was forgiven; Lucy beamed on me. "You're the first to know."

I thought of Vivian Malkin, sitting inside, alone, with her glass of wine. "Don't you think it might have been nice to tell your gran before you told me?"

Lucy's jaw jutted. Again I was confronted by her mother's younger face, the Janet I both knew and could never have known. Lucy's sea-green eyes, like Janet's, gleamed beneath her dark tumbled hair.

"How can I tell that lady anything?" she said. "I don't even know her. She doesn't know us."

"Are you helping her?"

"Well, we took her to visit Henry yesterday, his grave, you know. We wanted her to, like, remember him, even if she never actually knew him. Have you ever tried to make somebody understand what another person was like, and you just couldn't?"

"I'm not sure," I said.

"So there we all were, trying to tell her about Henry. Like, stuff he did and said, stuff that was like, really *Henry*. When we do that, it's like we can see him. Who he was. The person. But when we try to tell her, all she sees is this weird little kid who probably should have been on meds. I mean, he was interested in ticks. I can see how that would seem sort of not normal. But he was *Henry*."

"It's difficult for her," I murmured. "Meeting you all so suddenly, and not having known—"

"She doesn't like us. We just want her to go away." Exultant a moment ago, now Lucy began to cry. Great tears spilled down her cheeks. She looked very young. Of course, when I was her age, I had been married to Ranse. Then, I had felt a thousand years old, dried out, used up, as dead inside my body as my child had been. Now I could see what a child I'd still been.

"We want her to go away, and Dad to come back," Lucy wept. "She made him leave. I know she did."

"I don't think that's true," I began, but Lucy only cried harder. Stiffly, the stoic Kane put his arms about her.

"She told him bad things about Mom. She made him wish we'd all never been born."

"I hope not," I said. "In fact, I was going to see him now, if I'm able. Your grandmother wrote down the address for me."

Lucy sniffled. "It's that place with all the weird animals, the emus and stuff. It just figures Dad would run away and find some zoo. That's the only way he'd ever feel at home."

Taking my leave of Lucy and Kane, I retraced my route through the Malkins' country neighborhood and turned into the drive of the house with the emus. As I got out of my car, the same little bat-eared dog who had chased me before emerged from beneath a gray tangle of forsythia, barking furiously.

A sharp-shouldered young woman in jeans and a black spaghetti-strap camisole emerged from the house. "Can I help you? Did you want to buy some eggs? Get over here, Roscoe." The dog streaked to her, and she picked him up, caressing his ears. In her arms, he continued to mutter under his breath.

"I was looking for Howard Malkin," I said. "Do I have the right address?"

She jerked her head towards a new-looking red barn beyond the house, clean and bright in the sunshine. In its gable a paned window refracted the late light. "He's out yonder. You have to climb a ladder," she added, regarding me uncertainly, for which I could hardly blame her. I didn't strike myself, either, as the ladder-clambering sort. "But if you stand at the bottom and holler up, he'll hear you."

It was my turn, then, to look doubtfully at the barn lot, inhabited by the emus and water buffalo, numerous goats, and a white rooster who high-stepped along the fence, cocking his mad eye here and there. I didn't fancy stepping through all that mud, let alone the exotica treading about in it. But even as I hesitated, Howard himself appeared in the barn doorway and, seeing me, began to pick his way to the gate. Evidently the animals were used to him. The little dog in the woman's arms folded down his ears and was quiet.

"Yonder he comes now," the woman said unnecessarily. "If y'all want to sit someplace, there's a picnic table under the trees around the side of the house." Carrying the little dog, she went back inside.

"You know," said Howard, breathing a little heavily as he

approached me, "I told my mother not to tell anybody where I was."

"Sorry." I thought it wise not to let on to him that Lucy knew. Lucy's knowing was tantamount to the entire world's knowing where to find him. "Not even Janet?"

"Especially not Janet." His large face still sagged as if he had lost twenty pounds overnight. "Not that she wants to know, anyway."

"What's this about?" I asked him.

He shuffled his feet. "I don't want to talk about it."

To this day I don't know where my next words came from. These were not the sorts of things I had ever said aloud to another person.

"Do you think it will all go away if you don't talk about it?" Gathering the rooster's fierceness to me, though I shook inside, I made myself glare at him. "Do you think you can walk off into the distance and start your life over, all new and untouched? If you do believe those things, Howard, you believe a lie."

"Maybe." He fixed his gaze on an emu as it pecked something unseen on the ground.

"I know you've suffered a terrible blow. But what good does it do you to abandon Janet? And your bairns? Why would you add to their grief?"

Howard was silent a moment, watching the emu. When he turned to me again, his eyes were terrifying in their emptiness. "I lost my little boy, Miss Kirsty. I pulled him out of that pool. He was cold in my hands. I couldn't bring him back. I was helpless. I was worse than helpless." He shook his head. "I can't even look at my living children."

What reply could I make to this? My one child had died inside me, nameless. And look at you, I told myself, O craver of loneliness. In that instant I wanted nothing more than to be away home, away from Howard, away from all the Malkins, away from grief. Still, Howard's living children wanted to look at him. I had been sent, it seemed, to tell him this.

"If I'd turned that damn pool upside-down like I should have. If I'd been paying attention. If I'd ever paid attention. If *Janet* had ever paid attention—"

His voice hardened.

Now I wanted to shake him, as I'd wanted to shake Father Schuyler. "Stop it, Howard."

"You don't think it's Janet's fault, just a little? All the kids? All the craziness? All those damn saint statues?" Still his empty eyes rested on me.

"People die. In the safest place imaginable, Howard, a child can still die." Didn't I know it?

He shrugged. "That's not what the CPS people think."

"They're satisfied," I said, hoping fervently that it was true for good and all. "They've seen Janet. They've seen the children. They've seen the house. You and Janet aren't bad parents, Howard. You're not negligent. You're just not God, that's all."

Again Howard watched the emu. He was blinking hard, an angry boy trying not to cry. "I'm really not in the mood for talking about God."

Well, then. We would not talk about God. "Your bairns miss you," I said to him. "They need you."

Howard was intent on the emu. "Kids are resilient. They'll get over it."

"But why should they get over it, Howard? Do you not think they've got enough to get over already?"

"Well, I can't do it. That's all." He turned back to the barn.

"Haven't you even seen your new one?" My voice then might have belonged to Granny Astrid, the berserker. It carried ringingly across the mud. "She's a bonny wee lass, Howard."

Howard turned to look at me for a moment. His massive shoulders sagged. Even at that distance, I could still see the emptiness in his eyes.

"A new life," I said. "And you are her father."

He shrugged and turned away.

Again I had to raise my voice. "Father wants to fix the baptism for next Saturday, Howard. The Feast of the Holy Family. In the evening, after the Mass. You'll come?"

This last he did not acknowledge. I watched him trudge, head down, through the shadowy doorway, to vanish among the chickens scratching in the mud.

As I drove away, I realized I'd set down the bag with the baby's book in the hallway at the Malkins' and had not thought about it again. In that house, who would find it? What would happen to it, the fragile thing? Well, it had been my Jesuit's way to fly into danger, hawking terms precariously in hand. He'd gone, always, not where he was safe, but where he was needed. Meanwhile, it was true enough, what Howard had said. That baby would not miss a book. After I'd got home, I found I'd forgotten, as well, the restaurant gift cards in my handbag.

9

I spent the long afternoon of Christmas Eve alternately dusting, roasting my defrosted chicken, and dozing in the rocker with a book on my knee. I dressed myself warmly for Midnight Mass, somewhat misnamed, beginning as it did at half-past ten with a wan round of carol-singing. This Mass had been advertised as a bilingual liturgy, which turned out to mean that the Spanish choir, with guitars, an electric keyboard, and a set of chimes, sang the responsorial psalm and two songs at Communion, and that the canon of the Mass was said in Latin. *He'll have us speaking Latin*, the church ladies had said, and lo, it had come to pass. But the poinsettias were banked like flames round altar and ambo, the Infant Christ smiled at us from His manger, and the Incarnation, as I reflected, was capable of celebrating itself without any particular help from the rest of us. Nothing could mar it. At the end, the Spanish choir struck up with *Feliz Navidad.* As Father processed from the church, he wore a look of exaltation.

When I came home again, I was wide awake. The kitten, bulging with chicken, rushed out to greet me and climbed my trouser leg with exclamations of joy. Pulling him free of my clothing, I sat down in the rocker with him and stroked his rumpled blue skin.

"Really," I said, "you ought to have a name. That should be my Christmas gift to you."

His eyeless face tipped toward my voice. His purring

accelerated. But think as I might, I could come up with nothing that seemed to suit him.

"Well, you'll just have to *be*," I told him. He put his paws on my shoulders and snubbed his cool little nose against my cheek.

All night we sat there, as I had envisioned, the kitten purring as he slept on my lap, the little heater also purring as it blew its dry warmth across my shins. Outside, the night was clear. Through my window I could see the stars prickling sharply in the dark-blue sky above the trees. One by one, the houses in the neighborhood down the way had switched off their lights; there was only the darkness now, and the gleam of starlight. I turned off my reading lamp and sat, too, in darkness, listening and waiting.

When I was very small, we did not go to Mass on Christmas. The sea was too stormy, the gales too apt to blow, my father too unwilling to ferry us and have us away from home. On that holy night, we sat quiet by our own fire. According to her doctrine Granny Astrid did not mark Christmas, or Yule, as she called it, as a particular day in the calendar. Like Easter, its observance was a tradition of men. On what day of the year, she demanded, would you not remember that the Lord of Creation had entered the human world? What was wrong with people, that they needed to set that essential fact apart from everything ordinary? Still, almost by accident, it seemed to me, after our supper—reestit mutton soup and bannocks, or else saat beef or herring—she read aloud one of the Gospel Nativity accounts. She grunted, though not too loudly, as, my mother guiding my hand, I laid the plaster Christ Child in the manger on the mantel.

After that, with her own hands she would bathe me from my head to my feet, an old Shetland custom for Christmas Eve, and tell me stories about the trows who would come and try to steal power from me as I bathed. In her own girlhood, she said, they used to drop burning peat into the water, too, as a caution against the trows, but fortunately by my time we had dispensed with that. I was put into a new nightgown, and my father showed me the knife he would set on the table beside the door, because the trows were afraid of iron.

In the half-light, his pale eyes gleamed intimatingly across the firelit room, as if he and I had some secret between us. As far as I knew, we had none. It was my mother, who stood with her back rigid to do the washing up, clanking and splashing to show what she thought of the old Shetland magics—my mother with whom I had secrets. With her I stood outside the ritual things the Shetlanders did. By the time I was born, those things were fading away like the herring shoals: the skekling at Hogmanay, for example, when the men of the town, and some of the children, too, dressed themselves in straw, as if they were sheaves out of the fields and not familiar people. At the edge of memory I can still see my father, his eyes alight with a bitter sort of fun, marching among them up the street. Seen from the front window, wearing his cope and miter of oat straw, he looked transfigured, like a trow himself, bishop of some diocese in the air. My mother watched him, too, as the straggling crowd passed our house. "Pagans," she said. She held my hand tightly, as if I would tear myself away from her and run to join them.

She might have found something to like in Father Schuyler. If I could step back to that moment and take her hand again, I might suggest to her that like the dance for Our Lady of Guadalupe, with which I'd grown so familiar, perhaps this too was a way of redemption-minded tale-telling. I suppose in the end all these tales recount their own passing-away, to proclaim the triumph of what comes next. Or always has been, and has waited for its moment.

After my father and Granny Astrid were dead, there was no more ritual bathing on Christmas Eve. Instead, on that night, my mother and I sat down to tinned soup and pork pies from the shop. On Christmas Day we ate turkey, tinned peas, and mince pies, exactly like the rest of the British Isles, though my mother did, for a time, continue to make cloutie pudding, as my distant and unknown Aberdeen grandmother had done. Then my mother spoke no more of pagans; to her those categories had ceased to exist.

That final December, I stayed in college past the end of my term's work, until at last we final hangers-on were turned out of our rooms. By then I'd nothing to do except bicycle the lanes round Dermott's college, which I am ashamed even now to admit that I did, round and round, over and over, with a look of purpose on my face and, in my mind, a list of places to say I was going, should I encounter Dermott. Of course I never did encounter him. The streets lay quiet in the dark, wet winter afternoons.

Once I ran into my own Senior Tutor as she stepped out of a bakery by the Market Square, a crisp white bag in her hand. "Still here?" she remarked cheerfully. "Getting a start on next term already, are you?"

I agreed that I was. In a way, I felt, it was true.

"Have you any interesting plans for the holidays?"

I considered. To her, my village undoubtedly would look interesting, though its most starkly interesting inhabitants, like my Granny, were long since gone. My mother might look interesting as a character in a television drama. She certainly smoked and brooded at windows in a way that might be construed as intriguing.

"I'm only going home," I said at last.

The Senior Tutor's ruddy face brightened. She was wearing, I recall, a tweedy pork-pie hat that mashed her grizzled curls into her eyes. "Oh, lovely. My warmest regards to your family, my dear." I could see that she imagined me, girl of the far north, as the scion of some noisy, joyous, Fair-Isle-knit-clad clan, which would hail me and clasp me to its collective bosom.

Instead, not wanting to walk right in, I beat on my mother's door with my fist for some time—the bell had broken since the summer—before it opened.

"Oh," said my mother.

"Hello, Mother," I said. "Happy Christmas."

Her slaty eyes rested on my face with no glimmer of recognition. "You'd better come along in, then."

That was how it was. Later I reflected that I might have sent the Senior Tutor a postcard: *Interesting holidays here.* They were interesting chiefly in that more people than usual spoke to me in the street or the shop, saying things like, *She's all right, then, is she?* They didn't have to say who it was they meant. Yes, I always said, she seemed right enough. I'd a notion she'd have wanted me to say that, though I knew, and the people I spoke to also knew, that I was lying. Still they nodded as if I must know best.

But there was I, buying food, because there was none in the house. There was I, baking a chicken to leather on Christmas Day, because my mother seemed not to have thought of a meal. There was I, on Hogmanay, drinking a glass of bitter in the kitchen while I fried up potatoes and rashers of bacon for us both. By then I'd exhausted my limited store of cookery ideas, and I couldn't bear to think of tinned peas or fish fingers. I didn't know how long to cook the potatoes, so they were hard in the middle. That was a grim meal, the two of us gnashing away in the silence, my mother smoking, me getting up to replenish my beer, growing more sozzled by the minute and not caring. All I cared about was what Dermott might be doing right then, and with whom. I managed the washing up, then staggered to my bed, where I lay awake for a long time, studying the stolid ceiling through my tears. At midnight there came some halfhearted clattering and shouting from down the way, then absolute quiet fell. It was the new year. Things I'd no notion of would happen to me, I told myself. As indeed they had done in due course.

The final morning, I was up in the blackness to meet Ezekiel Wilson, son of Magnus the boatwright, who was to ferry me back to Lerwick. Ever since I'd come I'd been dying to get back. I was wrung out now with the effort of pretending that I wanted to be at home. I longed for my college room with its white walls, to which I hadn't tacked the first rock-concert poster or art print. I longed for the quiet that wasn't another person's silence. I longed for the university town where I could lose myself in medieval lanes, between walls of limestone or clunch, in alleys with bookshops, in places where nobody recognized me or said to me, with a sidewise glance, "You've been long away."

Mostly, of course, I longed for Dermott. I longed for the scent of his sharpened pencils and his pipe, the crinkle of his eyes, his long cool hands on my naked skin, the noise of the rain on the window as I lay with him of an afternoon. I longed for him in the way that you do long for one who is flesh of your flesh. He would not have seen it that way. But that Christmas, though I kept stifling the thought, his child lived in me. They speak of the tug of the womb; it was what I felt. But the girl with the blue-black hair had come. I had gone as if I'd never been. It was no good my crying my eyes out, I thought as I wept over my packing. I would go back, and nobody would be glad to see me. Nobody would say that I'd been long away. Nobody would have noticed. I would have made no difference at all to anybody: anybody who mattered to me.

So I told myself, weeping, as I bundled my clothes and

books into my rucksack. At the last minute I pulled out my volume of Southwell's prose from the tangle of my underwear and stuck it into an outer pocket, where I could reach it in the train. I'd this essay to compose, after all, and perhaps, perhaps, this time it wouldn't be *credulous*. Or perhaps it would. Perhaps *credulous* was what Dermott preferred. Perhaps it was better to be innocent as a dove, so that he could feel wise as a serpent. Some dove, I thought gloomily.

"I'm away, Mother," I said.

She raised the fag to her lips. I saw its end smolder against the darkness of the window. After a lingering second, she exhaled, a paler darkness.

"I'll come at Easter," I forced myself to promise. It was the last thing I wanted to do: to spend all my holidays in Shetland with this silent stranger, my mother. But I would do, I told myself stoutly. I would come and bear her company again, though as far as I could tell, it made no difference to her whether I was there or no. Still, I would take it on as a penance. *Penance:* a word I'd not thought of since sixth form and my last confession. But I thought it now. At Lerwick, boarding the ferry, I went inside the main cabin, sat down on a bench, and took my book from its rucksack pocket.

Having lost that light of her life, I read, *she desired to dwell in darkness and the shadow of death.* At that, I shut the book, and my eyes. I would be a long time traveling. On the train I would try to read again.

* * *

The kitten slept on my lap. My head lolled against the padded back of the rocking chair, and I fell into the shallow, breakable dreams of half-sleep, those dreams that are all the more vivid for their fragility. Again I was walking beside the river in the cold. I knew that river; it was there in real life. Even as I walked beside it, I knew that I had left it behind me, far away. Still, the rain, real as real, needled my face and made little pricks in the water's hastening brown surface. Bits of stick and sodden paper whirled with it, downstream to the weir where the swans were treading water.

With the hood of my duffel coat pulled up, I could see only what lay ahead of me, a round tunnelish view of wet black towpath, sodden grass, pollarded trees. I had to turn my head to see the river, the boats that bumped at their moorings along the bank.

So it was that although I became conscious of someone walking beside me, my hood obscured my view of him. I heard his footsteps, though: light for a man's, as if he walked out in the wet in fine shoes, not boots. I felt, rather than heard, his breathing. Ranse, I told myself. Who else cared to catch me up along the towpath? I thrust my hands into my coat pockets and walked faster. To avoid looking at Ranse, I looked at the river.

Again I saw it. This time I saw it first. The little blue-white body came riding on the current, face-down, its arms and legs bobbling.

Forgetting myself, I clutched at my companion. "That's a baby, there in the water."

Perhaps my hood fell back. Or perhaps I merely saw the way one sees in dreams: through things. It wasn't Ranse who walked beside me, but Dermott.

His eyes narrowed in amusement. "It's only a doll."

I peered at it. "Are you sure?"

"What would a baby be doing in the river?"

"Someone might have dropped it." I bent to unlace my shoes. "It might have fallen. There might be time." I was tearing off my coat. The wind bit at me and raked back my hair

The wind tore Dermott's words from his lips and whirled them away.

I was leaping. I, this time, not Ranse. Ranse was not there to care for the figure in the water. There was Dermott on the riverbank; there was I, myself, in my brief flight. Above me the white sky hung low. It was as if I leapt from an enormous height, from the cliffs at home with the furious sea below. The water came up to meet me with a noise like many wings.

I awoke then, or so it seemed to me. In the same needling rain, I stood at the door of my mother's house, knocking. At last she opened to me. Behind her, the unlit passage extended into blacker and blacker darkness. We regarded each other for a long time in silence. I realized that if anyone was going to speak, I would have to be the one to do it.

"Forgive me, Mother," I said. "I've been too long away."

She held out her hands, but before we could take hold of each other, a great wave of the sea arose, curling over at its foamed top and tumbling in clarity down its own silver slope. I could see the herring thrashing inside it, as they sometimes did on bright days. I did not feel the wave break over me. With a rushing noise it swept me off my feet. I fought it, flailing and kicking, tasting salt, to make landfall again. Before me the island rose and fell in its nest of sea. There, hidden, my mother still stood at the door, the storm wind blowing back her faded hair. Still she held out her hands to me. But the currents bore me away. Swim though I might, I could never go back.

The next instant, there was I, all dry, jerked awake in my chair before my pretend fire. The kitten, disturbed perhaps by my sleep-swimming, had gone away. At some point, in his roamings about the house, he had caught a mouse and left it on the hearth as a gift for me. In death it lay pathetically on its back, its little pink humanlike hands stiffly raised, as in blessing or supplication, beneath the heater's dry breath. On the mantel above, the golden-haired plaster Christ Child, too, reached out with stiff white hands, as if to catch hold of the world He'd just entered. A cold sun was tilting in through the window, and it was Christmas Day.

* * *

The week after Christmas lay like a fallow field, empty and waiting. I too felt fallow, empty, waiting. Saint Stephen's Day ran into Saint John, which in its turn bled into the Holy Innocents.

"What to do?" I asked the kitten, who lay fattening on the hearth before the heater. His enormous ears swiveled to catch my voice; his eyeless face tilted toward the sound. But he did not bother with any answer. What to do was not a question that plagued him in the slightest. He flexed and curled his downy paws in the heat. His transparent claws caught and held the sunlight. Occasionally he yawned, displaying small but fearsome teeth. *The Lord is a warrior,* I said to myself. *Lord is his name. Horse and chariot he has thrown into the sea.*

I stooped and stroked the kitten's velvet side. "Murr," he said, and I saw his teeth again.

That day, a card arrived from me in the post, in a sadly mangled state. The postman handed it to me himself, with apologies, though surely he was not personally to blame for whatever had happened to it. At some stage along the way, the envelope and its contents had got wet, then torn, and put into a plastic bag with a sticker on it proclaiming it to be damaged, with the regrets of the United States Postal Service. I opened the plastic bag; the contents exhaled a strong aroma of garlic, as if someone had spilled a tub of melted garlic butter, such as sometimes comes with a pizza delivery, all over a pile of post. The envelope felt not only wet but greasy, and the return address had been reduced to a shiny smear of blue ink. My own name and address were legible, just, but the hand was strange to me. When I tore open the envelope, gingerly, for fear of tearing what was inside, the paper fairly melted at my touch. The card inside, too, had become a sodden buttery mess, but it was undeniably a Christmas card.

On its cover I recognized a photograph of Our Lady of Guadalupe on which an image of poinsettias had been, by some miracle of technology, superimposed, so that the Lady appeared to stand in a nest of red flowers, rather than treading upon her customary half-moon and serpent. The writing on the inside had been spoiled by buttery accident. I could not make out who had written it, or what it said. But remembering my vision of Maricruz, driving in the dark and the wind, and the look of love on Wylie's face, I took it as a sign of their arrival. I could not know where, of course. I would never read what was written there or reply to the sender with my questions. I simply chose to believe that the most good thing was so. Though it smelled strongly of garlic, I propped the card—the only card I had received that season—on the mantel beside the Holy Family, as they awaited the coming of the kings.

The kitten cried for his supper. After he had polished his bowl, with many pink lashings of his tongue, he climbed my jeans and sweater to thrust his wrinkled head beneath my chin. Purr purr, he went. I had given up thinking of a name for him; whatever I thought of, he seemed to wriggle free of it and skitter away, unfettered by any word I might have chosen. He answered to the sound of my voice, that was all. His velvet skin rumpled beneath my stroking fingers. At night, when I went to bed, he tunneled down beneath the covers, and his warm body vibrated against mine.

In those quiet days I spent much time reading by my ersatz fire. I had read and reread my Jesuit's Christmas poems, a seasonal thing to do. I was struck now, as I could not remember having been before, by the exhortation that begins "New Heaven, New War," in which the speaker calls upon the denizens of heaven to "remove your dwelling to your God." What an odd thing, I thought, yet of course it was apt. Where God is, there those who praise Him should be. But had God vacated heaven to walk the earth? What of the Trinity, I wondered, the thunderous voice and the dove descending? I should like to have seen a Southwell poem on the Baptism of the Lord, to account for the whereabouts of those other Persons.

* * *

On Saturday, the Vigil of the Holy Family, I took myself again to Confession. In the unlit late-afternoon church I queued, as always, for my turn in the Reconciliation Cupboard. It was still the afterglow of Christmas, and only a handful of penitents waited, resting their backs against the cinderblock wall. Ahead of me in the shadows I recognized Lucy Malkin and her brother Moshe, who was to play godfather to my godmother later that evening. Instinctively, lighting on Lucy, my gaze sought out Henry, who should have been leaning at her hip, his bright eyes roving here and there in quiet observation. I felt his absence, then, as intensely as if it were itself a presence, watchful and good, but always just out of reach. It was a vocation, I thought, to be sent into the world to marvel at its strangeness. One could make a whole life of such work: Henry had done it.

Since the day before Christmas Eve, I had not seen the Malkins at all. Nor had I heard from them. I had merely assumed that things at home were progressing however they'd been going to progress, and that meanwhile, the proposed baptism was on. Nobody had told me otherwise. I had said to myself: *I'll go to Confession. I'll go to Mass. I'll stop a wee bit after. If nobody shows, I will go home again.* Part of me had hoped that nobody would show. I was tired, after all. I felt, rather, that I had done my bit. How would Ranse have put it? I had *pulled my oar.* I had *taken one for the team.* I had *gotten up in other people's business.* Even now, my predominant impulse was to mind my own. Though I'd done nothing but lounge about all week, that evening I felt that above anything else, I wanted a lie-down. Steeling myself, I had put on a nicer grade of dress than usual, the green wool I'd worn for my directory photograph, and with much inward groaning, to church I had gone. Now I stood waiting. It seemed to me that except for lounging about, I had done nothing for weeks except wait. Lucy slipped into the Reconciliation Cupboard. Moshe, hands in his pockets, eyes closed, leant against the wall. This was my answer. If I wanted a lie-down, I would have to wait for that as well.

My turn came. I went into the cupboard and knelt. "Bless me, Father, for I have sinned," I said, exactly as if the person on the other side of the screen were truly hidden from me, his personal sins and human foibles a cipher behind the mask of Holy Orders. Well, and so it was, though as always I struggled to put away my mental images of the empty refrigerator, the shining toilet, the sacristy door clicking shut behind a fleeing figure. Nevertheless, *in persona Christi*, the presence behind the screen waited in quiet expectation as I brought out my handful of sins and counted them like small change. He was waiting, I knew, to pronounce the absolution, in a voice that both was and was not the voice I had come to know, the voice that said, "I'm not good with people." Perhaps he wasn't good with people. Perhaps he would always stumble there. But he could, and he did, extend grace to me. He was good at that. The grace itself was good at that. The few coins that were my sins bought me nothing. They simply evaporated. What I came away with from this transaction was something not purchased—not by me, at any rate—but given. Though the same thing happened to me every week, still as I returned to the darkening church to pray my penance, I marveled at its strangeness.

The Christmas-Eve poinsettias still flamed about the ambo and the altar. White fairy lights twinkled round the tabernacle. Christmas seemed a century ago already, yet it occupied the present, twelve fleeting and endless days. At Mass, as Father Schuyler stood in his white chasuble before the altar, his back to us, facing God, his image seemed to me to melt into the image on my card at home, the Virgin with her feet in flames of flower. Old age was making me fanciful. In any event, the Virgin of Guadalupe wore blue and rose, not white. But she and the priest alike were bearing, always, the body of Christ into the world. At the strangeness of that, too, I marveled, as I went up to receive that hidden body on my tongue, to be hidden again in me. To what purpose? As always, I'd no idea, but there it was.

After Mass, in the narthex, the lights jarred tinnily against the softness of the early night, pregnant with more rain. It wasn't cold, only moist, the sort of damp that penetrates your joints. Mist hung round all the car-park lights. Stiff in my joints after an hour of sitting and kneeling, I wanted nothing more at that moment than my cup of tea, my whirring heater, my book and my kitten on my lap. It was with some envy that I watched the rest of the congregation filter away. Besides Moshe, Lucy, and Kane-the-fiancé, no Malkins had appeared for Mass. Perhaps they would fail to materialize. At that moment, I wished them all at home. Or if not at home, at least away from me. Then I wanted to kick myself, for had I not just come from

Confession? Here I was again, doing the very thing for which I had, only an hour earlier, expressed sincere contrition, promising to amend my life. So much for *firm purpose,* I rebuked my less-admirable self.

Moshe and Kane came out of the church and drifted over to the wall of bookshelves which constituted our parish library, talking quietly together. Possibly Moshe was telling Kane what he was in for. Through the door I could see Lucy still kneeling at her prayers. Perhaps they were only waiting for her. Perhaps then they'd all go home. If they did, then I could go home as well.

But when Lucy emerged, she came and stood beside me. "Are you ready?"

Ready for what, I was going to say, but at that moment Father appeared from the sacristy in alb and purple stole. Over his arm he carried a white stole as well. He went into the church, and through the doors I saw him genuflect and hang the white stole over the arm of the front pew. Rubbing his hands together, he rejoined us in the narthex. "Everybody here?"

The four of us, manifestly not everybody, blinked back at him from where we stood.

"Malkins always run late," said Lucy with complacency. "Right as we're going out the door, something always happens. There's always some disaster."

"Well, I hope not." Father was leafing through his red service book.

"Dominic's driving," Lucy went on. "He always has to check the oil four times before he starts the car. And then go inside and wash his hands again. And then Margaret has to yell at him, because she just got her permit, so everybody else's driving makes her crazy. I hope Dad comes," she decided to add.

Father glanced up, alarmed. "Is he not coming?" He fixed me with a burning look. "Kirsty, you told me you'd speak to him."

"I did speak to him, Father. But—" What could I say about that conversation, especially before Howard's children?

"He wasn't sure about coming." Moshe spoke from across the room. "He said he'd see."

"How do *you* know?" said Lucy.

"Because I went and talked to him today, that's how."

"Well, fine." Lucy flicked a curl out of her eyes. "Good for you. Of course, Dad doesn't know what he's saying. That's what Grandma Vivian keeps telling us. But legitimately, he's acting like a jerk. Like a legitimate asshole, sorry, Father." Her voice rang out across the linoleum.

Father sighed. "Remember where you are, Lucy."

"I know, I'm sorry. But what do you say when there's literally no other word?"

"*Jerk* was sufficient. I knew what you meant."

Grandma Vivian: I noted that. I noted the present tense. However Howard had decided to behave, whatever she had to say about him, *Grandma Vivian* sounded a heartening development.

"Anyway, we're all disgusted with Dad," said Lucy.

Moshe looked up again. "Speak for yourself."

I found myself noticing Moshe, more or less for the first time. For the grand event of a baptism, he had worn the black shirt and tie I had seen him wearing before—or perhaps he was on his way to work once the baptism was over. He had sleeked down his unruly black hair with some sort of gel, so that the curls, drying and springing up again, had a curiously repressed, shellacked look. His eyes were dark and hooded like Howard's, not Janet's sea-glass green. Still, in his quietness, I could see what Henry might have looked like. I wondered whether, in time, Henry too would have said, *Yeah, yeah,* and slicked down his hair, to make himself older, polished and knowing.

Though Moshe must have been at least twenty-two, he appeared, I thought, altogether too young, earnest, and vulnerable to make solemn promises on behalf of a helpless child. As godparents, what a pair we made. Young Moshe, old me. Him with his life before him, me with mine closing behind me, a door with no key. Being so young, naturally Moshe would miss his father. I recalled, too, that he had been the one to revive Henry, however briefly. Anger flashed through me: he was entirely too young for any of this. Too young, yet older than I had been, that watershed winter of my life. *Yawp,* I said to God. Surely the vulnerability Moshe telegraphed was simply hurt, grief compounding grief. Older than I had been, but still too young. He should not have had to bear these things. Still he stood talking, man-to-man, with Kane, who also had put on a tie and looked like a boy trying hard.

At that moment, the doors banged and Janet was swept in on a tide of rushing children. They came in mid-cry, all of them clamoring to hold the baby, clutched in a huddle of blankets to Janet's breast. Again, in all that tumbling crowd, my eye sought Henry's quietness and missed it. His absence announced itself more stridently than his presence ever had.

Janet caught my eye. "Yeah, yeah, we're here."

She shifted the baby in her arms, cradling her so that the blanket fell away from her sleeping face. I glanced at the round flushed cheeks, the upright stand of dark hair. It—she—looked to me like any brunette baby. In my observation, there were blond bald babies and dark hairy ones, but within either of those two phyla, one baby looked much like another. At some point, I supposed, you began to see the person. But I did not know when it happened, or how.

"Has she got a name yet?" I asked.

"Didn't I tell you? Howard names them."

So many questions rose to my lips, I hardly knew which to ask first—so I asked none of them.

Janet's glance swept the narthex. "And he's not here, obviously."

"Lucy says Malkins always run late." I tried to make light of things, but my neck prickled with anxiety.

"No," Janet said, "that would be me. *I* always run late. *I* make everybody else late. By himself, if he wants to be somewhere, Howard is *prompt*."

"Ah." Again the questions crowded in. I asked the first one that made itself clear. "Have you thought what you'd do for a name, if you had to—"

"Make something up, I guess," said Janet.

"Well." Father took Isaac by the shoulders and propelled him in the direction of the sacristy. "Go get vested if you want to serve. Remember to take off those sneakers. There's a pair of black shoes to fit you, right? The ones you wore last Sunday? In the cubbies by the servers' cassocks? You know where to find them." Isaac scurried away, and Father turned back to the rest of us. He rubbed his hands together and said with forced heartiness, "The gang's all here. Where is this baby?"

Now, for the first time, I took in how Janet was dressed: in a flowing black pantsuit like Vivian's. Vivian must have chosen it for her, I thought. Vivian must have made her wear it. Who else? Someone with a good eye had twisted her hair into a soft roll at the back of her head; at the front, black and silver curls had escaped in tendrils to frame her face, with its large light-filled eyes, their color chafed as by the sea.

How had I not seen before that Janet was beautiful? Vivian must have seen it, Vivian of all people. Vivian must have cajoled her into these clothes, this hairstyle. Vivian, perhaps with the help of the daughters, who had only needed the right sort of nudge. I could see Vivian commanding Janet to sit still, then steering her out of the door, closing it upon her, to keep her from fleeing back into the house. Had such a transformation been wrought for the glory of God, to come into His presence in His own holy house? For the solemnity of a baptism? No, I concluded. Vivian wasn't here now. She wouldn't have come to church with them; that would have been, like pork chops, a bridge too far. Although Vivian would know what was appropriate to any occasion, I suspected that Janet's clothes and hair had been chosen not with God in mind, but Howard. Howard, who wasn't here. *The assurance of things hoped for; the conviction of things not seen.* Well, indeed, at the moment, there were things we did not see.

Isaac emerged in cassock and stiff white cotta and stood where Father directed him. When Father opened the book, Isaac put up his hands to receive it. Turning a gold-leafed page, Father began to read out the traditional baptismal rite in Latin. I had been baptized, myself, with those same words, longer ago than memory. There were no photographs of the occasion. Auntie Lass had stood godmother, that I knew, but had my father been there? I had never thought to wonder before. Only one parent's consent was required for an infant's baptism—but had he consented? Had my mother been able to persuade him, or shame him, an unbeliever in sacraments, into seeing the rough place in my soul made plain? I would never know the answer. Everyone who might have been present that day was dead: silent as the grave itself. Time had washed over them, as the sea rubbed out its own patterns, over and over. Not that it mattered. One way or another, the thing had been accomplished. I had gone forth from that place not knowing what had been done to me, but clothed with grace, nevertheless, for the life ahead. Strange grace, I thought -- but when was grace not strange? Its thoughts were not my thoughts, nor its ways my ways. Somehow, still, we had rubbed along together, that grace and I. Now here we stood together, to see the pattern repeated.

Moshe took the baby. He held her as if he had been born to hold babies. She slept on in his practiced arms: her godfather. Some godmother I would be, I thought, more like the Bad Fairy of the old tales, bursting in to bestow her gift of darkness and death. If only I'd had my cat with me, my naked familiar, then they might have seen me for what I was. They might have risen together to cast me into the night where I belonged. Instead, they stood in silence as Father read, in English now, the old and ageless formula for salvation.

"What do you ask of the Church of God?"

"Faith," said Moshe and Janet and I, obediently and automatically.

I thought of that Easter Vigil years ago, when in the flickering candlelight Wylie had bent his slick head above the same font in the same church, wreathed then in lilies, to receive the water of life. Again I wondered where Wylie was. Again, half-hopelessly and without words, I prayed for him.

I remembered too that other Easter Vigil, Howard at the kindling of the fire, the longing kindled in him. Well, I must pray for Howard, too. Pass over, I said to the angel of death. Pass over, you bloody bastard. Go back where you came from. Fold your wings. Be still.

Three times Father Schuyler breathed on the baby, to recall the Spirit moving on the face of the deep. The baby's own face wrinkled, her eyelids fluttered, but her sleep remained unbroken.

"Thank God," whispered Janet at my elbow. "She screamed all the way here in the car."

Father signed the baby with the Sign of the Cross: forehead and breast. More Latin prayers, the words—familiar and strange to me, all at once—pattering like rain. Then he touched her tongue with salt. Again her face rumpled. Her small red mouth worked experimentally.

We moved by degrees into the church. The baby was exorcised, Satan renounced. Go home, old gargoyle, I thought. Depart. Begone. Get thee behind us.

By the soapstone font before the altar, Father removed his violet stole, took up and kissed the white one draped on the arm of the front pew. He turned to the gathered Malkins and said in English, "Do you believe in God the Father Almighty, Creator of Heaven and Earth?"

"I do," we said, most of us. Janet's lips moved over the words, but that was all.

"Do you believe in Jesus Christ, His only Son our Lord, Who was born and Who Suffered?"

"I do," said Janet's children.

"I do," I said.

"I don't know," said Janet abruptly and loudly. "I don't know anymore."

The children, craning round, gaped at her in horror.

"I'm sorry," said Janet. "I thought I could do this. But I can't."

Father's pastoral smile became strained. Before him, Isaac stood rigid, proffering the open book with its gold-edged pages, its red ribbon marking the baptismal ritual. For a moment Father's eyes lit on the words, as if to seek refuge there. Then, with obvious effort, he moved his gaze from the page to Janet, who was glaring at the floor. Having relinquished the baby, she cradled herself in her own arms and rocked, shifting her weight from foot to foot, as I'd so often seen mothers do in church, to quiet a child.

Father was looking at her with his old stunned anxiety. "What do you mean, you can't?"

Janet didn't look up. She hugged herself and rocked.

"Talk to me, Janet." Father Schuyler kept his eyes, wide and frightened, on her face. She evaded his gaze. Though Father pressed his hands together as if in prayer, I could see them trembling. I was proud of him.

In Moshe's arms the baby's eyes fluttered open, and she began to fret. His arms joggled her up and down. One of the little girls opened her mouth and cried, great loud retching sobs.

"Well," said one of the older girls in a strangled voice. "*Now* what?"

Father cleared his throat. "I would like to baptize this child."

"Not so fast." Janet clenched her jaw. "I'm not going to stand here by myself and just say things."

In all the days since Henry's death, I hadn't seen her cry. Now, though, her voice broke. The lid was off, all the sorrows loosed. She put her hands to her face.

Father appeared to count silently to ten. He shut his eyes, then opened them again. "You're not by yourself. And we're more than halfway there. What do you want me to do?"

"I don't know." Janet spoke into her hands. Children on either side were patting her: arms, hips, shoulders, hair, whatever they could reach. "I don't know, I don't know, I don't know—"

Lucy's voice, carrying as always, cut her mother short. "Hold the phone. I'm sick of this. I'm going to go find Dad. We are. Me and Kane." She clutched at Kane's arm, ignoring his startled glance. "We'll track him down. We know where he lives. We have to talk *sense* into that man. *Now*."

"Lucy," Father Schuyler began in a flustered tone.

Janet's hands fell from her face. She looked at Lucy. Lucy looked at Janet. For an instant, it seemed to me that each of them looked into a mirror: the same black curls, the same luminous sea-beaten eyes, the same stubborn chin. Then Janet tossed her head. In that gesture I could see her so clearly, her younger self. Her hair glinted with silver in the candlelight.

"That's not your job, Lucy." The words might have been spoken gently, but Janet's voice was icy.

"Then whose job is it?" Lucy said.

"You can put the book down now," Father told Isaac, still upright in his cassock, a little stricken statue. To Lucy he said, "I don't think this is a situation you can fix with a conversation, tonight. And your mother's right. It's not your job."

"Maybe not," Lucy said, "but you have to start somewhere. And *she*—" It was Lucy's turn to toss her head. "—won't even speak to him."

Janet hugged herself again. "You got that right. I'm not speaking to him. Not until he straightens himself out."

"Are you still in *middle school*?" Lucy's voice rose and rang in the stillness of the church. The other children gazed at her, enraptured by the spectacle of her rage. "Is this how you behave? You have a *marriage* here, Mother. You are an adult. That means you have to *adult*."

"Dammit to freaking hell, Lucy," said Janet.

"Mama, we're in *church*," one of the little girls cried. She jabbed a desperate hand at the tabernacle. "God is *right there*."

"Then God had better hear me." Janet held out her arms to Moshe. He handed the baby back to her. For a time she studied the little startled face. When she spoke again, her voice was gritty. "Because if this isn't what Daddy signed up for, then how does he think I feel about it? You think love is all fun and games in the bushes, but it's not." She rounded on Lucy. "Hear me? It's not freaking *that* at all."

"I never said it was," said Lucy primly.

"And I'm not in middle school, or high school, or grade

school, or kindergarten. But neither is your father. We are not in goddamn middle school. We are not in goddamn *love*, either. I'm sorry, but not any goddamn more, we're not."

"*Mama*." The children were dragging at her sleeve.

"It's true. You think love is all holding hands, missy." Her sea-glass eyes met Lucy's across the surging children. "But I'm here to tell you, it's not. It's a goddamn sword through your heart." She glared at Lucy as at a mortal enemy; Lucy stepped back as though her mother had struck her. "You better look out, Luce. Get ready. A goddamn *sword*."

"*Mama*," cried the children. Lucy's face was stony.

"Don't you think Howard hurts, too?" said Father quietly.

"*Howard*." Janet snorted. "Howard is absent, in case you hadn't noticed."

"I don't think any of us could have helped noticing." Father sighed and fingered the fringe of his stole. All about us, the candlelight stuttered. "But you're here, Janet. And your child is here. That's something. Isn't it?"

For a long moment we all watched Janet waver. She clung to the baby as to a plank in a vast tossing ocean.

At last she spoke, in a small, depleted voice. "Could we—Father—could we just go and talk—maybe? Somewhere? Now?" A sob escaped her. "And you could—maybe—hear my confession? Or not, it doesn't matter. Or—Look, I'm sorry. I need something. I don't know what. Just—maybe—I'm so sorry. I don't understand anything anymore."

"Don't be sorry," Father said with infinite gentleness. "I mean, yes, of course I'll hear your confession if you want, but—whatever. Just whatever. Really. It'll be okay."

"*Right* now?" said Janet. Her voice was a child's, with a child's urgency. "*Now*, Father?"

"Yes, yes, of course, right now. Why don't we go to the Reconciliation Room? We can talk there, and take your time, and just, it's all right—whatever." As he spoke, he was laying his hand on her shoulder, turning her towards the door.

Holding the baby, Janet let herself be turned. Then, pulling free, she stopped and looked back. Drawing a jagged, sobbing breath, she let her eyes rove over the children, who had begun already to edge away, out of the church, out of sight. She looked at me, as I stood beside the font. "Take this baby?" She held out the wrapped bundle. It mewed a little in drowsy outrage.

I backed away. "What? *Me?*"

"You're her godmother." I must still have hesitated; she looked at me imploringly. "Please. Please hold her for me. Just for a little while. You can take her out in the narthex, whatever. I don't care. Please just take her. Quick, before I lose my nerve."

Like that, the baby was in my arms, not a weight but a lightness. The small round head, with its drifted dark hair, nested in its fold of blanket. The crying stopped. The slaty eyes blinked open and peered about in wary curiosity.

There's a mind in there, I thought. Even now it's gathering in all it wants to say: one day, when it's ready. Perhaps one day it will want to talk to me.

* * *

After that, we didn't know what to do. There was the font before the altar, the water still shining in candlelight. Lucy was straightening her crooked mantilla. I took in, with what felt an incongruous twitch of amusement, her short dress, her bare white thighs. There was something comforting in the changelessness of Lucy, though even that was an illusion. Soon enough, she would be changed. We were all being changed, every minute, without our noticing it.

Now, though, familiar, even predictable, she genuflected, crossed herself gigantically, and slipped into a pew. "*I* am going to pray. And so is Kane."

Jarred out of whatever thoughts he was having, the silent, ponytailed Kane dropped into the pew beside her. After an instant's hesitation, he bent to the kneeler and rested his face on his folded arms. Did he know what he'd got himself into? Undoubtedly he did not, but I hoped that he would learn. The big boys, Moshe and Dominic, sat down as well, their faces expressionless. The other children had dispersed. Save for us, the church was empty. Beyond the candles, the tabernacle's bright brass doors glimmered their wordless answer. On either side of the altar, the four evangelists waited in darkness.

Love is the fire, I thought. Again, in the bad lighting and the smell of winter, I could hear Sister Bede's voice. The baby lay warm against my heart. *And Mercy blows the coals.* I remembered what Janet had just said: *Love is a goddamn sword.* Yes, it was. Just now I seemed to heft its weight in my hand. Those other words of my Jesuit's washed over me, the words I'd received in the train, on that long-ago day that had changed the course of my life. *Sorrow is the sister of mercy, and the maker of compassion. Woman,* he asked, as if for the first time, *why weepest thou?*

Holding the anonymous baby, all her slight warmth and weight, I walked out of the church. The narthex was empty. The children had disappeared, though somewhere in the building, small as the rustle of mice, I heard running feet, hysterical half-suppressed shrieks of laughter, the muffled clatter of somebody falling down, people shouting, *Get up, get up!* They'd done that at Henry's graveside, I remembered: chasing, throwing pinecones, giddy as if a rope had been slipped from their necks, their lives given back to them. For them every sorrow went up like that, in a spontaneous burst, not knowing what it did. What would Ranse have said to all this? *Get in the taxi, ma'am.* Always and forever, that's what Ranse would say.

From where I stood in the narthex, I could hear Janet's voice in the Reconciliation Room: not what she said, but a murmur like the fall of waves on loose stone. The church doors stood open. In the church, all this time, whether we watched it or not, the water in the font held candlelight. Unseen, unwatched, untended, through the parish hall and classrooms, the children ran and shrieked. *Just whatever,* Father Schuyler had said to Janet. *Really. It'll be okay.* If his words were not poetry, and slipped from me like water, still my mind would hold the gentleness of his voice.

"Well, then, you peerie lass," I said to the baby. She blinked up at me, a little old woman with a pink claw of a fist. "One of these days I'll know your name." Through the glass doors the car-park lights shone. Each light wore a white halo of finely falling water. I held the baby to my heart, and she was quiet. For a long time I looked out from that bright place into the night and the rain.

This is a work of fiction. Any resemblance to events or to persons, living or dead, is coincidental. Although it would be disingenuous to insist that people and places known to the writer did not in some way contribute their DNA to a given story, in an imaginative work the fictional people and places are themselves wholly, not clones or caricatures of something more real than they are. Their histories and experiences are their own. At the same time, I would be remiss if I did not acknowledge my friend Father Matthew Buettner of the Catholic Diocese of Charlotte, who long ago, as a new priest in a country parish, noticed a house with a mystifying Latin sign in the front yard. That story is his, but I hope he won't begrudge my more hapless Father Schuyler his own glimpse of the Latin sign. Unlike Father Buettner, Father Schuyler has yet to learn to laugh at himself, but he'll get there someday.

My research for this novel, particularly the portions pertaining to the Shetland Islands, was perhaps embarrassingly non-academic. For details of Shetlandic dialect and culture, I am grateful to a variety of online sources, notably the *Shetland ForWirds* website, which is a repository of information and audio related to the islands' oral and musical traditions. I also particularly wish to acknowledge the visual artist Ruth Brownlee, whose Instagram account provides daily visual images from the islands, as well as illuminating commentary about life in Shetland, flavored with everyday vocabulary peculiar to that place. I also found helpful a 2017 article by the poet Christine de Luca, who writes in Shetlandic: "'Recognizable yet Strange: A Guide to the Shetland Dialect," which appeared in *Voices,* the online magazine of the British Council. Like Annesdale, North Carolina, Kirsty's unnamed Shetland village is wholly an invention, but I am grateful to these resources which helped me to ground my invented place in a plausible world.

Books which contributed to the making of this novel include but are not limited to the following: Caroline Gordon's classic *How to Read a Novel*, James Woods' *How Fiction Works,* Charles Baxter's *Beyond Plot: The Art of Subtext,* Joan Silber's *As Long As It Takes: The Art of Time in Fiction,* and George Saunders' *A Swim in a Pond in the Rain.* I also found *The Letters of Flannery O'Connor and Caroline Gordon,* edited by Christine Flanagan, illuminating and helpful. In addition to Robert Southwell's own prose and poetical works, Alice Hogge's *God's Secret Agents: Queen Elizabeth's Secret Priests and the Hatching of the Gunpowder Plot,* provided additional details of my Jesuit's life, ministry, and martyrdom.

I am grateful to Joshua Hren and Wiseblood Books for the gift of time and support in the form of a two-week residency, during which this novel approached completion. Joshua's editorial insights have been invaluable in helping me to clarify the novel's vision; his belief in that vision has been a sustenance to me. I wish as well to thank Belmont Abbey College, which hosted me during the two weeks of my writing residency. I am especially grateful to Abbot Placid Solari and the monks of Belmont Abbey for the daily gift of the Mass in that beautiful place, and for their continual witness to the goodness of a life ordered by prayer.

Finally, I owe a debt of gratitude to my dear family: my husband Ron and our four children, Ada, Joel, Ben, and Rachel. Their love, cheerleading, and forbearance sustain me always in my writing life. Yes, yes, I know it's funny to ask me questions while I'm typing, just to hear how randomly I answer, but without you all, nothing I do would be worth doing.

Made in United States
North Haven, CT
20 November 2022

26987189R00147